OVERDOSED

AMELIA KAPPE

THE VERGOOSSENS SERIES, BOOK I

Copyright © 2022 Amelia Kappe
All rights reserved.

No part of this book may be used or reproduced in any form or by any means, electronic or mechanical, including photocopying, recording, or by any information storage and retrieval system without prior written consent of the author except where permitted by law.

Any references to historical events, real people, or real places are used fictitiously. Names, characters, and places are products of the author's imagination.

Published by Amelia Kappe
Editing & Proofreading by My Brother's Editor
Cover design by Ever After Cover Design
Formatting by Amelia Kappe

To all the girls who need to hear this,
You're a warrior.
You're a powerful woman.
You may not see it yet but you have it in you!
All you need is to believe.

PROLOGUE

Her eyes were swollen, eyelashes wet and heavy with tears. Her body was quivering, and her breath ragged. It was breaking my heart. "Melanie, I love you. You have to believe me," I pleaded. "Everything we've had was true. I wasn't pretending my love for you. If I could go back in time—"

"But you can't," she cut me off, her voice cold and stern. "That's the thing, Shane. You can't!" She started crying, punching my chest with her fists, and I let her. "I hate you! God, I hate you so much! I trusted you. I told you everything I went through, and even that didn't stop you from playing your role! You're sick!"

"Melanie, you know that's not true." I gently grabbed her wrists in my hands, pressing them to my chest. I watched the woman, who I swore to protect, break down. I clenched my jaw, fighting back the tears in my eyes as she desperately cried. I knew I was the reason for it, and I couldn't stand that thought. Her pain was tearing me down. "I've regretted agreeing to my father's fucked-up plan every fucking day since I met you. And I hate myself for it. I'm fucked up. I know that. But I was raised that way. My father was fueling me with goddamn revenge as if it was the purpose of my life. Until I met you." My voice was breaking. I held her hands in mine and, for the first time in twenty years, cried. Last time I shed a tear, I was five and at my mother's funeral. "You freed me from this, Melanie. You freed me from the heavy chains keeping me in the past. And I love you. I so fucking love you, Melanie. You're my life. I'm lost without you."

"I don't believe you," Melanie sobbed, struggling to catch a breath. Fuck, I wanted to take the pain away from her. I just didn't know how. I felt so fucking helpless. I broke the woman I loved the most.

"You have to believe me," I whispered, grabbing her chin in my fingers and tilting her head back so our eyes locked. "Ever since I laid eyes on you, I knew I couldn't hurt you. And you kept proving me right every single day. Everything I've done after was to protect you."

Melanie pulled back, taking a deep breath as she wiped her tears. Her eyes turned black with lethal hatred. "If you wanted to protect me, you should've stayed away from me."

"Melanie, please… give me a chance to prove that I love you." My voice cracked.

"No, Shane. What we had was lust, not love."

"Don't say that."

"But it's true. We've mistaken lust for love."

"No, Melanie. Only love can be this strong. And only love can hurt so damn much that I'm suffocating."

"Well then… Love is lethal," Melanie whispered, staring numbly into my eyes. I didn't understand her words, but I felt cold shivers washing over me. I felt fear.

"Because whatever this was… I overdosed, and it killed me."

I shook my head, her words cut deep like a knife, tearing my heart apart. "Don't say such things."

Melanie looked at me with contempt, her eyes glistened with tears. "Stay the hell away from me," she shrieked before she turned on her heels and got back in the car.

Ledford instantly drove away, and I felt like I was drowning. Suffocating. I stood alone on an empty street, surrounded only by the darkness of the night, immersing in the excruciating pain and questioning every decision I'd ever made that led me to this point.

Did I regret anything? Hell yes.

Would I change anything? No.

AMELIA KAPPE

ONE

Melanie

A couple of months earlier.

"Are you crazy, Theo?!" I pushed my boyfriend away, fixing the clothes he'd tried to take off of me. "Did you think I would have sex with you in a storage room?"

He rolled his eyes at me, making that weird sound he always did to express his frustration. "I'm so tired of it, Melanie!"

"Of what exactly?" I frowned, crossing my arms.

"We've been dating for over a year now, barely having sex," he snarled.

"Oh, you thought I would let you screw me between my legal analysis and procedural law classes?" Sarcasm dripped from my voice.

Theo and I started dating in our senior year of high school, winning the titles of king and queen of the prom. Although, I could never tell if Theo was more of a friend to me or a boyfriend because as much as I enjoyed his company, I'd never felt the burning lust everyone was talking about. We had our first sex after eight months of our relationship, and only because Theo was pushy, but no fireworks for me. I felt terrible because I cared about him and our relationship. At the same time, no matter how hard I tried, I didn't feel the spark. I thought it might've been caused by my bad experiences haunting me from my past. My former boyfriend hurt me in the worst possible way, leaving an irreversible strike on my soul forever.

After graduation, Theo and I chose the same university. Or rather, it'd been selected for us. As the daughter of this year's candidate running for the governor of California, Derick Atwood, I couldn't decide about my own life. In my case, everything was already planned for me. The course of my education and my future career. Even my boyfriend, which at first, I had no idea about. So yes, I was one of those rich kids who got into Stanford University because of their societal position. And even though I had no desire to get a law degree, my father believed it would be best if I followed in his footsteps and became a lawyer or, even better, a politician.

"I don't know what you want," Theo growled, snapping me back to reality. "But it frustrates the hell out of me that my girlfriend won't let me touch her!"

"Theo—" Before I could finish, he stormed out of the dark, dusty storage room, slamming the door behind him.

"Very mature." I let out a deep sigh. I had no time or energy to deal with this crap. I was up all night cramming for that legal analysis exam. I fixed my clothes and left for the next dry as dust lecture.

AFTER SCHOOL, I TUCKED myself under a soft, white blanket. I'd had one of those bad days when you wanted to sink into your bed, hoping no one would ever find you. But despite the thick walls of my bedroom, I could still hear my parents arguing—*again*. I covered myself with a furry pillow, pushing it onto my head. Even that didn't make their shouting or throwing dirty names at one another stop ringing in my ears. I hated their fights, and those would happen daily. My parents' marriage was of convenience, not love. And I was their only child, so I was stuck in this toxic swamp all alone. Or maybe it was better I had no siblings? At least there was no extra person who'd have to suffer everything I had. I could never understand why my mother wouldn't just drop everything and run away from that monster, a.k.a. my father, burning all the bridges after her. Especially after everything he'd done to her. Or maybe, I wish I had done that myself? And yet there I was, trying to survive yet another day in this luxurious life of mine… that behind the closed doors of this hell of a mansion called our home wasn't luxurious at all.

I heard a loud door slam, followed by my mother's heels clicking on marble stairs as she headed downstairs—finally, no more screams. I took a deep breath, crawling out of my bed that felt like my fortress, helping me survive all the wars this house had witnessed. I reached out for my phone and saw a few missed calls from Theo, and one text from Scarlett, my best friend. I chose to ignore the calls from my boyfriend and, heading up to the bathroom, unfold the entire message Scarlett sent me.

From: Scar

Hey, boo! Will u make it to the party tonite? We're at Mike's.

Sent Friday 5:52 PM

I sighed, not feeling the Friday night vibe as a nineteen-year-old girl like me should. But the truth was, I'd rather go out than stay in this dreadful place, risking being an invisible partaker in yet another quarrel. I quickly freshened up and was ready to leave about an hour later. I glanced at my reflection in the mirror, amazed at how a little bit of makeup and a sexy outfit could boost one's self-perception. I tended to be very insecure about myself. I blamed my emotionally unsteady childhood for that because my mother would never tell me I was beautiful like my friends' mothers would do. I'd been struggling with my low self-esteem ever since I recall. It felt like I was fighting my own war with the demons. Demons slumbering inside me, waiting for the least convenient moment to come out and destroy the self-confidence I desperately tried to build all over again. But that wasn't the case tonight. I smiled at myself, satisfied with how I looked. I slipped a black minidress, with a straight neckline cut out in the middle, over my naked breasts, pleasingly tightening them. The V-cut on the left bottom gave some sultry to its design. I brushed my lips with my favorite Dior gloss in a medium nude shade and drew a simple cat line over my eyelashes, enhancing my look.

To: Scar

I'm on my way, S.

Sent Friday 7:18 PM

I typed the quick response and hit *Send*, leaving for the party.

"Do you want me to wait for you, Miss Atwood?" my chauffeur asked as we were approaching Mike's place.

"No, you can go back home," I answered as he pulled over in front of my friend's house. Music was playing so loud I bet all the neighborhood could hear it.

"Are you sure, miss?" Gregory peeked at my reflection in the rearview mirror, and I met his hazel eyes. The freckles forming around his eyelids implied he was smiling.

Sometimes it felt like he worried more about me than my parents did. I'd never seen him only as my chauffeur. We had a connection, something like a grandfather and granddaughter would have. And something I'd never experienced because I'd never gotten to know my grandparents. But even though it felt nice, it still hurt that a stranger would care more about me than my mother or, let alone, my father would.

"Yeah, I'm sure. Thanks, Gregory," I said and got out of the car.

I looked at the two-level loft with massive windows through which I could spot my friends having wild fun, and suddenly, all the confidence in me faded away. I took a deep breath as the overwhelming feeling of anxiety rushed over my body. I forced myself to smile and somehow moved forward.

"MELANIE!" SCARLETT SPOTTED me from afar and, squeezing between some people I'd never seen before, greeted me with a hug. "I was worried you wouldn't come."

Unlike me, Scarlett was a life-of-the-party girl who adored being the center of attention. Taking a sip of her martini, she scanned my face with her extraordinary emerald eyes, perfectly matching her fair, freckled complexion and wavy hair dyed a copper shade of red.

"Haven't you seen my text?" I arched my eyebrow, smiling.

"Oh, God, no." She giggled, struggling to swallow the sip she'd just taken, her cheeks flushed. She was tipsy, no doubt. "Sorry. I don't even know where my phone is."

Scarlett grabbed me by my elbow and led me to an enormous living room. There was an open drink bar, a leather couch by the see-through glass wall, and at least three hundred square feet of space in the middle where some people were dancing. The room was dim, with a few colorful flashing lights glistening against the ceiling giving the club vibe to this place. I glanced across the area, searching for Theo. I spotted him drinking his whiskey. He seemed immersed in thought, not paying much attention to people cheerfully laughing around him. Among others, Mike, who was overly gesticulating while enthusiastically telling something, and Audrey, one of my friends. She stood by Theo's right arm, cooing at him. Scarlett quickly picked up on my mood as I involuntarily clenched my jaw, watching my so-called friend hitting on my man.

"You're not jealous of Audrey, are you?" Scar said, biting on her lower lip teasingly while a sarcastic smirk formed on her face. She grabbed a drink from a bar countertop behind us and fetched it for me.

"I'm not," I said dryly, drinking the martini she handed me in one go. My eyes were still on Audrey, whispering something into Theo's ear, and a playful smile appeared on his face.

What did she tell him that he suddenly looks so amused?

"You know that Theo is head over heels for you, Mel." Scarlett nudged my elbow.

"I know. It's just… I don't trust Audrey."

Scar chuckled softly as if what I said was funny. But I hadn't felt like laughing. I was anxious because I'd had a bad feeling haunting me that night. And in most cases, my female intuition was pretty reliable.

"Well, why don't you just go over there and get your man?" my ruby-haired friend asked, but I didn't even have to answer. It took her only one glance at me, and she knew. "Oh, you two fought?"

She must've noticed the distress on my face.

"Yeah," I sighed, casting my eyes downward to the ground.

"You guys have been fighting a lot lately." Her gaze was penetrating me. "Wanna talk about it?"

"Nope," I said shortly and looked up to face her. From the corner of my eye, I noticed Theo was now looking in my direction.

His gaze lingering on my skin made my stomach clench. My heart was telling me to go over and kiss him to end our infantile quarrel. But then, something stopped me, urging, it was him who should make the first move. And that something, whatever it was, won. I turned on my heels and headed to the backyard. As I was squeezing through the crowd of people, I heard two random dudes shouting to one another, obnoxiously checking me out from head to toe.

"Have you seen Melanie Atwood?" A pale-skinned guy with sunflower-blonde hair leaned toward his friend before gulping his beer.

"Who wouldn't notice that ass, bro?" the friend scoffed. "Fucking hot!"

And I knew Theo heard them too because when I fleetingly peeked in his direction, he was glaring at me with the kind of gaze I knew far too well. He was seething with jealousy.

I STOOD ON THE PORCH, deep into my thoughts with my eyes glued to the starry sky. Chilly air was sweeping across my cheeks, causing goose bumps on my body.

"I'm sorry for earlier," I heard a familiar voice whispering in my ear as warm hands slid around my waist from behind. I didn't even have to turn to know who it was. I knew the scent of sandalwood with a hint of geranium hitting my nose by heart. I turned to face Theo. He looked like a lost puppy begging me to help him find his way back home.

"I'm sorry, Melanie. I acted like a dick earlier today," he said with an apologetic tone.

"You did act like a dick." I smirked, gazing into his coffee-colored eyes. The moonlight illuminated his wavy, fair hair, ideally done in a tapered way. But even his gorgeous face wouldn't make up for his behavior earlier today. I still had in mind how he left me in that gross storage room looking like a five-year-old baby that hadn't got the toy he desperately wanted. That was one trait that I genuinely hated about Theo. Whenever he didn't get what he wanted, he would just sulk.

"Can I make it up to you somehow?" he said, caressing my cheek with his thumb.

"Well… I might forgive you if you kiss me now." I smiled at him, and his face lightened up. I couldn't be mad at him for too long. It just didn't sit right with me. I wasn't the one to hold the grudge, even if, at times, I should have.

He slowly leaned in, sliding his hand at the back of my neck. His warm lips gently brushed over mine. "You look so hot tonight. I couldn't take my eyes off you," he whispered against my lips, our breaths mingling before closing the tiny gap with a kiss.

"Hey, lovebirds!" Mike's raspy voice broke in our tender moment. "Get a room!" he joked, showing off his white teeth beautifully contrasting his ebony complexion. One of his dark dreadlocks fell onto his forehead as he took a few deep gulps of his beer.

"Are we good?" Theo asked me after slowly pulling away, setting his eyes on mine.

"I get you can't keep it in your pants, bro! But you guys are gonna miss out on the party!" Mike's teasing comment made me blush. I turned my gaze back to Theo, who rolled his eyes with annoyance.

I smiled and grabbed his hand. "We're good." And I led him back inside.

ABOUT AN HOUR LATER, I was on my third drink and I felt dizzy. Usually, I avoided alcohol, so I didn't need much for it to kick in. The party was in full swing, and I was chatting with Scarlett and Teresa, a friend with whom I had legal analysis workshops. I searched across the room for Theo but couldn't spot him. I wanted to ask him to drop me home. I knew his driver was waiting for him because we'd always been doing that. I'd dismiss Gregory, and Theo's driver would stick around.

"Have you seen Theo?" I asked the girls.

Teresa quickly checked out the room before replying, "Nope."

"Maybe he went somewhere with Mike? I can't see him either," Scarlett added.

"Yeah, I'll check outside. Maybe they went for a smoke."

"Yeah, probably." Scarlett smiled. "Want me to go with you?"

"Nah, I'm fine. I need to use the toilet on my way there." I gave the girls a reassuring look and set aside the drink before following toward the restroom.

The toilet on the ground floor was occupied, so I decided to go upstairs. I knew Mike's place because he used to throw parties nearly every Friday. Besides, he was my boyfriend's best friend, and sometimes we hit his place.

With each step up the stairs, the loud music playing downstairs seemed to fade away. I could finally hear my own thoughts. I was about to get inside the washroom, but something stopped me. I heard moaning coming from one of the rooms. It wasn't something unusual. People hooked up at parties, but this time was different. I felt a cold shiver sweeping down my spine, realizing it was Audrey's voice whining my boyfriend's name.

My heart started racing like crazy as I walked over to the door leading to Mike's bedroom. The closer I'd get, the louder I'd hear the moans. I grabbed the doorknob and slightly opened the door. My hands were shaking. I was not ready for what I was about to see. My eyes grew wide, and I gasped in shock. I saw Theo and my narrow-waisted friend making out. Both half-naked.

"Shit! Melanie?!" Theo's face fell as soon as he spotted me, gawking at them with my jaw dropped. "It's not what you think!" He tried to devise some ridiculous excuse while hurriedly buttoning his fly, but before he managed to put himself together, I stormed out of there faster than a speeding bullet.

TEARS WERE RUNNING down my face as I was running down the street. I didn't know where or for how long. I kept running, holding my expensive Louis Vuitton high heels in my hands, and my perfectly done makeup was likely ruined. The picture of my boyfriend's hand sliding down Audrey's tanned belly, disappearing underneath the silk fabric of her panties, her shiny, chocolate-brown hair falling at her arched back as she sighed in pleasure while running her fingers through Theo's golden hair while he planted hungry kisses down her neck, kept haunting me all the way here, whenever I was. With each passing second, the excruciating pain tearing my heart apart intensified. I'd never felt so broken before, and believe me, my life had been fucked up just enough to make me experience all kinds of shitty feelings. I could barely see through my watery eyes, and I hadn't noticed the car approaching me from across the street. Then just when I thought it would hit me, I heard a loud screech of brakes as the driver managed to stop an inch before me.

"Are you fucking crazy?!" he shouted at me before he even managed to step out of the car. I couldn't guess if he was more shaken because he almost hit me with his speeding car or more furious that I ran right in front of it, risking destroying his brand-new, shiny black Bugatti. But, as soon as our eyes met, he kind of… froze.

And that's when I met him. The most handsome man I'd ever laid my eyes on with the kind of piercing blue eyes that told me I should run the other way.

TWO

Shane

A few hours ago, I was in New York, where I lived. But because of my task, I had to come here. I was on my way from the airport when some batshit crazy girl ran in front of my speeding car, and I managed to stop at the last minute.

Fucking great. I rolled my eyes and got out of the vehicle to see... *her*. I recognized her the moment I saw her. My father had been preparing me for this task since I was five. Yet, it was so random that the first person I met after landing in LA was none other than Melanie Atwood. My target.

You lucky bastard.

"Are you okay?" I asked, making sure my car hadn't hit her.

"What a sudden change of heart!" she said sarcastically. "Just a second ago, you called me fucking crazy, and yet it was you who was driving like a fucking madman!"

I smiled at her sassy comment. She was fierce, and I liked it.

"Now what? Cat got your tongue?" she snapped at me. "Didn't you see a speed limit of thirty miles per hour here? You had at least sixty on the clock!"

"My bad." I smirked. "Let me make it up to you." I indicated she should get in the car.

"Do you expect me to get in the car with my potential murderer?!" she exclaimed, irritated, and I couldn't help but chuckle.

"Like I said. Let me make it up to you." I went to the other side of my car and opened the passenger door, gazing at her expectantly.

She looked like a mess. Well, like a fucking hot mess. Her big brown eyes that, I bet, usually would glimmer like diamonds were now red and puffy. Her mascara was all over her face indicating she'd just cried. She was standing barefoot, holding her heels in her shaky hands. But despite it, she still looked like a fucking goddess. Her shiny, platinum-blonde waist-length hair was twisting in the wind. Only some shorter strands fell on her face, covering its beauty.

"Come on. I see you don't know what to do with yourself. Let me drop you somewhere." I got no response. "Unless you want to march barefoot for God knows how long and risk getting hit by some fucking madman," I said, alluding to her previous phrase, and she smiled.

"Alright. Just because you owe me for nearly killing me," she said and got in the car.

I smiled, satisfied, and closed the door after her. This was going to be a long night.

WE'D BEEN DRIVING for about half an hour, and the roaring of the accelerating car engine was the only thing muffling the deadly silence. I pretended to be focused on the road but still could feel her gaze on me.

"Like what you see?" Knowing she'd been gawking at me all this time, I couldn't help but tease.

"Don't flatter yourself!" she said, unfazed, and I chuckled.

"Well, stop biting your lip while staring at me, so maybe I'll stop flattering myself," I said, with my eyes still focused on the road, and she gave me a kind of "*How the hell did he notice that?*" look.

"I was just wondering what's your name." She cleared her throat to sound more convincing. "Nothing more."

I briefly glanced at her before setting my eyes on the highway again. She looked pretty adorable with her blushing cheeks.

"It's Shane," I said, and she nodded, acknowledging.

She turned, leaning her head on the backrest, and focused on the sweeping landscapes of bustling LA. We'd been driving along US Route 101, a.k.a. the Hollywood Freeway.

I could see her reflection in the mirror. She seemed down, and I wondered what had happened before we met, which led to her running desperately ahead like she was trying to escape the brutal reality.

"Where are we going?" she asked shrewdly as if something awakened inside her, and I smiled.

We entered the gleaming lobby of the Beverly Wilshire, a Four Seasons hotel, and I noticed Melanie got tense. She bent down her head as if wishing she could've been invisible.

"What's wrong?" I asked, slightly concerned.

"Nothing," she hesitated. "I just... don't want anyone to recognize me," she whispered. She was frowning and bit her lower lip anxiously while gazing up at me from under her lengthy, black eyelashes, and my lips curled in a soft smirk. I found it cute that she was so... innocent.

"Why does it matter?" I asked, trying to hide the amusement.

"Oh, stop acting like you don't know." She seemed embarrassed, covering her face with her hand. "I saw my reflection in the car's window on our way here. I look like complete chaos."

"That's not true. You look... cute." I caught myself smiling at her like a fool. "Besides, you're here with me. I'll punch anyone who dares to say something that would offend you."

That was so damn lame. What am I now? Her knight in shining armor?

But she smiled, and for some reason, it felt nice. "You don't understand. They know me here. And I no doubt remind them of some kind of a pickup street girl now. Just go to check-in, and I'll wait here. Please." She gave me puppy eyes, and I gave in.

"Okay. I'll be right back."

I went to the reception, but all I could focus on was her. I glanced in her direction and saw a tiny, petite woman anxiously hiding from the world, wondering how I was supposed to see someone this fragile as my enemy?

I watched Melanie lean against the wall, reeling in embarrassment, when a desk clerk's voice snapped me out of my thought, "Here you go, Mr. Vergoossen." A beautiful brunette in her twenties said as she handed me the key to my suite, smiling politely, "Enjoy your stay."

"Thank you," I grabbed the key and headed toward Melanie, my gaze focused on her the entire time.

"We can go." I took hold of her hand and led her toward the elevators.

I pressed the top floor button, and we watched the elevator door closing in silence.

"So?" She paused, hesitant. "You're staying at a hotel?"

"Yeah, I'm not a local."

"So I've figured." Her eyes were carefully scanning my face. "What brings you here?"

"Business," I stated, without the intent to elaborate.

"What kind of business?" She tried to drag something out of me, but I just smiled. I heard the elevator ring, and we headed to my presidential suite.

"WHISKEY?" I ASKED, holding a scotch bottle.

"Yeah, please," she said quietly. "Why exactly did you bring me here?"

"I told you," I said casually. "I wanted to make it up to you somehow."

"It?" She raised an eyebrow and curled her lips in a soft smile.

"That I nearly hit you with my car."

"It wasn't your fault," she reluctantly admitted. "You don't have to feel obligated to babysit some batshit crazy chick who ran in front of your car in the middle of the street, you know?"

I smiled, fetching her the drink, and she tilted her head to the side, frowning, again with a soft smile.

"What's so funny?"

"That's what I was thinking about you a while ago." I'd been struggling to hide the amusement.

"Thinking what about me?"

"That you're batshit crazy," I scoffed. "But now—" I paused, contemplating my words.

"But now?" she demanded an answer.

"But now I see you're not some crazy chick, but a fragile human being dealing with some shit." She seemed surprised, and we kept staring into each other's eyes for what felt like an eternity. It felt weird. As if no words were needed. As if I could read right through her. As if we had some kind of an instant connection.

"Yeah, well," she was rubbing the back of her neck with her long, slender fingers while biting her bottom lip anxiously.

She drank the whiskey I fetched her in one go while I slowly took a few steps toward her. I overlapped her hand in which she was holding the glass with mine, and our eyes locked. I gently took the drink away from her and set it aside on the glass table behind us. I tilted her chin with my fingers, and my gaze dropped down to her slightly parted mouth. I couldn't fight the urge and brushed my thumb over her soft lower lip, and I noticed her body was shivering. Fuck, she was so gorgeous. Was it wrong of me that at this moment, all I wanted to do was rip off her silky dress, lingering against her sultry body, and fuck her against the wall behind her, so hard that all the hotel guests would hear her screaming out my name in pleasure?

"Melanie…" I whispered, leaning in with every intent to taste her luscious lips.

"Wait!" She stepped back. "How the hell do you know my name?"

Fuck!

She never told me her name. I knew I couldn't afford such rookie mistakes. It could ruin everything. And the last thing I'd want was to ruin anything. Especially at the very fucking beginning of my task. It was just those tempting lips of hers, begging me to lick, suck, bite them, or all at once for that matter, that kept distracting the hell out of me.

"You've mentioned your name." I kept my cool.

"No, I haven't," she objected, staring intensely at me.

I sneered and turned to sip my whiskey. "Well, maybe a cold shower would help. The toilet's on the left." I was trying to throw her off the scent.

"Excuse me?" I hadn't been facing her, but her petulant voice gave away that she was nettled.

I turned to look into her eyes. "You're not thinking clearly."

She bit her lower lip and shifted her eyes to the side, clearly stunned. Apparently, that was what she did when she was anxious—bit her lips. And for some fucked-up reason, it turned me on. She seemed confused, deep in thought, like she was trying to replay the last hour we'd spent together to dispel her doubts.

"Anyway, you might want to wash off your…" I paused, examining her smeared makeup, trying to find the right words to name it.

"Yeah, I could use the toilet," she said sheepishly. "It's about time I make myself look civilized again."

I sipped my whiskey, satisfied that I'd managed to disorientate her enough to drop the "name" topic. It was easy, but her mind was troubled with some other stuff that night. I was aware of it, and I knew I'd have to be more careful.

"Make yourself at home," I said, gazing straight into her timid eyes.

She turned with no word, and I watched how effortlessly she swayed her hips as she headed toward the restroom. Damn, her ass. Her sexy, round butt was driving me insane. I imagined ripping off that fucking dress covering her body of a goddess from my sight and fucking her senselessly.

Yes, I've got a dirty mind.

I SCROLLED THROUGH dozens of the emails I'd gotten during my flight concerning some business shit when Melanie came back and instantly caught my attention. She washed off her face and obviously didn't use any cosmetic products or whatever the hell they're called, so she had no makeup. She pulled her hair up in a high bun, revealing her baby-doll-like face. She was so fucking naturally gorgeous. Sure as fuck, it would've been way easier for me to follow my plan if she wasn't such a goddess. It was distracting as fuck. Especially that she had that angelic kind of beauty. She had those luminous, big eyes many would die for. Or her slim, long fingers she bashfully played with every time she was uneasy. Don't even make me start on her sultry body that made her look so fragile and innocent and at the same time hotter than hell. Melanie Atwood was a mix of everything any man could ever dream of.

"I should go home," she whispered. Her voice was so quiet it felt like she was afraid the words would hurt if she said them loud enough.

"You can stay here if you want," I instantly second-guessed what I'd just said. Melanie's dark eyes grew wide as she glanced at me, astonished, probably questioning my nonsensical offer as well.

"Believe me, I'd love that, but—" she said, her suddenly gloomy gaze dropped down to her fingers she still nervously played with. I wondered what she meant by that? I thought she led an ivory tower life, considering she was a billionaire, influential daddy's only little girl.

"But your father would be worried," I said assumingly, trying to pick up track of what was going on in her life. I hoped she'd take off the lid once I hit the right spot.

"I bet!" she scoffed, rolling her eyes. "Anyway, could you order me an Uber or something? I had to leave my phone at my friend's place."

"I'll drive you home myself." Words just blurted out of my mouth.

What the fuck is wrong with me?

She tilted slightly to the side, frowning, scanning my face with her eyes.

"Making sure you get there safe and sound," I added with a teasing tone, trying to play it out. "How else will I be sure I don't hear about the girl who jumped in front of a speeding car in tomorrow's news?"

"Oh, screw you!" She sneered, her hand on her hip.

Yeah, screw me

THREE

Melanie

Shane insisted on driving me home, and at some point, I gave up. Apparently, he was a very stubborn man that had to have things his way.

Walking up the stairs of our lavish mansion that'd never felt like home, I realized we hadn't exchanged phone numbers, so I most likely would never meet him again. And, for some strange reason, that thought sucked. *Something* about Shane pulled me toward him as if he was a magnet. *Something* I craved to explore.

I FELL ONTO my bed and closed my eyes to dive into images of him floating in my head. His dark hair contrasting his pale complexion, perfectly matched his strong jawline, and relatively narrow lips smirking to the side alluringly wouldn't leave my mind. He was so fucking handsome. I sank my teeth into my bottom lip as the memory of his firm, broad arms tightly hugged by his shirt with tattoos underneath his slightly folded sleeves as he casually shifted gears popped into my head. I wasn't sure if it was his to-die-for azure gaze or a hint of darkness emanating from him that attracted me immensely.

I let out a deep breath.

Shane.

I liked the sound of that name, and I found it fit his irresistible, luring-me-in personality.

Fascinating how the black-haired, mysterious stranger made me forget about my cheating boyfriend. I tucked myself into bed and fell asleep thinking of my newly met prince, hoping I'd see him again.

THE FOLLOWING MORNING, I woke up earlier than usual. The night was pretty restless as the images of Theo and Audrey haunted me in my dreams. Or rather nightmares. I reluctantly crawled out of my king-size—*way too big for one person*—bed and slid into my white, silky robe. I hated weekends because they meant more time spent in this prison. And no, unfortunately, moving out wasn't an option. My father wanted to detain me here until I graduated or got married. Whatever would come first. I knew he was counting on me marrying Theo and being useful to our family, as he used to say, but I didn't mind before. In a way, I loved Theo, and I was looking forward to marrying him. Or maybe it wasn't love but a coping mechanism helping me survive in this hell and a way to free myself from the devil's claws?

"Melanie! Let me in." A few loud knocks rumbled through my room. *Speaking of the devil.* "Melanie!" My father shouted, still banging at the door.

"What did I do now?" I asked sarcastically, through a slightly ajar door. But he didn't reply. Instead, he looked at me with a gaze that could kill before grabbing me by my elbow, squeezing so hard it hurt, and dragging me after him.

"Let me go!" I yelled, trying to yank out of his grip, but in vain.

As we were approaching the living room, I could hear the TV. My father pushed me inside the bright and spacious room and stood behind me with a deadly gaze. He was clenching his jaw, seething. Not that this kind of behavior was something new to me, but I didn't understand what enraged him this morning. That was until I heard the lady on the news.

"Melanie Atwood, the daughter of this year's candidate running for the governor of California, Dedrick Atwood, was spotted entering a hotel room with a mysterious, handsome man. The man's face hasn't been caught in the pictures one of the paparazzi has taken, but we've confirmed it wasn't her long-term boyfriend, Theo Ledford."

My blood ran cold. I looked at the 100-inch TV showing pictures of Shane and me entering his suite with shock on my face. My heart was pumping so heavily that it felt like it would jump out of my rib cage. Icy shivers continued to sweep up and down my spine. I turned to face my father, who was staring at me spitefully. He had never loved me. He only cared about his reputation—especially a few weeks before the elections. And my relationship with Theo suited him. Robert Ledford, Theo's father, was the current governor, and because of his son and partially because of me, he was endorsing my father in his campaign. Now, I understood my father's outrage after he saw the news. And I knew the fact that my boyfriend had cheated on me with my fucking friend wouldn't have any meaning to him.

"Robert called me a few minutes ago, disgusted with the whole situation," my father hissed through clenched teeth. "He hopes it's just a fatal misunderstanding, and you have a fair reason why you entered a stranger's room in the middle of the night."

"Maybe he should ask his son." I scoffed, boiling inside at the thought of Theo getting into Audrey's pants just a few hours ago.

"Listen, Melanie." He took a few steps toward me. "I don't care what happened yesterday."

I cut him off, "Of course, who would care about their offspring?"

"I'm not done speaking!" He clenched his fists and hit on the marble countertop of a square table standing in the middle of the living room. "You are all over the news, young lady! Not Theo! And I haven't put so much effort into raising you in vain! You won't ruin my life because of some teenage drama!"

"Excuse me?" I couldn't help but mock him. "Effort into raising me? You haven't done shit for me except for providing me with money for my education! But at what price?"

"Shut up, Melanie!" he shouted aggressively, barely holding back from hitting me. A rash caused his pale rosy cheeks to turn a deep shade of red. "Listen carefully because I'll say this only once. You're going to marry Theo, and your engagement party will be held in a week."

WHAT?!

I stood there, speechless. My eyes wandered all over my father's flushed face, hoping I'd find even the slightest trace of something that would imply he was joking. He couldn't be serious. He had no right to make such significant decisions for me. I glanced over at the TV screen that no longer showed the pictures of my pictures with Shane, and I swallowed a huge lump in my throat. Just a few days ago, I would react a hundred and eighty degrees differently. I would be counting the days to marry him, elated that I'd escape this Hades. But that was before I caught Theo with Audrey—and *before I met Shane.* So moving out from the tyrant my father was to a cheater my *ex*-boyfriend was, wasn't an appealing option anymore.

"Over my dead body!" I stomped my feet for the first time in my life, so determined to finally stand up for myself.

"Don't tempt me," my father scoffed.

I took a step back, and my jaw fell wide open. I couldn't believe how effortlessly my own father would trade my happiness for his own benefits. I'd always wondered what I did that he was refusing me his love. I'd heard bits of my parents' quarrels about something that had happened in the past, but suddenly, their mouths would seal up whenever I'd bring the topic up. I found it odd, but I'd never dug too deep because I knew it was pointless. I knew they would tell me nothing. Or maybe, I was too tired of this life to care?

"You don't have much of a choice, you know?" He continued, mockingly, as if my misery was entertaining to him. "Everything is already arranged. As we talk, guests are invited, and the official announcement will go viral at noon." He took a few steps toward me, locking his dark eyes with mine. Then he hissed in a low tone that caused goose bumps on my skin. "And don't try any tricks with me, Melanie. I'm warning you. I had to bribe the head of the TV stations to stop airing the news about you. You cost me way more than you're worth." *No matter how many times I'd heard that it always hurt just the same.*

"I will n—" I tried to object, but he put his finger over my lips. His cold touch felt paralyzing.

"Theo is going to propose to you, and you will say yes. Understood?" He smiled in the most cynical way I'd ever seen before moving back. He fixed his well-tailored grayish jacket and reached for his phone from the pocket of his matching pants. He ignored me completely, having his eyes glued to the digital screen, so of course, he didn't see the pain written all over my face. "You may go now. I guess you have yoga in an hour. You don't want to be late."

Wow, what a caring father. He knows his daughter's schedule by heart.

I'd heard that too many times. But the truth was, he demanded I report everything I did to him. And I felt like a princess imprisoned in a high tower, waiting for her knight to come and rescue her. Too bad my knight turned out to be a cheating ass.

"Earth to Melanie!" Teresa's articulate voice snapped me out of my thoughts.

We were at the private gym, doing yoga together. That was our Saturday routine. Yoga in the morning, followed by Pilates and then lunch together. Healthy and vegan. I felt like my life had already been so rotted that at least my lifestyle could be blossoming. Besides, working out was an excellent way to eliminate all destructive emotions. Thanks to it, I managed to keep my sanity. And the fact that it helped me stay in shape was a nice addition.

"What were you saying?" I breathed, wiping away the sweat from my forehead before fixing my ponytail.

"I said, you seem odd today." She looked me up and down, frowning. "Did something happen?"

"I guess you'll find out at noon."

"What do you mean?"

"My life is doomed, T." I let out a deep breath. I sat on the floor, resting against the wall, staring blankly at my reflection in the mirrored wall ahead of us. Teresa gave me a worried look before she sat beside me.

"Mel, what is it? You know you can trust me, right?" She squeezed my shoulder in a friendly, comforting manner, and I forced a smile.

Teresa might've been a kind and gentle soul, and even though we hung out a lot together due to our similar likings, I hadn't fully opened up to her. She didn't know any of my struggles or how much of a tyrant my father was. No one knew what was happening behind the closed doors of our luxurious mansion. Not even Scar, who was closest to my heart. I led my glamorous life carrying the darkest secrets alone. Pretending. Acting to the whole world that I was okay when I wasn't. Why? Maybe I wasn't strong enough to face the brutal reality, so I chose to keep lying to everyone, including myself.

"It's nothing. Don't worry," I said softly, smiling. And usually, it worked. People gave up the second they heard what they wanted to. Because no one likes being engaged in the dark side of your life, no? But to my surprise, Teresa didn't give up.

"Is it about that guy from the news?" she asked hesitantly, knitting her brow. She didn't want to seem nosy but was genuinely worried about me. *Was I failing on my acting skills?*

"Well, partially," I sighed.

"Are you having an affair with him?" She gazed at me apologetically, her mahogany-toned face inflamed with shame.

"No." I couldn't help but chuckle. She looked so adorable with the unnecessary guilt written her eyes. "Although, I wish I had."

"What?" She didn't hide the astonishment. I didn't blame her. After all, everyone at Stanford called Theo and me a "golden couple." They perceived us as a perfect match, made for each other, cut from the same cloth. And until yesterday, I believed so, too.

"Never mind." I brushed it off. Knowing I had no choice but to follow my father's "orders," I didn't want to tell her what I'd witnessed the night before. I knew she wouldn't understand why I agreed to marry a guy who fucked my friend behind my back. The truth was, I wasn't sure of that myself. I guess it's called fear. Weakness. "We should get going." I stood up and grabbed my backpack.

ABOUT HALF AN HOUR LATER, freshened up, we headed toward the building exit. I grabbed the doorknob, only to see Theo through the glass door. In an instant, a smile washed off my face, and a stone-cold gaze took its place.

"Theo!" Teresa exclaimed enthusiastically, but I couldn't tame my anger. I pushed the door with all my force, nearly hitting my ex in his face, but unfortunately, he managed to step back just in time.

"Melanie, wait!" He took hold of my arm, stopping me. "Baby, please, let me explain," he said pleadingly, and

I closed my eyes, clenching my jaw and fists. I let out a heavy breath, trying not to lose it. "I tried to call you—"

"Leave me alone, you fucking asshole!" I hissed, firmly yanking out of his grip, and Teresa gave us a "what the hell" look. "And don't you ever call me baby again."

"I'll give you guys a moment," Teresa uttered.

"No. It's okay, Tess," I objected, giving Theo a spiteful look straight in his lying eyes. "We're done here." I rushed to leave, but Theo seized my arm again, not letting me go.

"Thank you, Tess." He glanced over at my friend, who nodded uncertainly.

"I'll see you around, Melanie," she muttered, giving me an apologetic look, and left.

I set my gaze on a random object ahead of me and kept tapping my foot, exasperated. "I don't want to listen to your stupid excuses, Theo."

"Give me five minutes," he whispered, somewhat annoyed, somewhat pleading.

"Fine, five minutes," I sighed, disappointed at myself. But I knew I didn't have any other choice anyway. My father was dead set on arranging that marriage for me, and I bet the announcement went viral while we spoke. And there was nothing I could do to prevent it from happening. I was just a pawn in my father's games. A puppet that gets eliminated if it makes the wrong move or becomes redundant.

"Good. Come on." He turned to open the car door for me. "Get in."

THEO CHOSE A SAFE PLACE, ensuring I wouldn't make a scene because he took me to my favorite outdoor restaurant and ordered a coffee that I always chose—*playing a loving boyfriend, huh?*

"Melanie, it was a fatal misunderstanding." He reached for my hand that I nervously played with on the wooden table, and I instantly removed it.

"A fatal misunderstanding?" I scoffed, shaking my head. "I always knew she'd set her eyes on you, but I didn't think you were fucking her behind my back."

"Lower your voice, please," he hissed, and I burst into derisive laughter.

"Or what?"

"I guess you don't want to make a scene here, do you?" I knew he brought me here to avoid a real confrontation.

"How long, Theo?" I looked him in the eyes, and even though I tried to hide the pain he caused me, I knew he could see it. "How long have you been cheating on me?"

"I'm not cheating on you, Melanie," he replied firmly, adjusting himself on the chair. "It was a mistake. I was drunk and frustrated. Guys kept mocking me that they get laid more than I do even though they're single."

"Oh, poor you." I pouted my lips, making a sad face. "Of course, it's a good reason to cheat on your girlfriend. Why am I even mad?" I was dripping with sarcasm, and he rolled his eyes. *Why did he even talk about our sex life with his friends?* Pathetic.

"Baby, I'm sorry, okay?" He tried to sound repentant, but I couldn't spot even a trace of regret on his face. "But nothing happened. I swear."

"Nothing happened because I interrupted you." I sneered.

"Okay, I won't lie." He rested back on the chair, sighing. "I don't know what would've happened if it weren't for you, but I'm so glad you found us, Melanie. I don't want anyone else but you, and I couldn't forgive myself if I lost you."

"Too late, Theo," I said dryly. "You already lost me. No matter what happens next, I'll never be yours again." Even if it meant leading an unhappy life beside the man I didn't love. Just like my mother.

"But we're getting married—"

"So you knew about it." I scoffed, looking away. The more time I spent with the man I used to see my future with, the more sheer disappointment rushed through me. How could I be so blind before?

"My father mentioned that to me some time ago," he admitted reluctantly.

"So you're just like them. You take part in their games. Let them manipulate me."

"It's not like that, Melanie." He furrowed his brows, trying to grab my hand again, but I didn't let him. I didn't want him to touch me. I was disgusted that I trusted him while he played me this whole time. "I thought you'd be happy. And I didn't tell you because I wanted to surprise you. Baby, I've always wanted to marry you. I love you."

"Save it, Theo." I threw a napkin that I kept squeezing in my hand and stepped away from the table. "If you loved me as you claim you do, you wouldn't have put your hands down my friend's pants."

FOUR

Shane

"We have confirmed that Melanie Atwood, this year's candidate running for the governor of California, Dedrick Atwood's daughter, and Theo Ledford, the son of our current governor, are getting married." I heard a familiar voice of the lady from the news and put away the weights before I sat down on the training bench, breathing heavily after the killer workout. I wiped the sweat from my forehead and reached for the remote to turn the sound up. "The engagement party is to be held this Saturday in the private estate of Mr. Atwood. We wonder…" She kept talking about Melanie and Ledford, but I couldn't focus. I saw her picture on the TV screen hanging on the wall in the gym I had in this house I'd just got the keys to a few hours prior. I assumed I'd stay in LA for longer due to my task, and I wasn't the type to stay at hotels. Cameras in every corner of the building, nosy staff or guests. Not my thing. But this information hit me like a wrecking ball. Were they getting married? She hadn't mentioned anything. Besides, the last time I saw her, she didn't look like someone about to get engaged. I knew every other woman wouldn't stop rambling about the upcoming engagement or wedding. White dress and all this shit. But not her. She instead looked like someone who just heard a death sentence.

I ran up the new, shiny granite stairs to my vast bedroom. I could get used to this place. It had everything I needed and a stunning view of the soothing, sunny beach—something I didn't have back in New York. I looked across the room for my phone. In my twenty-five years of existence, I could never get used to having it around.

"Boss?" I heard my right-hand man's deep voice.

"Callan, I need you to get me an invite for Melanie Atwood's engagement party." I went straight to the point. I wasn't the one to waste my time on superfluous courtesy, even if Callan was not only a member of our Mafia but my most trusted friend.

"How do ya think I can do that?" He scoffed. He was the only one of our men who wasn't shitting his pants in front of me, and I liked that. I think that's why I blurred the boss-subordinate line with him. "That's fuckin' impossible. They'll never let ya in. Should I remind ya, you're a freakin' Vergoossen?"

"I don't care how you do that. You do that," I said, unfazed. "Or you're out."

I heard him sighing heavily before he replied, "Fine. Consider it done."

I smiled, amused he took me seriously, and I ended the call. I threw the phone on my king-size bed's black silky duvet and headed to the bathroom for a long, cold shower.

The week had passed in a blink. I got caught up settling in my temporary new home and enjoyed the night charms of lustful LA. I felt like I was on a vacation I'd never had. No rules, no duties. Away from the dark side of my life. I glanced over at my reflection in the mirror and ran my fingers through my hair, putting it back into place. I wore a black tailored suit over a slightly unbuttoned black shirt, revealing my two olive branches inked above the word PURE on the front of my neck. No tie. I grabbed the keys to my Bugatti and headed down the stairs to the garage. I got in the car and soon enjoyed my favorite sound of the running engine–music to my ears.

"ELLIOT WRIGHT." I looked straight into the butler's eyes, who nodded before searching for the name across the guest list.

"Welcome, Mr. Wright," he greeted me with a polite smile. "Have an unforgettable evening, sir." I knew Callan wouldn't fail at finding a way to get me in.

I nodded my head, smirking.

AMELIA KAPPE

Sure as fuck it's going to be an unforgettable evening, I thought as I walked past the older man, entering the gleaming entryway of Atwood's residence. I was greeted by a long-legged gorgeous brunette who fetched me a glass of champagne. She smiled alluringly before leading me to a grand and opulent, lofty room with round tables decorated with white flowers and a live band playing classical music in the background. I drank the sweet and bubbly liquid in one go and put the empty glass on a silver plate that a walking-by waiter was holding. I squeezed through the crowd of overdressed people to the back of the room and rested my body weight on my left arm, leaning against a wall shimmering from the crystal chandeliers spiraling down the high ceiling. I put my hands in the pocket of my pants, not too elegant of a move, but I was bored as fuck.

People around me were chatting and laughing, jamming my own thoughts. Suddenly, the hall fell silent, and everyone gasped. And I saw her. *Melanie*, accompanied by her to-be-fiancé, his hand on her back. The guests started clapping, and she blushed. Her gaze dropped to the ground, and she nervously played with her fingers. I couldn't grasp why she seemed so timid. I thought she'd be used to such show-offs by now. Besides, she looked stunning. Breathtaking. She wore a black, long dress, glimmering in silver, perfectly tightening her slender body, and with a sexy high cut on her left leg. She had her platinum waves half up, half down, with two shorter strands left loose on each side of her beautiful face. Her long, sparkling nails perfectly matched the white-gold

OVERDOSED

rings, bracelets, and a double-layered long choker falling right into her cleavage, bringing attention to the deep *V* neckline embracing her round breasts. My cock stirred against my zipper, and I straightened up. *She looked like a fucking goddess that I'd die to fuck.*

"Thank you, everyone, for coming," Ledford said, wearing a shit-eating grin. "It is a meaningful evening for us. I'm going to ask my beautiful girlfriend, Melanie, one of the most important questions, and we want you all to be here with us when it happens." I narrowed my eyes as I watched the golden boy giving the speech proud as a peacock. He pulled Melanie's body closer to his, grinning like a Cheshire cat, but she… She seemed upset as if it was a performance, a shit show in which she was forced to participate.

Melanie hesitantly looked around the room until her gaze met mine. Her gleaming yet sad eyes grew wide with pure shock and confusion. It was apparent the sight of me had taken her aback. Suddenly, everything around me was a blur. It felt like there was only Melanie and me, staring into each other's eyes like hypnotized, helplessly trying to break the invisible, electric attraction between us. She bit her lower lip involuntarily, and her chest was moving up and down heavier and slower.

"Enjoy your evening, everyone! We'll gather here again at eight!" Theo exclaimed, and the guests applauded before the band started playing music and everyone was off to dance.

I rushed toward her. My gaze never left hers as I approached her. I could sense her heart beating faster and stronger with every step I took. Her petite body was quivering.

"Hello, Miss Atwood," I said, nodding slightly and smiling. "It's a pleasure to see you again." Melanie was rooted to the spot. It seemed like she wanted to say something, but no words would come out of her mouth. She just kept glaring into my eyes.

"I don't believe we've been introduced to each other, Mr....?" Ledford slid his hand around Melanie's waist as if my presence alone felt like a threat to him, and I smirked.

I switched my attention to him. "Wright. Eliot Wright," I said, unfazed, and from the corner of my eye, I noticed a puzzled expression written all over Melanie's beautiful face. "May I say your date looks ravishing?" I stated, looking back at the face of an angel.

"She does," he replied dryly. "Excuse us, Mr. Wright, but I need a moment alone with my fiancée."

"Future fiancée," Melanie cut him off, and it was the first time I'd heard her soothing voice this evening. Ledford's face went red. He clenched his teeth, seething. I barely refrained from laughing.

"Melanie—" He started, but I cut him off before he could continue.

"May I have this dance?" I said, loud and clear, my gaze fixed on Melanie's as I reached my hand to her.

"With pleasure." She rested her slim palm on mine, and I smiled, unable to fight the urge to run my thumb over her soft skin.

I led her toward the dance floor, leaving the redundant piece of this puzzle with his jaw wide open. I twirled Melanie around, admiring her perfect curves embraced by the shimmering dress, before sliding my hand on her waist from behind, pressing her body tightly against mine. I seized her by the slender forearm as she tightened her fingers on my collar, tilting her head to the side and back to look me in the eyes, leaning in on my chest, melting in my arms. I cast my gaze down and locked it with hers. Our lips just inches away, our heavy breaths mingling. Her other hand rested on her waist, just below mine, our fingers touching.

"Why are you doing this?" I asked, swaying our bodies to the rhythm of the music.

"Doing what?" She whispered, her voice shivering.

"Marrying a man who you don't want to marry."

"How can you know what I want?" She objected before I whirled her around again. She fell into my arms, and I slid my hand to the small of her back, claiming her as if she belonged to me. I didn't give a fuck that all the guests kept glancing at us, whispering, gossiping. Melanie didn't care either. She set her gaze on mine again, resting one hand on my arm and the other left cupped in mine as we kept dancing. "You don't even know me."

"Hardly," I said before leaning down to whisper against her ear, "But I know you feel it too."

"What exactly?"

"The attraction," I stated, satisfied like the cocky bastard I was. "I see how your body trembles at my touch. Even though you try to hide it, I can see it, Melanie. Feel it."

"Who the hell are you?" She stepped back to look at me.

I moved closer to her and gazed down into her puzzled eyes. "Tonight, I'm Elliot Wright, whoever the hell he is. I'm also your savior."

"My savior?" She scoffed. "What are you going to save me from?

"The biggest mistake you're about to make," I stated firmly, unfazed. She gave me the most perplexed look I'd ever seen and said nothing. The music stopped playing, and I nodded, thanking her for the dance before kissing her hand. As I lifted my head to meet her luminous eyes, I whispered, "Meet me upstairs at the library in fifteen minutes," before leaving her, completely flabbergasted, to her boyfriend heading her way.

FIVE

Melanie

"Melanie!" Theo's enraged tone rang in my ears, but all I could focus on was *him*.

I watched Shane walking away, admiring the nonchalant way he took each step. He looked like a Prince Charming in his elegant, well-fitted black tuxedo, yet at the same time so dark, *dangerous*.

"Melanie, for fuck's sake!" My fiancé-to-be squeezed my arm painfully, leaning down to my face, hissing through his clenched teeth. "Is this some twisted retribution?"

"Retribution?" I asked, still perplexed by Shane's words. I could still feel his electric touch lingering on my skin. His magnetic sky-blue glanced before my eyes.

"Don't play dumb! You know what I'm talking about," Theo whisper-yelled against my ear, peeking around anxiously. "Who was that man?"

"I don't know…" I let out a quiet sigh. I was asking myself the same question.

Who is the mysterious man with the captivating touch and an electrifying gaze?

What is he doing at my engagement party?

It can't be a coincidence, can it?

"You don't know?" Theo scoffed. "Well, okay. I'll tell you who he is not." He was seething. "He's not your fucking fiancé. I am!" He barely kept his voice low before letting go of my arm's tightening grip and trotting toward the exit, grabbing a glass of champagne on the way that he drank in one go.

It was so unlike Theo. He'd never acted so disrespectfully toward me. What had changed then? Had he felt that he was losing the ground beneath his feet?

I looked around to spot people staring at me, but I didn't care. For the first time in my life, I wasn't burning in shame. Instead, I was occupied by Shane's husky voice ringing in my ears. *"Meet me upstairs at the library in fifteen minutes."* I was occupied with figuring out a way to escape this ridiculous engagement party that shouldn't have taken place, a way to sneak out to the library to meet my mysterious man.

I WAS CLIMBING UP THE STAIRS, and the clicking of my heels against the polished marble stone was the only thing masking the sound of my pumping heart. I headed to the library to meet Shane. I had to know who he was or what he wanted from me. I had to see him once more before making a lifetime commitment to another man. The adrenaline was rushing through my veins like never before. I felt like a thief breaking into someone's property, sneaking out of my engagement party to see a man I knew nothing about. It felt so wrong yet so right at the same time.

"Where do you think you're going?" I jumped out in fear hearing my father's harsh voice as I reached the end of the stairs.

I swallowed, peeking behind him at the door leading to the library where I knew Shane was supposed to wait. Was I busted? Did my father find him? My hands started shaking, and I felt like I was suffocating.

"Melanie?" He said, his tone raised, watching me.

"I'm going to my room to change," I managed to blurt the words, swallowing the lump in my throat.

"Change?" He stood there like a firewall with his arms crossed and frowning.

"Yes." I cleared my throat to sound more convincing, straightening up. "I have another dress prepared for the proposal."

"Women." He rolled his eyes obnoxiously before heading down the stairs.

I slowly took a few steps toward my room, turning back to check if my father had walked away, nervously playing with my fingers.

"YOU CAME," SHANE SAID, entirely composed, holding his hands behind his back as I entered the library.

"I was hesitant for a moment, but I had to come," I stated, my voice trembling.

Shane slowly took a few steps closer, reaching his hand behind me to close the door. His gaze fixated on me, and a soft smile curled up in the corner of his tempting lips. He rested his hand on the doorframe and leaned down to look at me, holding me semihostage between his toned body and the heavy wooden door behind me. I kept holding my breath as if scared to let myself indulge in his intoxicating body scent combined with his smoky and spice cologne of musk and patchouli, which was like an aphrodisiac to me *or a drug*. Yes, definitely a drug. His scent alone made me feel like I was on the highest dosage of the most addictive drug that ever existed, the one that, once tried, made you crave more.

"You had to?" he teased, grabbing my chin with his fingers and running his thumb over my slightly parted lips as our gazes locked.

Shivers danced down my spine, but I tried to play it cool, pretending that his touch didn't have such an overwhelming effect on me. "Yes. I need to know who you are and why you're here. Are you a reporter? Did someone send you to snoop around?"

He scoffed, still hovering over me. "You really don't recognize me?"

"Should I?" I was taken aback. Had we met before? I was sure he was just a stranger nearly hitting me with his car, but now I wasn't sure anymore.

I scanned his face carefully, starting from his side-shaved, raven-dark hair pleasingly falling onto his forehead, down to his beautifully gleaming aquamarine hooded eyes, straight nose, and dark stubble enhancing his sharp jawline and narrow lips. Inch by inch, but I still hadn't remembered meeting him before. I was pretty sure I would recall the beauty of this man. I took a deep breath, fighting the growing urge to taste those alluring lips of his. I cast my eyes to catch him hungrily gawking down at my lips. But unlike me, he was composed, his breath slow and steady. I could tell he knew how to control his emotions. I, in turn, was barely restraining myself from throwing myself at him like a beast unleashed from its cage, devouring him. My body refused to obey me, trembling under his touch as he ran his fingertips down my bare arm. Hell, I wasn't sure if I could bear the sexual tension between us. Deep down, I begged him to break finally and kiss me. Or even better, fuck me. I was craving his touch underneath the clothes lingering against my skin. He leaned down even farther so that our lips were parted by nothing but our warm breaths. He rested his forehead on mine, trapping me with both his arms.

Was he fighting the urge to kiss me like I was?

"You don't know what you're doing," I breathed against his lips. "If my father sees us here, he will hurt you."

He didn't seem to care about what I'd said. Instead, he scoffed, smirking provocatively, which was hot to me. It was the first time I met someone indifferent to my father. Before, everyone else had always been so tense, petrified even as soon as I mentioned my father. Or even worse, when he was around. But Shane didn't give a damn, which attracted me even more to him.

"I'm not afraid of your father," he whispered, slowly stepping back before looking piercingly into my eyes. "I'm not afraid of anyone, Melanie."

I looked at him, somewhat intrigued. "Who are you?"

He stood still like a statue, focused on me before stating, "I'm Shane Vergoossen."

Vergoossen.

My blood ran cold. I should've run away after hearing this surname, but of course, I didn't.

The Vergoossens were the most powerful family I had heard of in the United States with Dutch roots thus the unique last name. The business magnates and investors owning a variety of companies. According to Forbes, the wealthiest family in the world. Although the Vergoossen family was well known, I did not recognize Shane. Yes, I heard that name often, but they tended to avoid media and stay low-key. There were some rumors they had associations with the Mafia, hence why they were so rich and influential, but to me, it sounded surreal. Supposedly, Shane, being Karl Vergoossen's oldest son, was the heir to the Vergoossens' empire. I had no idea if any of this was true. All I knew for sure was that Karl Vergoossen was the greatest enemy of my father. It all made sense to me why Shane wasn't afraid of him. The Vergoossens did not fear anything or anyone. On the contrary, people feared them. But what was he doing at my house? At the lion's den?

"If you want to get out of this ridiculous engagement thing, be at the back of the service entrance." His raspy voice snapped me out of my thoughts. "Eight o'clock, sharp," he added before turning on his heel and leaving through the other door leading to a reading room no one ever used and through which you could reach the back stairs.

How the hell did he know about it?

TIME PASSED, AND I got back to my engagement party. Theo dragged me to join his parents, who, as he claimed, were dying to talk to me. I sat by the round table beautifully decorated with white cloth, golden ornaments, cream, and pale-rose peonies. The dinner was already served, and a delicious smell of food was reaching my nose. I had Theo making jokes on my right and my parents laughing at his every comment on my left. In front of me were Theo's parents grinning proudly at their son and his sister, who definitely didn't enjoy her evening. *I could relate.* I glanced across the room, wondering what was going through the heads of all the guests. A lady in red that I'd never seen before was flirting with a man in a dark suit, not paying attention to his date sitting just beside him. I wondered if that was how my life would look if I married Theo? Once a cheater, always a cheater, no?

I scanned the room further, realizing all the important figures were there. Nothing new. My father was a famous politician and businessman. Another question ran through my head: was the rich people's world so rotten? Was it a standard for them to cheat? Did love even exist in this world of money, power, and fame? Even though I was raised among the wealthy, I'd always felt I didn't fit into this world. Maybe because I knew I had nothing. Everything belonged to my father, who, for some reason, despised me. I wasn't a "spoiled rich girl" like other girls from society. I knew I was on my own.

I took a deep breath, focusing on what was happening at my table. Despite the chatter and laughter, I couldn't concentrate on anything but Shane's image before my eyes and the unconventional suggestion he made at the library.

"You look phenomenal in that dress, darling," Victoria, Theo's mother, exclaimed before taking a long sip of her champagne. She looked so much like her son that it was impossible not to guess they were family. She had golden waves the same shade as her son, fair skin, and hazel eyes. She was gorgeous with exceptional taste in fashion and particularly attentive to her appearance. Although she was in her forties, many had mistaken her for Theo's sister on plenty of occasions. Even her own daughter, Natalia, who was only sixteen, sometimes looked more mature. Natalia, in contrast, favored their father. Long thick hair in the deep chocolate shade, golden skin tone, and amber eyes, just like Robert.

"Thank you, Mrs. Ledford," I replied timidly. Victoria had the overwhelming kind of aura that made it impossible for me to feel comfortable around her. She craved attention and loved being in the spotlight, unlike me.

"I agree with my mother, Melanie." Theo slid his hand around my waist, smiling. "You outshine the brightest of the stars tonight." *Cliché.*

"You should go to powder your nose, sweetie," my mother squeezed my arm gently, semiwhispering into my ear. "It's nearly eight. It's time for the proposal. You should look your best."

"Eight?" Suddenly my heart started pumping heavily again. Everyone looked at me, somewhat puzzled. I was barely composing my nerves because I knew I didn't want to marry a man who just a few days ago was fucking my so-called friend. I didn't want to live my mother's life unhappy and without love. At the same time, I was hesitant about whether I could trust Shane Vergoossen or not. Most likely not. But could it stop the invisible, irresistible pull toward this man?

Be at the back of the service entrance. Eight o'clock, sharp.

Shane's husky voice was rumbling in my ears. With each passing second, my heart was beating faster, more forceful. My breath was unsteady, heavy. What was I supposed to do? I had no idea why he showed up in my life at my engagement party. What were his intentions? I was damn sure he had some ulterior motives, yet the scent of this man, his lingering touch, and mesmerizing eyes held me captive. Intoxicated. Craving more.

My mother nudged me discreetly, whispering, "Melanie?"

I cleared my throat and put down the napkin that I was nervously squeezing in my hand. "Excuse me. I need to powder my nose," I said before leaving the table.

I was rushing toward the restroom, adrenaline growing in my veins. Everything around became a blur. I couldn't hear the tittle-tattles or the slow classical music. All I could hear was my heartbeat.

"Melanie." I felt a firm grip on my left elbow and turned to see my boyfriend. "Do you want me to accompany you?"

"To the toilet?" I breathed heavily.

"Yes, you look pale."

"No," I huffed. "I'm just a little stressed. That's all."

"Are you sure?" He frowned. His eyes darted back and forth between mine.

"I'm sure, Theo." I managed to steady my breath. "I'll be right back." I gave him a reassuring yet fake smile before turning on my heels and heading down the hall.

I FOUND MYSELF RUNNING through the long hallways of my father's residence with a thousand questions crossing my mind. I looked at the vast clock hanging in the middle of the beige wall to check the time. It was almost eight. I grabbed the lower part of my dress to make it easier for me to run faster. Until I finally took a breath of fresh air, inhaling and exhaling heavily, looking at Shane sitting on a motorcycle.

My eyes grew wide in pure shock. I had never ridden on a motorcycle before, and he expected me to do it in a ball gown? It was crazy.

"Jump on!" The running motorcycle engine muffled his husky voice.

I spotted my fiancé-to-be's best friend, watching me, baffled, with his jaw dropping to the ground. He must've grasped what was going on. That was when I knew if I didn't make a move now, I'd have to go back to my engagement party and say *yes* to the man I didn't love.

"It's now or never. Hop on!" Shane shouted, and for some reason, his voice tamed my rumbling heart.

Without a second thought, I dashed down the stairs of my father's luxurious mansion, jumped on his Harley Davidson bike, and rode away with the sexiest, most dangerous man I'd ever met, a Mafia heir, *Shane Vergoossen.*

SIX

Shane

We entered the main hall of the mansion I bought for myself in LA for the time being, and Melanie seemed to be taken aback. She scanned the spacious foyer, the latte-colored walls lighted by the crystal chandeliers. The polished marble floor looked like a sheet of glass. She took a few slow steps and gently rested her hand on the fancy black railing of the wooden espresso staircase leading upstairs.

"No longer staying in a hotel?" she said rather more assumingly than questioningly before turning back to face me.

"I value my privacy," I replied. "That's something I can't get in a hotel."

She only nodded slightly, setting her gaze on the paintings hanging on the wall.

"Want something to drink?" I asked, admiring her angelic beauty. Her hairstyle was messy from the helmet and the wind after driving here on my bike, but she still looked like a goddess.

She sighed quietly before replying, "Yes, please."

"After you," I said, pointing her toward the kitchen.

She swallowed hard before following my lead. I bet she had crazy thoughts running through her head. I bet she had been wondering what the hell she was doing there with me. To be frank, I had been wondering that myself. I hadn't expected she would run away from her engagement party with me. A stranger. An enemy to her family. I had expected a spoiled rich girl, too puffed up with her own vanity. Instead, I met a fragile woman full of fear and pain in her eyes. The pain she so desperately tried to hide. That made me wonder, what was going on behind the closed door of her luxurious life?

But also… *How the hell was I supposed to stick to the plan?*

I COULDN'T HELP but check out Melanie's sexy curves, which were more exposed as she leaned against a shiny whitish countertop that contrasted the black design of the kitchen. I fought a smirk that desperately was forming in the corner of my mouth at the thought of fucking her in this position. My cock twitched in my pants, and I shook my head before following to the fridge, leaving the sinful thoughts behind.

"Are you hungry?" I asked, searching through the full refrigerator. Gladly, I had hired a housekeeper that took care of the grocery shopping.

"Starving, honestly." She smiled. Her voice was so soothing. "I haven't eaten anything since yesterday."

I looked back to face her, alarmed that she hadn't eaten in a day. I frowned, and she straightened up as if anxious.

"I couldn't force myself to eat anything." The words were blurting out of her mouth. "I've been under a lot of pressure lately."

Melanie was nervously playing with her fingers, just like that night in the hotel room. She sank her teeth into her lower lip, and her gaze dropped to the tile floor. I was good at reading body language. It was a part of my training to read your enemy's emotions. I could tell Melanie was dealing with overwhelming anxiety. Again, that was not what I expected. That was not what I signed up for.

I approached her slowly and gently grabbed her chin with my fingers to make her look into my eyes. "Hey," I whispered. "Don't do this."

"Do what?" She gave me a startled look.

"Don't be afraid. I'm not going to hurt you." I caressed her cheek with my thumb, and for a second, it seemed like she let herself indulge in my touch.

She took a deep breath, swallowing hard. "Why are you doing this, Shane?"

I narrowed my eyes, my voice soft. "What?"

"Playing a knight in shining armor. Pretending that you care about me." She stepped back, taking a better look at my face. "We both know who you are."

"So I am a villain in your story?"

"No," she objected. "I mean… we both know who we are to each other. Who our families are."

"Who are we, Melanie?" I said, challenging.

"You're a Vergoossen, and I am an Atwood," she said dryly. "Everyone knows there's a running battle between our families. My father would—"

She hesitated, and I cut her off. "I don't care, do you?"

Her eyes grew wide as she looked at me, astonished. Her lips slightly parted.

"Why are you so scared of your father?" I asked, setting my eyes on hers, but she avoided my gaze.

She cleared her throat, looking down at her fingers, nervously playing with them again. "That's… not something that should concern you."

I inhaled heavily before moving closer to her, gently grabbed her hands, and cupped them in mine, caressing her long slender fingers, her skin so soft.

"I don't know what happened between you and your father, and I respect that you're not ready to tell me," I said softly, and she cast her thick black lashes to meet my gaze. "But it's evident that you live your life in the shadow of fear and the rules he set. That's not how it's supposed to be."

I felt like a hypocrite telling her that she should live her life like she wanted to, not caring about the rules, while I myself had been living my whole life driven by vengeance, following the rules of our crime ring to one day take the reign. That moment with Melanie made me stop and wonder, was it how I wanted my life to look like? Was taking my father's place in the dangerous world we lived in what I wanted? That was what I'd been prepared for, ever since I was born. But that was not what I chose myself. At the same time, I knew there was no escape. Not for me—*my father's oldest son, his rightful heir.*

"I'll cook something," I said, figuring it would be best if we changed the topic.

"You?" She smirked, her tone somewhat sarcastic.

"Why? Can't a man cook a tasty meal?" I teased, and she chuckled. Her luminous almond eyes brightened up.

"No, that's not what I meant," she said with an apologetic tone, her cheeks flushed red.

"It's okay. I'm just teasing you." I tried to dispel the shame in her. In some twisted way, I wanted to change that she was so shy and insecure. I tried to find that hidden within her self-confidence and unleash it, bring it to the surface. "Now come on, sit and relax while I make magic." I winked at her flirtatiously, and she chuckled freely.

I took off the blazer and tossed it onto the high stool next to the kitchen island. I undid a few buttons of my white shirt and rolled up the sleeves. Melanie watched me as if mesmerized until our gazes locked, and she cupped her face in her hands, laughing.

"MMM, IT'S DELICIOUS." Melanie purred like a kitten, chewing the first bite of sweet and spicy tofu served with vegetables I'd prepared.

She sat across the table, keeping her distance, and frankly, I was thankful for that. She had something in her that had awakened the wicked beast in me. I watched her licking the sauce that dripped down her luscious lips, barely keeping myself from kissing her. I had imagined how she would purr underneath me while I licked her sensitive skin. My breath quickened as I pictured devouring her, wondering what she tasted like. I shook my head, annoyed how this woman made my blood drain from my brain straight to my dick.

"Why aren't you eating?" She wiped her lips, this time using a napkin. Thank God she hadn't licked her lips as before because I wasn't sure if I could tame my lust again. "You didn't have to cook vegan if you don't like vegan food."

"I don't mind," I replied before clearing my throat, dispelling the lascivious thoughts consuming my mind. "So, are you a vegan? For how long?"

"I wouldn't call myself a vegan."

I raised my eyebrow, smiling. "Why did you ask if I have something vegan?"

"I like to eat healthily. However, I love seafood too much to give up on it completely. Hence, I wouldn't label myself as a vegan." She smiled, looking straight into my eyes. "More like a fan of a healthy lifestyle. I have some crazy rules I like to stick to regarding how I treat my body."

Oh, you have no idea how I would treat your body.

"Intriguing, Miss Atwood," I said teasingly, taking a sip of red Bordeaux. "Tell me about those crazy rules."

"No." She smiled sheepishly. "I wouldn't want to bore you."

"You don't bore me, Melanie. I insist."

"Okay." Her face brightened up.

I watched her talking about her habits with so much passion in her voice and glimmering sparks in her eyes. It was nice seeing her like this for a change. She told me she loved to start her day with a glass of water with freshly squeezed lemon and porridge with fruits, then yoga, Pilates, or a run. No wonder she looked like a model, leading such a lifestyle.

WE KEPT CHATTING, joking, and flirting, and hours passed without us realizing it. It felt so new to me and refreshing to have such a connection with someone that made me forget about the crazy world around us. And most likely, the world went insane after she had disappeared from her engagement party.

"Shane?" she asked, slightly hesitant, her big brown eyes looking in my direction. "Could you please give me something to wear? I'm sick of this dress."

"Of course," I said quietly. "Although I have not been prepared for having a female in need of some comfy clothes, I can only offer you my shirt, and maybe I'll find some shorts in which you won't drown."

She laughed softly. "A shirt will do." She looked into my eyes, and suddenly her face went dark again.

"What is it?"

"May I…" She hesitated, her voice trembling. "Stay for the night?" Her eyes darted between mine as she awaited an answer.

"That was the plan," I joked, hoping it would lighten the mood.

"Oh, so you have planned that I would stay the night, yet you haven't prepared yourself with any female stuff?" I loved when she would tease me. I loved seeing that side of her. Frisky, perky like she should always be.

"My bad." We both chuckled when my phone rang, breaking the oblivion bubble we'd been hiding in for the past few hours.

I checked my phone, and the very second I saw my father's number, I reminded myself who I was and what purpose I was supposed to serve in all of this. I took a heavy breath, realizing I was getting too comfortable with my target.

"I need to answer this," I stated firmly.

Melanie gave me an abashed look. "Of course." She looked down and bit her lower lip nervously.

"Hey, chin up," I said while walking toward her. I hated seeing her anxious. I hated myself for caring when I wasn't supposed to care. I wasn't supposed to feel anything toward her. On a day-to-day basis, I was as emotionally annihilated as my father. Then why did she manage to somehow bring emotions out of me? It wasn't who I was.

I grabbed her chin and lifted it to lock our gazes. "You may go upstairs. The second door on the left, you should be able to find a shirt in my closet." I smiled, and so did she.

"Thank you, Shane," she whispered before taking a deep breath and vanishing from my sight as she left the dining room and headed upstairs.

I turned on my heel and headed to my office before locking the door behind me. I couldn't risk her overhearing the conversation I was about to have. I walked past the wooden desk and stood by a wall-size glass window. I exhaled, feeling doubtful about my task. I hadn't expected Melanie to be so… *human.*

I unlocked my phone and searched the missed calls, picking the last incoming number.

"Hello?" My father's harsh voice rumbled through the speaker.

"What's new?" I asked, anticipating.

"What have you done?"

"What do you mean?" Judging by his cold tone, I sensed something had happened.

"Every station is airing the news about the kidnapping of Melanie Atwood from her damn engagement party." He kept a straight face even though I'm sure he was seething. But that was how he was. He was designed to keep a cool head even when all hell broke loose. That's how he wanted me to be.

"Wasn't that the plan?" I couldn't help but mock him. "Wasn't I supposed to get close to her?"

"Get close. Not kidnap," he retorted.

"I haven't kidnapped her," I said, which I was sure calmed him down. "She came here out of her own will."

I heard a deep sigh. "Stick to the plan, Shane. Don't let me down."

"I won't," I stated firmly, even though, at this point, I was questioning this fucked-up plan. "Is that all?"

"Not quite. I have intel."

"I'm listening."

"Her relationship with Ledford's son was a part of Ledford and Atwood's contract. Ledford's boy knew about it. He has been fucking another girl for months now. Our lovely Miss Atwood found out her boyfriend cheated on her and broke up with him, but her father had other plans. Hence the sped-up engagement."

"How do you know this?" I asked, my voice harsh. I knew this kind of intel shouldn't have had any effect on me, and yet, my blood boiled. I quickly put two and two together, realizing it must've been the reason why Melanie ran away with me from her engagement party. What I didn't understand was the fact that her own damn father had been treating her like a bargaining chip.

"It's not a conversation over the phone, son."

"Agreed." I inhaled deeply, wondering what else had been happening in Melanie's life.

"You have a card, now's the time to play it."

I went upstairs to my bedroom to find Melanie sitting on the edge of my bed, only wearing one of my shirts. Her back turned to me, her gaze fixed on the starry night sky through the window. Her long waves were now let loose, falling down her arms, reaching her waist. It was odd, so unlike me, but I enjoyed that view — the view of her waiting for me in my bedroom.

"Melanie?" I said softly. I didn't want to startle her, and she seemed deep in her thoughts.

"Shane?" she whispered, turning slightly to look at me. She had washed off her makeup, exposing her natural beauty.

God, she was so fucking beautiful. I loved seeing her, just like she was, without any makeup, fancy clothes, and her hair down and messy. But it wasn't just her appearance that got me hooked. It was her purity. Innocence. Kindness. She was so different from all the women I used to be involved with. Despite all the money, power, and fame, she remained vulnerable. It was rare. She was rare.

I leaned against the doorframe, admiring her beauty, watching her like a wolf watching its prey. Thirsty, hungry, big bad wolf. She stood up, turning to me, and I could marvel at her from head to toes. Her petite body was drowning in my shirt that she had left slightly unbuttoned, exposing her perky, round breasts brushing against the woolen fabric. My shirt reached her midthigh, revealing her toned, tanned legs. I swallowed hard, trying to tame my raging lust.

"Is everything okay?" she asked, her voice soft and quiet while she walked past the bedroom and moved closer to me.

"The way you look in my shirt," I said, devouring her with my gaze. "God. Do you have any idea how attractive you are?"

She blushed, smiling sheepishly, and I wondered how such a sex bomb could be so coy.

"Shane…" she whispered hesitantly, looking at me in a way that I couldn't figure out her thoughts. Her eyes darted between mine expectantly while she unwittingly licked her bottom lip.

"Don't, Melanie…" I hissed, fighting the temptation she was. "Don't bite your lip like that or else—"

She cut me off. "Or else?" She took a few more steps closer to me, not breaking eye contact. She stood in the doorway, right before me, breathing heavily. Although she could boast a model height, me being six-two, I still hovered over her by at least five inches, which gave me a perfect view into her exposed cleavage.

I clenched my fist, taking a deep breath. "Melanie, I'm barely restraining myself."

"Restraining yourself from what?"

"Ripping my shirt off of you and fucking you senseless," I rasped, looking straight into her eyes that, to my surprise, turned black with desire.

"Do it," she whispered without thinking twice. Her gaze fixed on me.

Do it.

It was enough to break all the boundaries I set for myself. It was crazy how attracted I was to her, how her presence alone made me burn with lust. I'd never felt such a pull toward anyone else before.

I threw myself at her like a starving beast at his prey, crashing my lips onto hers, kissing her hungrily. I grabbed her hand and pinned it against the wall she was resting on and above her head. I moved my other hand between her thighs, reaching the hem of her lacy thong before sliding my fingers beneath the lacy fabric. I felt her body tremble as I rubbed my fingers around her hard bud. My hard shaft twitched against her belly, aching to be inside her. I glided my fingers lower, reaching her dripping-wet center before slipping my finger through her juices, and she moaned loud against my lips.

"Oh, fuck," she breathed as I kept pulling my fingers in and out of her, fingering her faster and more forceful. At this point, I lost all the control I'd been restraining, unleashing the savage beast inside me.

I lusted for her. I craved her like a madman. And I was going to get her. There was no way I could resist the wild desire.

I held her hand tighter to keep her steady on her shaking legs. Her whole body was trembling from my touch, from the wicked pleasure I'd been giving her. Her walls squeezing around my fingers, coating them with her moisture completely. I watched her fighting the growing ecstasy, her sheepish gaze replaced with a sultry, seductive, sinful one.

"Don't come yet," I commanded into her ear before I pulled back, licking the taste of her off my fingers, and a deep growl escaped my throat.

She watched me burning, begging for more. I grabbed her by her ass, kneading it with my fingers, and lifted her, biting her lip playfully before kissing her, hard and demanding, our tongues tangling up. She slid her hands to the back of my head, running her long fingers through my hair, pulling me closer, deepening the kiss. I carried her to the bed before tossing her onto the dark, silky duvet. She lay there with her lips swollen, ragged breath, seductively unbuttoning my shirt she was wearing, exposing her body to me in its full glory.

"Take me, Shane," she pleaded, and even something so wicked sounded so innocent coming out of her luscious lips.

I ripped the shirt I wore off and threw it somewhere on the floor before jumping on top of her. She placed her trembling hand on my cheek and wrapped her leg around my waist, her sultry eyes staring into mine. I didn't want to rush. I wanted to savor every moment, every inch of her sexy body. I ran my tongue over her slightly parted lips, and she let out a quiet sigh of pleasure. I trailed wet, warm kisses down her neck and prominent collarbone, sucking her hardened breast before moving lower until reaching her most sensitive spot. I licked her dripping sex, and a loud moan filled the room. She arched her back, giving me better access to where she craved me the most. I sucked and licked her sensitive bud alternately, making her moan and breathe heavily. She slid her hand at the back of my neck, pulling my head closer, and I growled. I loved when she lost herself to lust. I loved when she took control of what she wanted and became selfish and dominant when her insecurities and shyness wouldn't overshadow her needs.

"I want you," she breathed. "I want all of you, Shane."

I moved back, licking the remaining juices off my lips. Fuck, she tasted so good.

I reached into the drawer of my nightstand for protection, but before I took it out, Melanie whispered, "I'm on the pill."

I was satisfied hearing that. I preferred sex without condoms, it was a whole different experience. I jumped on top of her, resting my body weight on my arms so that she was trapped underneath me.

"How do you want me, Melanie?" I wanted to hear her saying that. Admitting that she wanted me to fuck her.

She stared into my eyes, her body trembling before she whispered, "I want to feel you inside."

I leaned down to kiss her, adjusting myself between her thighs. "Fuck," I growled, pushing my cock deep inside her, and she let out a sweet moan as if in sync with me, spreading her legs wider to accommodate my full length.

SEVEN

Melanie

I opened my eyes, still groggy, to see the sun was already up and its rays peeking through the enormous window, brightening up the dark room. I was snuggled into Shane's broad chest, inhaling his addictive scent. I bit my lower lip and felt my cheeks burning at the flashes from last night. It was wild... *and oh so good.* I traced the firm lines of Shane's abs with my fingertips, wondering when I'd had such mind-blowing sex last, realizing that... never. I'd wondered if that was just a dream, and I would wake up from this oblivion any minute now. I wanted to savor this moment while it still lasted. I gently pulled out of his embrace and sat beside him, covering my naked body with the silky duvet, staring at the piece of art he was. He was so devilishly handsome. No doubt he would tempt a saint into sin with no effort. His body was too perfect to be real, yet there he was. I scanned every inch of it carefully, engraving the sight of him deep into my memory. I'd realized he was heavily inked, but a rose underneath the word MERCY tattooed on his hand caught my attention. I peeked over at his right hand to see a whole sentence inked above his knuckles, and I slowly leaned in to read what it said, "Destruction is a form of creation," with three crossed swords above the phrase. I wondered if his tattoos had any meaning to him.

"Good morning." His still sleepy, husky voice murmuring in my ear snapped me out of my thoughts. He put his hand at the back of my head, entangling it with my hair, and pleasant shivers swept down my spine. "What are you looking at?"

"Your tattoos," I admitted, slightly abashed. "Do they have any meaning to you?"

He took a deep breath before pulling up and resting his back on the cushioned headboard. "Most of them, yes."

"What does the rose one stand for?" I asked, and it seemed like I hit the wrong spot.

He looked away, and his eyes filled with pain.

"I'm sorry." I quickly picked up on the mood change. The atmosphere suddenly became so heavy and dark. "I shouldn't have asked."

"It's okay, Melanie," he said softly before gazing at me. "Let's get us something to eat." *A way to escape the topic.* "There's a nice restaurant nearby that may serve porridge with fruits."

I was taken aback, he remembered. I thought he was just pretending to listen to my rambling the day before.

He cleared his throat, looking around the floor with the pieces of our clothes scattered all over it, and I bet my cheeks flushed the deepest shade of red.

"Shane?" I said timidly, and he turned to face me. "About last night…" I felt the urge to clarify this to him. I wasn't myself the other night. Not that I regretted what happened, but it was so unlike me. Usually, I would never end up in bed with a man I hardly knew. But with Shane, it was different. It felt like an irresistible attraction between us, pulling us to each other like magnets, pulling me to him in ways I couldn't grasp. It felt like we had shared a bond, tying us to one another before we even said *hello*. Whenever I was close to him, the world around me seemed to fade. Let alone my body's response to his touch. It was always the same, set on fire, every inch burning in need of him. Whenever he was close to me, it felt like I was losing control over my senses. It felt like he was my drug I failed to resist. Instead, I kept craving more.

"I'm sorry if I overstepped your boundaries," he cut me off, slightly troubled.

"No," I protested. *It was the best night I'd ever had.* "I just want you to know that I'm not a one-night stand kind of a girl. Usually." My cheeks burned, and I looked down at my ring finger, remembering that if it weren't for Shane, I'd wear an engagement ring on my hand. An engagement ring from a man who cheated on me and whom I didn't love, yet I couldn't help but feel guilty.

Shane reached for my hand and cupped it in his. "Who said it was a one-night stand?"

I looked at him, surprised by his words. "Shane, I have no expectations. You don't have to—"

He brought his hand to my face, running his thumb over my lips before whispering, "Don't overthink, Melanie. Let's just go with the flow. At least, for now."

I nodded, looking into his eyes that gave me a sense of security before he stole a tender kiss from me. He then got up out of bed, covered his crotch with a pillow, winked at me, and I giggled, watching him with my cheeks flushing as he headed to the bathroom.

I SCOUTED THROUGH SHANE'S FRIDGE, grabbing eggs and bacon. I put them down on the countertop and rooted around multiple shelves before finding a frying pan. I broke the eggs on the pan, sprinkled them with some neatly set herbs standing beside the stove, and added a few slices of bacon. The kitchen was filled with the smell of fried bacon and coffee that I brewed in the meantime in a fancy coffee maker. I took out ground flaxseed I'd noticed while searching for the pan from one of the shelves and smashed a banana, mixed that with vanilla, olive oil, and some water to make vegan pancakes. I might've been a fan of vegan food, but I wasn't planning on changing Shane's habits, so I've decided to prepare a regular dish for him and something vegan for myself.

"Mmm, what is that delicious smell?" Shane entered the kitchen, dressed in a white T-shirt revealing his tattoos and black pants. He grinned widely, revealing his perfect, white teeth while running his fingers through his wet hair, making my knees turn to jelly.

"I'm making us breakfast." I smirked, turning over the bacon.

"I thought I was taking you out." He leaned against the countertop opposite me, his eyes set on mine.

"And how do you think I was supposed to go? Wearing this?" I teased, indicating the oversized white shirt I was wearing.

"I have already handled that issue." He gave me a provocative wink.

"What do you mean?" I was puzzled.

He walked around the kitchen island and embraced me from behind, taking the spatula out of my hand. His intoxicating scent and warm touch, combined with cold water droplets dripping from his hair, raised goose bumps on my skin. "See for yourself," he whispered in my ear. "Go upstairs. Some bags are waiting for you in my closet. You know where to find it, right?"

Startled, I turned back to face him. "Have you been to the mall? When?"

"I haven't." He laughed. "I had Mrs. Dorothy, my housekeeper shop for me this morning. She dropped off the bags here while we were still sleeping."

"Wow." That was all that my stunned self managed to say. That was how Shane Vergoossen was. Before I even thought of something, he had already dealt with that. He was always a step ahead. "When did you contact her?"

"Yesterday," he said before moving me back from the stove. "Go. I'll take care of everything here."

I bit my lips, smiling as I watched him flipping the pancakes.

"Mmm! Banana pancakes, my favorite," he teased, and I burst out laughing before trotting upstairs.

I climbed a few stairs when a doorbell rang out through the foyer. I turned around, hesitating whether I should answer the door or hide upstairs. My heart started pumping heavily, and adrenaline rushed through my veins. I had a hunch it was my father. I was scared that he had found me.

"I'll handle it." Shane emerged from behind the wall dividing the foyer and the living room. His voice was cold and firm, and I knew something was off. "Go upstairs," he added, but I couldn't move. I stood still like a statue, rooted to the spot, with my heart beating crazily.

"I'm here for Melanie," I heard Theo's raging voice, and my blood ran cold.

How did he find me here?

"She doesn't want to see you," Shane replied with an icy tone. Although he was facing Theo, standing with his back to me, I could imagine his stone-cold gaze.

"Give me back my fiancée!" Theo hissed through clenched teeth, seething, but Shane seemed utterly unfazed.

"She's not your fiancée," he said callously, yet with a touch of sarcasm. "Besides, she's not an object that I can take or give back to you. She's a lady that can do whatever she pleases."

"Very funny, Vergoossen," Theo sneered. "I knew you seemed familiar when I saw you at my engagement party."

"The pleasure is all mine, Ledford." Shane's deep voice rumbled in my ears. I was impressed how he kept his cool while Theo looked like he was just a step away from exploding.

"Listen, dude. I am not scared of you," he hissed, clenching his jaw. "The fact that you are a Vergoossen doesn't mean a damn thing to me."

Shane scoffed. "I'm glad you don't see me through the prism of my name. Yet, I'd advise you to be careful with me." He moved closer to my ex and leaned to whisper something into his ear. I didn't catch what he said, but Theo's face went pale. I wasn't sure if it was because he spotted me, watching them half-naked in Shane's house, or because of what Shane told him.

"Melanie?" Theo said, jaw dropped, looking at me. "Did you sleep with him?"

I hadn't gotten the chance to speak when the sound of police sirens echoed through the hallway.

"We have company," Shane stated, his gaze fixed on something outside. I didn't see what or who he was looking at, but I felt it in my bones that whatever that was, spelled trouble. "Melanie, take Theo to the living room." Shane turned to face me, and I didn't even question him. I just nodded and followed his order, my heart pumping heavily and a huge lump forming in my throat.

I climbed down the stairs, grabbed Theo by his arm, and led him toward the living room, confusion written all over his face. Shane stepped outside, closing the door behind him.

Theo wandered around the room, rubbing his temples, his breath ragged before snapping at me, "What the hell, Melanie?" His eyes turned black with rage, and his voice sent dire chills down my body as he shouted, "Did he fuck you?!"

I didn't respond. I stared at him blankly, wondering how a single gaze, mere touch, or a faint scent of Shane Vergoossen had ignited a flame within me while months with Theo would make me feel nothing. I stared at the man I thought I loved, not recognizing him anymore.

"You're such a hypocrite!" he scoffed, shaking his head. "You've accused me of cheating while you're the one fucking another dude behind my back! And you played innocent."

"Don't you dare, Theo!" Something in me broke, unleashing all the resentment I'd been caging within me. "I won't take all the blame! You slept with my friend! You fucking broke my heart!"

"Broke your heart?" he mocked. "That's why you jumped into another man's bed during our fucking engagement party?! You're such a—"

"I wouldn't finish that sentence," Shane's deep voice rumbled from behind.

I turned to see Shane gazing sinisterly at Theo, and my father clenching his jaw as his eyes met mine.

EIGHT

Shane

I went out of my house, closing the door behind me. I didn't want Melanie to see him. Her father, who had arrived here with cops. *Pathetic.* I tilted my head to the side, watching him whisper something to one of the officers, who then nodded and ordered his colleagues to leave. I remained unfazed, not breaking eye contact with Dedrick Atwood, my worst enemy. A man who I wish I could kill right then and there.

"What do you want, Vergoossen?" he hissed through his clenched teeth, slowly approaching me.

"Who said I want something from you?" I smirked at the sight of him seething.

"We both know you wouldn't have shown up in California if your father didn't order you to." He looked into my eyes, breathing heavily, angrily, his hands in the pockets of his gray jacket, and whispered, "It's all about Rose, isn't it?"

I heard a noise coming from the other side of the gate surrounding my place, and I'd notice a flash of the camera. *Fucking reporters.*

I rolled my eyes, sighing. "If you want to avoid this going public, you better come inside."

"It's too late. Haven't you seen the news?" he retorted. "The whole state is talking about my daughter's kidnapping!"

"Kidnapping?" I scoffed. "Whatever, come inside, or your story will lose its credibility, and so will you." I smiled and opened the door for the man I intensely despised.

"What?" He seemed confused, but it didn't take long until he followed my gaze, realizing we'd been watched. "Fucking paparazzi." *On that, we agree.*

I LED DEDRICK toward the living room, where I heard Ledford shouting at Melanie, and my blood boiled. I wasn't supposed to, but for some fucked-up reason, I wanted to save Melanie. In a twisted way, I noticed I was chasing the wrong prey. I'd seen she was already surrounded by deadly predators, sucking the life out of her, and so, I'd become her protector.

"I wouldn't finish that sentence," I said, and both Melanie and her ridiculous ex had turned to face me. As soon as Melanie's troubled eyes met her father's, her face went pale. That was when I knew I was wrong. My whole life, I'd been told the Atwood family is my enemy, my target, with Melanie being the main pawn, prey, a key to our revenge. But it wasn't the truth. Melanie Atwood wasn't my enemy. She was my ally in a war against her father, who, I was sure, had hurt her too. She was a prisoner kept hostage in this wicked world of deceit. She was broken, damaged, and needed salvation, not destruction.

"Melanie," Atwood said, barely keeping his composure. "It's about time you end these ridiculous games of yours. We're going back home. Now."

I glanced at Melanie, who looked like she'd just seen a ghost. She swallowed hard, her hands shaking. She couldn't bring herself to open her mouth. The sight of her father was paralyzing for her. That only added to my conviction. I was after the wrong Atwood. Melanie was the only one innocent in all of this. She didn't deserve to be dragged into all this swamp. I couldn't be against her.

"Come, Melanie." Ledford grabbed her by her elbow, dragging her with him, and something inside me broke.

"Not so fast, boy." I stepped between Melanie and her ex. "You will tell her the truth, or shall I do it for you?"

He frowned, puzzled. "Fuck off, Vergoossen!"

I scoffed.

"What truth?" Melanie looked at both of us, agitated. I didn't want to break her because she was already in pieces, but I knew I had to use this card. I still had a task to do—just a different aim.

"I'm sorry, Melanie. I didn't want you to find out like this." I was genuinely sorry, which surprised even myself.

"You're on thin ice, Vergoossen," Atwood hissed warningly, but I knew he was shitting his pants, losing the ground beneath him.

"No! I'm sick of all these games!" For the first time, I saw Melanie as determined. For the first time, I didn't see her as the victim but as a fighter, a fierce warrior. "Someone tell me what's going on here, or else... I'm going to tell the press what you've done to me!" She shouted, her gaze focused on her father, and my blood ran cold at the thought of all the possible things he'd done to her.

I turned to look him in the eyes, restraining myself from putting a bullet in his head. It wasn't easy to push my buttons, but this man... fucking fueled my rage to its limits. I clenched my fists, taking a deep breath. I wanted to punch him repeatedly, savoring the feeling of life draining out of him right under my hands. Kill this fucking bastard for all he'd done to my mother... and Melanie.

"Shane?" Melanie asked pleadingly.

"Don't interfere, Vergoossen!" Ledford hissed, anxiously clenching his teeth.

"Shane, please..." Melanie moved closer, looking deeply into my eyes. For fuck's sake, I felt it in my bones that this news was going to break her. But I didn't assume that telling her would break me twice as much.

"He only dated you because of an arrangement between your father and Robert Ledford."

"What?" Her gaze dropped down, her breath heavy and ragged. I watched her beautiful brown eyes welling up with tears. "Is it true, Theo?" She looked at him, barely standing still. "All of it was just a lie?"

"Melanie." He went to grab her hand, but she yanked it away.

"Don't... touch me," she hissed.

"Enough, Melanie!" Dedrick stepped in, boiling. "We're leaving!"

"No! I'm not going with you! I'm staying here. With Shane."

Atwood clenched his fists, hissing, "You clearly don't know what you're dealing with, Vergoossen. You want war? You'll have one. We'll see who gets the last laugh." He switched his gaze to Melanie, who looked like she was breaking, and I slid my hand around her waist, pulling her tight as if she was a fragile piece of art, it's shattered pieces I was holding together, not letting her crumble. "And you, my beloved daughter, will crawl back on your knees, begging me to help you after he smashes you so hard that you won't get your shit together ever again! Mark my words." His hoarse voice rumbled through the walls before he turned on his heel and walked away, shutting the door behind him.

"I'll ruin you, Vergoossen!" Ledford yelled, reminding us of his miserable existence.

"Good luck." I smiled, and he made a hilarious sound before following Dedrick like the good dog following his master.

Melanie took a heavy breath, cupping her head with her trembling hands. She turned to look out the window, now rubbing her temples. It pained me to see her hurt. I slowly moved closer and rested my hands on her arms, inhaling the sweet scent of her hair.

"I'm sorry, Melanie," I whispered, hoping the cliché phrase would make her feel better.

"How did you know about this, Shane?" she asked, her eyes blunt, set on the clear sky.

"I had my employer look up Ledford's family," I stated.

She turned to face me, frowning. "Who are you, Shane?"

"You know that already." I looked deeply into her eyes.

"I don't think I know." She shook her head before rubbing her temples again.

I took her hands and enclosed them in mine. "Hey," I whispered before grabbing her chin with one of my hands, still holding hers in the other. "You're safe with me, Melanie. I promise. I won't let anyone hurt you. You're under my protection now."

"Why?" she asked, her eyes full of confusion and pain.

I let out a soft sigh, wondering what I was supposed to answer. The truth was, I wasn't sure myself. I couldn't explain why, but I felt the need to protect her. That was when I knew I was fucked up. I was never supposed to care about her, and yet, in such a short period of time, I did. I fucking did, and that could only spell trouble. Since Melanie Rose Atwood somehow found a way into my soul that I didn't know existed. I fought a constant battle between my inexplicable, irresistible attraction toward her and my life's mission, my duty, the fucked-up plan, *revenge*.

Melanie's eyes darted between mine. Her brows furrowed before she took a heavy breath and rubbed her face with her hands. She walked over to the table standing in the middle of the living room, grabbed the remote, and turned on the TV.

A news reporter's deep voice filled the room. "Allegedly, Melanie Atwood was kidnapped during her engagement party to Theo Ledford. The police…"

The man kept rambling, and Melanie looked like she was about to cry. I approached her and gently took the remote out of her hand, turning the sound down. I reached for my phone from my pocket and dialed the number of the station airing the news.

"What are you doing?" She glanced at me, puzzled.

"I'm calling the station to get this straight," I said, smiling.

"What do you mean?"

"I'm going to tell them the truth."

"The truth?" A soft smile curled her lips, and a tiny spark glistened in her eyes.

"Yes. That you were not kidnapped but ran away to avoid the biggest mistake of your life."

"But…" She hesitated, crossing her arms nervously, frowning again. "I'll cause a scandal."

"I don't care. Do you?"

She shook her head, chuckling softly. "No."

"Good."

"Thank you, Shane," she whispered, her eyes welling up with tears.

NINE
Melanie

I locked myself in the bathroom and stepped into the shower, overwhelmed by the prior events. I let the cold water wash away my tears. I didn't want Shane to see me miserable like this. I felt like I was wearing out my welcome in his house. But the truth was, I didn't know what to do with myself, with my life in general. I felt like I was about to break; at the same time, I was trying so fucking hard not to. I closed my eyes, letting the tears drip down my face, mingling with the water stream. Shane's words echoed in my head.

He only dated you because of an arrangement between your father and Robert Ledford.

I finally broke. I let myself cry, not holding back my tears while I washed my body inch by inch, trying to erase any memory of Theo touching me. I was so hurt that Theo, despite knowing that my father had never loved me, never cared about me, and only kept using me for his games, agreed to plot behind my back with him, my father, my worst enemy. How could I be so stupid? So blind? How did I not see it was all a part of their game? I should've known better.

I WASN'T SURE how long I spent there in the shower. A few minutes? Half an hour? More? I took a few deep breaths and stepped out, resting against the granite countertop and looking at my reflection in the mirror. My hair was wet, drops of water dripping down my bare arms until sinking into a white towel I wrapped around my naked breast. I stared at myself, feeling numb, torn, hurt, uncertain, depressed, and furious all at once. I felt like people around me never noticed what I was going through. Everyone had always assumed I led a rich and glamorous life. Many envied me for money, fame, and position. But no one had ever noticed how damaged I was. No one had seen those dark demons I fought with every single day—the kind of demons invisible to the eye, living inside you. Inside your head, broken into pieces, haunting you when you talk, laugh, eat and even sleep. But just because you couldn't see those big, sharp teeth or the scary claws didn't mean they weren't real. But that was the bare truth. That was the world I lived in. People refused to see your suffering until it went too far. They just didn't care. Until Shane… he showed up in my life at my lowest, offering me something I'd never had—a sense of security, care, and attention. I didn't understand why. Maybe I was too hungry for any of that to refuse him, despite the warning signs I chose to ignore. The fact that a man I knew for a few days gave me something my family, friends, or boyfriend failed to offer was breaking me even more.

"Melanie?" I heard soft knocks followed by Shane's husky voice rumbling through the door. "Are you okay? I'm worried. It's been an hour since you've locked yourself in there."

An hour?

"Yeah." I cleared my throat, wiping the tears away before adding, "I'm okay. I'm sorry. I'll get dressed and be gone in no time."

"Are you kidding me?" I wasn't sure if he sounded more sarcastic or troubled, but before I could reply, he unlocked the door and stepped inside, giving me an affected look.

I turned to face him, jaw dropped. "How did you—"

"It doesn't matter." He took a few steps closer to me and cupped my cheeks with his hands, looking down into my eyes. "You're not going anywhere."

"Shane, I can't wear out my welc—" I protested, but he cut me off.

"You're not. Stop overthinking, Melanie."

"Easier said than done," I sighed, my tone somewhat sarcastic, somewhat drained. "It's not you occupying a stranger's house."

"A stranger?" he asked. "That's what I am to you?"

"Shane, I…" I didn't know what to say. Frankly speaking, despite knowing this man for just a mere few days, I'd felt a deeper bond with him than with any other person I'd ever met before.

His eyes darted between mine expectantly. "Tell me, Melanie. Am I just a stranger to you?"

"What am I to you, Shane?"

"Definitely not a stranger," he replied without hesitation. "Not after last night," he whispered, running his thumb over my lower lip where he set his hypnotizing eyes.

He traced his fingertips down my wet, bare arm, leaving goose bumps on my skin. My lips parted involuntarily as I fixed my gaze on his tempting lips. In an instant, I was burning—burning with lust. I could never explain the effect Shane had on me, but whenever he was close, I wasn't capable of thinking straight. Unable to fight the temptation. One spark was enough to ignite the flame of pure lust, electrifying desire setting my body on fire in just a fraction of a second. There was a strong physical attraction we both failed to resist.

"Take me, Shane," I whispered, brushing my lips against his as I slid my hand at the back of his neck, pulling him closer.

"Melanie…" he muttered, trying to combat the dark cravings.

"Don't, Shane. Don't fight it," I both demanded and pleaded. Our breaths were ragged, mingling against our lips. "Make me forget."

And so he did.

He moved his hand to the back of my head, entwining his fingers in my wet hair, and crashed his lips onto mine, hard and demanding. He put his other hand on my waist before gliding it down to my thigh, kneading it. I slid my hands underneath his shirt, grazing my nails against his bare, toned body, and his muscles tensed. He started kissing my neck, moving his hand up to my tight nipples underneath the towel, my body quivering under his touch. I swiftly took his shirt off above his head and threw it away before kissing him again, our tongues tangling in need. He grabbed the hem of the towel and, with one swift move, ripped it off me, revealing my naked body to him.

"You're so fucking beautiful, Melanie," he hissed, trailing heated kisses down my body, and I let out a soft moan.

I searched for his belt and unbuckled it, impatient. He looked at me, his lips swollen and eyes black with sheer lust, ready to devour me. He grabbed me by my ass and lifted me to position me on the cold countertop behind me before kneeling down between my legs. He started licking and sucking my core, and penetrating me with his tongue, driving me crazy with desire. I lost myself to the mad arousal he was causing to my body, grabbed his hair, and arched my back, resting my head against the mirror. I heard a deep growl escaping his throat before he stood up and looked at me. His eyes were dark, hungry, filled with savage lust. He unzipped his fly, freeing his hard manhood.

He wiped his mouth with his hand, never leaving his inflamed gaze off me as he hissed in a low tone, "Are you ready to be fucked?"

I bit my lip, looking at him with pure lust in my eyes, spreading my legs wider. Shane put his hands on my hips, and I wrapped my legs around his waist before he shoved his penis deep inside. A loud moan slipped from my lips, and I moved my hands around his neck, digging my nails in his back as he kept thrusting, fast and rough, leading me to mind-blowing savage ecstasy.

"Good evening, Mr. Vergoossen." An elegantly dressed, beautiful dark-skinned woman smiled as we entered the chic lobby of Mastro's in Beverly Hills. "Miss." She nodded, greeting me.

"Good evening, Charlotte. Is everything ready?" Shane asked, holding his hand at the small of my back.

"Of course, our luxurious private dining room is waiting for you. Please follow me," she said before leading the way.

"You have booked a private dining room?" I whispered as we followed the gorgeous woman, and Shane chuckled.

"Haven't I told you I value my privacy?"

I raised my eyebrow before shaking my head, chuckling.

We entered a completely empty, large dining area. It was set amid a wine cellar that created a sophisticated vibe. Now I understood why Shane asked me to dress elegantly. I wore a white, tight dress with one long sleeve and one open arm, reaching my ankles, and high heels that Shane bought for me. I was surprised that everything fit perfectly, and he didn't even ask for my clothes size. I had my long waves down, falling loosely on my back. Shane, in contrast, was dressed all in black—an elegant black blazer, shirt, no tie, and tapered pants.

"Please." The lady smiled, pointing to the table.

There was a single wooden table in the middle of the area, covered with a white cloth, and only two chairs beside it prepared for us. Shane had pulled out the chair for me, smiling before walking around and sitting opposite me. We had oysters on the half shell for appetizers, Caesar salad and jumbo lobster tail for me as a main course, and a fifty-day, dry-aged strip for Shane, complemented by a bottle of fine red wine. The evening was passing by in a charming atmosphere. We talked about our likes, joked, laughed, and flirted. I'd felt like I'd known Shane for ages. I had never felt so good in someone's company. It was magical. Until reality hit me, I realized I would have to return to my everyday life.

"What's on your mind?" Shane asked, scanning my face carefully. It had always amazed me how attentive he was. He had never missed my mood change. And that was news to me; because before Shane, no one had ever paid so much attention to me. Not even Scar or Tess.

I let out a soft sigh. "Tomorrow is Monday. I have to get back to uni."

"And you don't feel ready?" His gaze was still on me.

I nodded. "You know, most of my peers are, let's say, hard to keep up with. They live for drama. And I guess after I ran away from my engagement party, I will be the talk of the month. Or even a whole year." I rolled my eyes, annoyed at the thought of all the gossip I'd have to face.

"Frankly, I thought you'd be like that too," Shane stated, taking a sip of wine.

"Like what?" I frowned.

"Entitled." He tilted his head slightly to the side. "But you aren't. You're so different from what I assumed."

The last sentence made the warning bells start to ring. "You had assumptions about me? I thought it was a coincidence we met."

"It was," he replied without blinking, composed like always.

"But it couldn't have been a coincidence that you showed up at my engagement party, right?" I tried to drag something out of him. I knew there was no chance he had come to my engagement party, seducing me out of this for no reason. I just couldn't figure out *the* reason, and whenever I brought the topic up, he would shrewdly find a way to escape it. And this time, it was quite an unusual way.

"Don't move, or I'm gonna shoot!" A well-built man in a leather jacket, an earpiece, dark sunglasses, and a scar above his left eyebrow shouted, pointing a freaking gun at us.

My blood ran cold, and I couldn't move. I got so scared I felt like my body was paralyzed. My heart was pumping so heavily that I thought it would jump out of my chest.

"Melanie, get behind me," Shane stated with stoic calm, and it was mind blowing how he kept his composure in a situation like this. There was a man ready to shoot us.

I watched Shane quickly pull out a gun from the inside pocket of his jacket and point it back at the man; the sound of its cocking sent icy chills down my spine.

"You have a gun?!" I shouted, panicking—my heart in my throat.

"I always have a gun with me," he hissed, angrily watching the lad.

WHAT?!

"What do you want?" Shane asked in a dangerously low tone, aiming at the man.

"The girl comes with me," the man replied harshly, and my eyes grew wide in fear.

"What?" I whispered, struggling to catch a breath. My body shaking.

"Over my dead body!" Shane said, and a loud sound of a gunshot rang in my ears.

Next thing I knew, Shane grabbed me by my hand and led me outside. I was running, tightly holding his hand. I was so scared that I didn't even know if he had shot the guy or not. Fear took control of all of my senses, and I just followed Shane's lead without question.

WE EXITED THE BUILDING using the back door, and we froze.

"Fuck!" Shane said, irritated.

We were trapped. At least a dozen men looking like clones in leather jackets with earpieces and dark sunglasses surrounded the exit and us. Shane took a firm hold of my trembling hand. I didn't know what was happening, but I was terrified—my heart kept racing like a hummingbird. A few seconds later, two men on our left side spread out, and a man in his fifties with grayish hair and pale skin in a black suit escorted by two more gorillas in leather jackets came in front of the rest before they settled in the line again. The whole situation looked like a scene from a thriller movie when a Mafia boss enters the room. Little did I know, it was exactly like that, except it wasn't a movie.

The man in a suit took off the sunglasses and looked at me with his icy-blue piercing gaze, just like Shane's.

"Karl Vergoossen?" I said, astonished and frightened as I recognized the most respected and feared man in the United States.

"Good evening, Miss Atwood," he said, his tone low and calm. His attitude reminded me of Shane's. "My apologies for this commotion, but we need to talk."

Cold shivers ran down my back.

"Leave her out of this," Shane hissed in warning.

"Oh, I wish," Karl said, his tone sarcastic. "But how could I if she's the key element in this whole mess?"

I didn't understand what they both meant, but at this point, I was sure it was not a mere coincidence that I'd met Shane. There was so much more to it, and I was sure I was about to find out.

"I said…" Shane pointed the gun at his father, and in an instant, every single one of the gorillas pointed their weapons at Shane, cocking them. Again, I froze.

"That wasn't a wise move," Karl stated before raising his hand in the air, and one of the men hovering over him shot Shane.

I screamed out in fear, covering my mouth with my hands, watching Shane struggling to stand still, losing consciousness. Two men rushed toward him and caught him just in time to prevent his body from falling to the ground.

"What the fuck?! Did you kill your own son?" I couldn't believe my own eyes that grew wider and wider in pure shock with each passing second.

Karl scoffed, an amused smirk curled up his lips, and his people took Shane's body and followed him to one of the black, armored Mercedes SUVs. "I wouldn't have hurt my firstborn, Miss Atwood. It was a tranquilizer gun."

"But why did you do this?!" I was shocked and in fear, but also damn mad. I couldn't grasp why he'd do that to his own son. As far as I was concerned, the Vergoossens were considered a family with strong ties, traditions, and values. Should anything happen to any of them, they would crawl through glass for one another.

"Because, young lady..." He paused for a few seconds as if building up the tension. His piercing eyes locked with mine. "We need to talk."

"After you, miss," a deep male voice rumbled from behind, and I turned to see two of Karl's gorillas flanking me.

I let out a quiet sigh, knowing I had no other option but to comply. I glanced over at Karl. He was watching me expectantly, his hands crossed behind. A man with hair dyed a platinum shade of silver opened the door for me. I couldn't see his eyes through the dark glasses, but I could feel his gaze, and I got goose bumps. I gave Karl a death stare before heading to the car, and to my surprise, Karl followed me and got in, sitting in the back seat next to me before the man with silver hair closed the door, jumped in the passenger seat and the driver drove away.

I wasn't sure how much time had passed or where we were, but I hadn't opened my mouth since we got in. I couldn't stop thinking about Shane.

Where did they take him? Why did they do this?

"Cat got your tongue?" Karl's mocking tone snapped me out of my thoughts.

I turned my head to look at him. He was sunk into the black leather seat, his right hand on the armrest, holding a glass of whiskey.

"What?" I asked quietly, not sure he could even catch my words.

"Are you always so quiet, love?" *Love? The nerve of that man.* "I'm starting to believe you're scared of me. Am I right?" He smirked softly to the side. *Was this amusing to him?*

The truth was, I was scared of him as much as I didn't want to admit it. You see, Karl Vergoossen was the kind of man who was effortlessly intimidating. He didn't have to do or say anything. His mere presence was just enough.

"Where's Shane?" I cleared my throat, trying to hide my fear.

"One of my men took him home," he replied, unfazed. "Don't worry about my son, dear. He's being taken care of."

I wondered if such situations were the bread and butter for them. I started questioning the gossip about them being a Mafia family. The way they behaved, the gorillas all dressed in the same way, guarding Karl as if he was the most precious person in the world, following his orders without blinking, seemed to be taken out of a Mafia movie.

Nonetheless, Karl's assurance that Shane was alright made me a little calmer. "Alright, Mr. Vergoossen. What do you want from me?"

"Your father called me this morning," he stated, and my heart stopped.

"What?" I swallowed. Knowing my father's hatred toward Karl Vergoossen, I'd never suspect he would contact him—his long-term worst enemy. I never knew what happened between them that they hated each other so much. I never really wanted to know. My father, being an ambitious politician, had many enemies.

"Hmm," he muttered, amused. "Imagine my surprise when I heard your father wants to talk to me. First time in twenty years."

"I don't think I follow, Mr. Vergoossen. What do I have to do with all of this?" I started getting annoyed by all the games. Besides, I'd figured that if he wanted me dead or to harm me, he would've done that already. He wouldn't waste his time if he didn't have any interest in it. "I assume you didn't shoot your son with a tranquilizer gun for no reason, right? My question is, what is the reason?"

He raised his brow, giving a single nod. "So you do have a feisty side. You should know I respect fearless and decisive people." He smiled before pointing to a glass filled with whiskey that stood on my side of the armrest. "Fancy a drink, Miss Atwood?"

"No, thank you," I replied dryly.

"Alright. Let's skip our chitchat and get to the point of our charming conversation. Excuse me a moment," he said before he turned to his men in the front seats, and they talked for a short while in a foreign language that I believed was Dutch before they clicked a button, and a dark window rolled up, dividing the space between his men and us.

I inhaled and exhaled deeply, feeling uncomfortable as hell. I was praying for this ridiculous encounter to end.

"We're enemies, Miss Atwood," Karl stated, turning his attention back to me. "I can't let my son get involved with the daughter of my great enemy."

I was confused. Perplexed. Dumbfounded. Shane and I… weren't involved. Yes, we had sex twice, but that didn't mean he'd want a relationship with me. I wasn't even sure if I would want that. At the same time, the thought of not being allowed to see him again was like a stab in my heart. That thought… pained me. I was unable to explain it, but something was pulling me toward this man like a moth to a flame. I guess that was why Karl's following statement made my heart skip a beat.

"Unless…" He paused, overseeing me.

So there's an unless? "Unless what?" I asked, dying to hear what he had in mind. Adrenaline rushed through my veins more intensely than when he'd forced me to go with him in an unknown direction with no further explanations.

"We make a deal."

TEN

Shane

I woke up to a throbbing pain in my head, and everything around me was spinning. My eyelids were so heavy I struggled to keep my eyes open.

"Fuck," I growled, squeezing my temples with my fingers.

I looked around, my vision blurry.

"I've been waiting for you to wake up, son." I heard my father's voice before I could spot him.

He was sitting on a cushiony light-grayish chair contrasting the dark walls with his legs crossed and both arms on the thick, soft armrests. The light was dim, and the curtains closed, so it was hard to tell if it was day or night.

"Melanie—" I muttered, some images from my dinner with Melanie flashing before my eyes.

"She's safe and sound in Atwood's mansion, where she belongs," he said dryly.

"What the fuck?!" I yelled, struggling to sit up. "How could you shoot me?"

"Don't be so dramatic, son." His tone was sarcastic, and his face emotionless like always. "We both know it was just a tranquilizer gun, so technically, I didn't shoot you."

"It doesn't change the fact you fucking did this without batting an eye," I shrieked. "I swear, I should fucking punch you." I leaned my head down, cupping it in my hands as my eyes were still sensitive to the light that came through the window after my father opened the blinds.

He then approached the sofa I sat on, resting his hands on the backrest.

"You gave me no choice, Shane." He articulated each word. "You pointed a gun at me. Your own father. Why? Because of a fucking woman who was supposed to be your target. Nothing more." He took a deep breath before walking around the sofa to look at me.

"Was the man who came after her in the restaurant one of yours?" I asked, slightly leaning up to look at my father, the most twisted man I'd ever known.

"Ah, yes. Alexander," he said, his hands crossed behind.

"Your ways are sick." I shook my head, scoffing.

"My ways are effective, son," he retorted. "That's why I always achieve what I want."

He took a few slow steps closer to me before leaning back against the heavy glass table standing in front of the sofa.

His tone was low and cold. "What concerns me, son, is that you think with your dick, not your brain."

"I had everything under control," I replied harshly. "I hope you didn't fuck it over."

"Hmm." He put his fingers to his chin. "Is that so?"

I rolled my eyes, my head still pounding in pain.

"Alright, son." He clapped his hands before following to the bar on the right side of my living room to pour himself a glass of scotch. "If you claim you have it under control, and her seductive assets didn't overshadow your way of thinking, I might have a new deal."

Fucking great, this can't be good.

"Care to elaborate?" I tilted my head to the right to look at him, my elbows on my knees and my hands clasped.

"You'll convince her to be our ally," he said before taking a long sip of his drink. "Convince her to help us destroy Dedrick."

I let out a heavy breath, running my fingers through my hair. *Fuck.* I knew he was twisted, but this? How was I supposed to persuade Melanie to go against her own family? Despite knowing Dedrick was wicked, and she didn't share a father-daughter bond with him, it was still her fucking father.

"What if I don't?" I asked, my voice dark.

"You know the answer," he stated. "Stick to our initial plan."

"Our initial plan?" I scoffed. "You mean yours. She's not our enemy, Karl. Dedrick doesn't even give a damn about her. Her death won't hurt him. Rather bring release." I was seething. I clenched my jaw, breathing heavily.

Our initial plan was to get close to Melanie, gain some shit on Dedrick to ruin his career entirely, and finish Melanie. That was my father's wicked way of taking revenge. He lost my mother because of Dedrick, so now he wanted Dedrick to lose the person most precious to him, to feel the same excruciating pain that my father had felt after losing the love of his life. And he'd been waiting nearly twenty years for this, fueling my head with hatred for the Atwoods ever since I was just a damn kid. How twisted was that? But he couldn't understand that getting rid of Melanie wasn't the right move. It wouldn't hurt Dedrick the way my father would want it. And I couldn't kill an innocent woman. I couldn't let him hurt Melanie. I couldn't lose her. I shouldn't have agreed to this in the first place, but I was brainwashed, believing my purpose in life was to fulfill my father's vengeance. Until I met her and she made me open my eyes.

"Tell me where your allegiances lie, Shane." My father's cold tone rang in my ears. "Are you with me or against me?"

I stood up and approached the island my father was standing behind. On its countertop was a bottle of scotch he poured himself and an empty glass. I filled the glass with brown liquor.

"I'm with you." I clinked his glass before taking a sip, my eyes on his.

"I knew I'd talk some sense into you." He smirked, finishing his scotch in one shot.

Yeah, you did. Now I know what I have to do.

"Good morning, Miss Atwood," I said after Melanie got into her chauffeur's black Range Rover. I smirked, looking at her astonished reflection in the rearview mirror.

"Shane?" Her eyes brightened up. "What are you doing here?" She giggled, and our gazes met in the mirror reflection. "How? Where's Gregory?"

"Well, your chauffeur seems to be very fond of you. He agreed to switch cars with me," I replied, smiling. The sight of Melanie being so joyous felt oddly good. "He drove to your uni already, so we can switch cars again once we get there. That way, your father won't suspect anything."

"You're insane!" She chuckled, her eyes gleaming.

"So I've been told," I teased before starting the car, leaving the Atwood's driveway.

Melanie hopped onto the front passenger seat, leaving a soft kiss on my cheek. I glanced over at her and couldn't help a smile forming on my lips. She looked gorgeous as always. Her long hair was tied in a high ponytail with two wavy strands embracing her oval face from the sides. She wore white sneakers, high-waisted blue jeans, a white sleeveless turtleneck, and little to no makeup. She was smiling all the time, gawking at me with her big brown eyes. She put her hand on my arm, raising weird goose bumps to my skin.

I swallowed hard, switching my focus back on the road, dispelling the devilish thoughts running through my mind whenever she was around.

"I'm sorry, Melanie," I said apologetically.

"Sorry?" She frowned, adjusting herself on the seat to face me.

"About last night—"

She cut me off. "It wasn't your fault, Shane," she said, her voice soft. "I've seen what your father is capable of. It looks like we're more alike than I thought."

"Meaning?" I asked, clenching my jaw at the thought of all the possible scenarios that could've happened between my father and Melanie yesterday.

"We both have twisted fathers," she said matter-of-factly.

I let out a heavy sigh. "What did my father want from you?" I looked at her fleetingly before focusing on the road ahead of us.

"He said…" She hesitated as if contemplating her words, and I caught myself clenching my jaw. "That we can't be together. That *he* can't let us be together." She quickly rephrased the sentence, dropping her gaze to the fingers she was playing with like she always did when she was nervous. "Because our families are enemies. My father called him—"

"What?" That took me off guard, but I quickly put two and two together, and now it all made sense why my father came to LA in the first place. "Did he say something else?"

"He mentioned a deal," she replied, casting her eyes upward to look at me.

"A deal?" I asked, my voice rough. "What about?"

"He never told me," she said quietly. "He drove me back to my house, saying we'll meet again."

Meet again, my ass! I exhaled deeply, not letting my emotions take control. That was not how I handled things. I'd been trying to keep my wits.

"Then he talked to my father, but I don't know what about. My father sent me away," she continued.

"I promise something like this won't happen again." I tilted my head to the side, locking my eyes with hers.

"Can I pick you up after school?" I asked, leaning down to peck the tip of her straight nose as we stood by the entrance to her campus. The day was sunny and warm, and most students were outside, chatting and laughing.

"Sure." She smiled, tilting her head back to look me in the eyes, our hands interlocked. "I finish at five thirty. Does that time work for you?"

I leaned down to whisper into her ear, smirking, "I'll be here at five thirty sharp."

I didn't see her face, but I heard a soft chuckle. I slid my hand at the back of her neck, stroking her smooth skin gently with my fingertips before leaning down to look her in the eyes. She cast her thick, black eyelashes upward, biting her lower lip temptingly, and I couldn't resist kissing her. I put my finger under her chin, tilting her head back, our gazes locked. She was breathing shallow, her brows furrowing. I brushed my lips against hers, and I could feel her body tremble before kissing her gently at first, but as soon as our tongues touched, swirling around with each other's, a chill ran down my spine. I started kissing her hungrily, barely restraining myself from pushing her against the stone fence and fucking her right there in front of everyone.

"I can't believe it!" A high-pitched voice articulating every word broke up our heated tangle. "Look! Melanie Atwood is cheating on Theo!"

I slowly pulled away, breathing heavily. Melanie seemed upset and embarrassed. I couldn't let her feel that way. Not because of me.

I tilted my head to the side to see a group of girls standing in a half circle, watching us. I glanced at the one with a squealing voice. "Melanie's done something she should've done a long time ago. She dumped him," I said, my tone low. The girl's mouth slowly parted, and her eyes grew wide. "She's now with a real man." I winked at the girls, who blushed, suddenly speechless. I switched my attention back to Melanie. Her cheeks flushed too. I put a section of her hair behind her ear and kissed her forehead. "I'll see you later, babe."

"Yeah." She smiled, somewhat embarrassed, somewhat satisfied. "I'll see you later. *Babe.*"

I turned on my heel and headed toward the parking lot.

"Was that…" I heard the girls gasping as I walked away. "Shane Vergoossen?"

ELEVEN
Melanie

"Melanie!" A familiar voice reached my ear as I rummaged through things in my locker to find my notebook. I closed the grayish metal door of my locker to see Scarlett resting against the neighboring one, her arms crossed.

"Are you for fucking real, girl?" she whisper-yelled at me, narrowing her eyes. "I've been trying to reach you the whole weekend. Where have you been? You got me worried sick!"

"I'm sorry, Scar," I replied, not knowing what to say or where to start.

"As you should!" She acted offended, but I knew it was just her teasing me. "Now tell me what the hell happened at your engagement party. Suddenly, you disappeared into thin air, and every station was telling the news about your kidnapping, and then they twisted it, saying that you allegedly ran away with your lover. I don't understand anything."

"Theo has been cheating on me," I said, and to my surprise, those words didn't even hurt anymore.

"What?!" She gave me the most puzzled gaze I'd ever seen, dropping her backpack to the ground.

"With Audrey," I added, my voice indifferent.

Scar stood there speechless, watching me with confusion. Her red curtain bangs slightly covering her befuddled eyes.

"Holy shit." Suddenly, her eyes grew wider with shock as she set them on something behind me. Or rather, someone. "You've got to be shitting me," she whispered, articulating the words slowly, stunned.

I turned back, leaning my body weight against the cold locker behind me, squeezing my notebook against my chest, watching Theo entering the hallway with Audrey by his side, holding her hand in his. People around us started gossiping, ping-ponging their gazes between Theo, his new girlfriend, and me. I hated being in the spotlight. And I deeply despised being the talk of everyone. I took a deep breath, wishing I could sink through the floor. Theo, in contrast, seemed to enjoy his little performance. His friends gathered around him and Audrey, and they started flirting with each other so obnoxiously it made me sick. I rolled my eyes, turning back to my friend, who was utterly dumbfounded.

"Are we going yet?" I asked her, sighing, slightly annoyed.

Scarlett shook her head, mouth open. "You don't care, Melanie? You were supposed to get engaged. How can you be so calm?"

"I met someone," I said, drowning in the memories of Shane's touch on my skin.

"The guy you left your engagement party with?" Scar's eyes darted between mine, but I found no judgment in her gaze.

"Yes, Shane." I smiled softly. "And for the first time in my life, I felt something…" I paused, searching for the right words but failed. "Something so rare, I cannot verbalize it."

My friend nodded, squeezing my arm reassuringly. "I hope you know what you're doing, Mel."

I hope so too.

But the truth was, I had no idea what I was doing. I just let things happen and went with the flow.

I SAT AT THE DESK where I always sat and searched through my notes to remind myself of the previous lecture. I tried not to pay attention to other students staring at me and enjoyed the gossip from the Saturday night until Audrey came into the classroom and headed straight toward me, taking a seat by the same desk.

"Are you serious?" I asked her, trying to keep my cool even though the audacity of this woman had me fuming.

"What's the problem, Mel?" she mocked, and I rolled my eyes, collecting my things from the desk. "After all, your relationship with Theo was fake, wasn't it?" She said it clearly and loudly, making sure everyone in the classroom could hear her.

"Fake?" I heard some whispers, but I didn't bother to comment. I wasn't going to play her wicked games.

I hung my bag on my arm and trotted toward the only empty seat next to Xavier, a guy I'd never spoken to but knew because he was extraordinarily clever and always gave comprehensive answers to the lecturer's questions. "Mind if I sit here, Xavier?"

He pulled the chair for me. "Not at all, Melanie." He smiled at me comfortingly, which I was thankful for.

"Thanks." I smiled back before sliding onto the chair. I searched for my phone in my bag and started a new conversation.

To: Theo :*

We need to talk.
Meet me after classes at the back entrance.

Sent Monday 9:02 AM

I typed fast, scrolled through my contacts to find my ex's number, and hit send. I was surprised how it took him only a minute to reply. I felt my phone vibrating, and I quickly opened the text.

From: Theo :*

We don't have anything to talk about.
U let a random guy fuck u.

Sent Monday 9:03 AM

I inhaled and exhaled a few times deeply before typing a response. I was dead set on not letting them get under my skin.

I noticed I still had his number saved with a kiss emoji next to it, so I immediately corrected that inadmissible mistake.

To: Fucker

At least I didn't cheat on u with ur fuckin friend.
Maybe I should hit on Mike. I'm sure he'd be up for a hookup.

Sent Monday 9:09 AM

Again, I didn't have to wait long for his response. It was so unlike him. Fucking hypocrite.

From: Fucker

I'll meet u there.

Sent Monday 9:11 AM

"Good morning, students." Mrs. Ortiz walked into the classroom, holding a few textbooks in her left hand and her big black bag hanging on her right arm. Her stylish glasses on her nose complemented her professional gray suit. Her short burgundy curls were put behind her ear. "Sorry, I'm late. Please take your seats. We're staring." The room filled with noise as everyone rushed to their seats, shuffling their chairs against the tile floor.

I put my phone back inside my bag and took out my notebook, trying to focus on the lecture.

I RESTED AGAINST the concrete frame support at the back entrance of the university building, impatiently waiting for Theo. My heart fluttered in my rib cage, my fingers fidgeting. I was quite restless because I wasn't the type to enjoy any kind of drama, but at the same time, I knew I had to confront Theo.

"Well, well. Who do we have here?" His mocking tone snapped me out of my thoughts.

I straightened up, clearing my throat. "We need to talk."

"What? Did you miss my dick already?" he taunted, dropping his backpack on the ground before setting his rage-filled gaze on me. "Or did your lover boy get bored with you yet?"

"Don't be such an asshole, Theo," I said dryly, rolling my eyes. I crossed my arms and looked him in the eyes. "I want your new girlfriend to stop spreading rumors about our relationship being fake."

He scoffed. "They aren't rumors."

"Theo, please!" I knitted my brows, sighing. "Neither of us is without blame here, but let's have some respect for each other."

He took a few steps closer to me, leaning against the concrete column behind me, trapping me between his arms. "You're talking about respect?" he hissed, his eyes filled with fury. "You're the one that disrespected me in front of the whole state!"

I clung to the support frame behind me. "Move back," I said, my voice shaky. He was scaring me. The rage building up in his dark gaze looked horrid. I'd never seen him fuming like this before.

"You should be mine, Melanie," he hissed through his clenched teeth, dropping his gaze to my lips, he brushed them with his thumb. "You are mine."

He grabbed my chin with his fingers so forcefully that it hurt. He moved his other hand to my waist, pressing me against the cold frame, caging me in. I tried to free myself from his grip but it was in vain. I was taken off guard. I didn't expect him to act like an abusive tyrant. He was too strong, and everything was happening too fast. He crashed his lips onto mine, forcing me to kiss him. I groaned, squirming as much as I could to set myself free, but the more I tried, the more he kept pushing me against the concrete support, squeezing my chin harder. Suddenly, someone grabbed Theo by his arm and swiftly pulled him away, and I could finally catch a breath.

"Shane?!" I cried out, watching how he punched Theo with a killer rage in his eyes.

"You shouldn't have done that!" Shane hissed, his voice cold with anger.

I jumped in fear, covering my mouth as I screamed, watching Theo falling to the ground, blood bursting out from his nose. I watched him struggle to stand up, ultimately rooted to the spot, my heart pounding.

"You fucking broke my nose!" Theo shouted angrily, wiping the blood away from his mouth.

"Stay the fuck away from Melanie," Shane threatened, his gaze deadly. "Or next time, I'll break more than just your nose."

He shoved past Theo and took my hand. His mere touch made me feel safe and secure. We headed to the other side of the building, leaving Theo swearing and shouting all kinds of names after us, but I didn't look back. I held Shane's hand tight, thankful he showed up in time. Not only there, but in my life in general.

He was my savior, razing down the carefully crafted realm of deceit and abuse that held me captive.

TWELVE

Shane

I was fuming. I was fucking furious. Raw rage flowed through me like lava. I clenched my fists on the steering wheel, accelerating down the highway. My gaze focused on the road but the images of this son of a bitch forcing himself at Melanie kept flashing before my eyes. I breathed heavily, trying to combat the towering rage. I should've killed this motherfucker right on the spot. I should've fucking put a bullet between his eyes, savoring the sight of life leaving his wretched body.

No one touches a woman like that.
No one touches my woman like that.

"Shane?" Melanie's trembling voice rang in my ears, snapping me back to reality. "Thank you." She furrowed her brows, nervously fidgeting her fingers.

"You don't have to thank me, Melanie." I tried to sound as calm and soft as possible. "Are you okay? Did he…" I clenched my teeth, taking a deep breath before continuing. "Did he hurt you?"

She shook her head no, but her gaze dropped, and she sucked on her cheek nervously. "He was acting mad because he was jealous, and his ego was hurt. But he wouldn't do anything."

I glanced at her, taking a deep breath to calm my raging anger. "Something like this will never happen again. I will not let anyone touch you, Melanie. I promise."

"Shane, it wasn't your fault." She looked at me, confused. "If there's anyone to blame, that's me. I made a horrible choice of a boyfriend. I—" She hesitated, and I grabbed her hand and cupped it in mine.

"Now you have me, and I promise to protect you, Melanie," I said, gazing into her eyes. "And I will not let a hair be harmed on your head."

Melanie watched me, slightly bewildered, but all I could think of was the sound of the bones cracking. I imagined breaking Ledford's neck, shooting his head, killing him in a hundred different ways.

Wicked? Maybe.

But that's who I was. A beast. Stone cold. Ruthless. Bad to the core. *A Vergoossen.*

WE ENTERED THE MAIN HALL of my house, and Melanie turned on her heel to face me. She set her uncertain gaze on me, watching me for a few seconds before bringing herself to say something.

"Shane, I'm sorry," she started, her tone apologetic.

"Sorry? For what?" I frowned, confused.

"I dragged you into this mess. I shouldn't…" She shook her head, her eyes sad.

I moved closer to her and cupped her cheeks with my hands. "Melanie, stop. Stop blaming yourself for everything," I said softly, caressing her soft skin with my thumbs. She cast her gaze upward, locking it with mine. "You didn't drag me into this mess. I entered it of my own free will. You know why?"

"No," she whispered, shaking her head. "I'm racking my brain to figure it out, but I see no rational answer to this. You have everything, Shane. You could have had anyone, yet you're here stuck with the lost daughter of an abusive monster and your enemy. Why?"

"Because you possessed me, Melanie," I stated, my voice low yet soft. "You fucking possessed me, my body and mind. My soul, I didn't know it even existed until I met you. You unleash something inside of me. I buried all kinds of fucked-up emotions inside me for so long that I thought they died, yet you brought them to life."

Melanie's eyes darted between mine, and I noticed a single, glimmering spark of hope in her gaze. The hope of a better tomorrow? Hope of not being alone anymore? I had no fucking idea, but this something danced in her eyes as a faint smile formed on her lips, making my heart skip a beat, and I knew I was fucked.

"You have me under your spell, Melanie," I whispered, brushing my lips against hers, and she sipped every word from my mouth like a thirsty man diving into a long-awaited oasis.

"Kiss me, Shane," she whispered pleadingly, seducing me with her gaze.

I slid my hand at the back of her neck and pulled her in for a kiss. A weird chill ran down my back as our lips touched. Something I hadn't felt in a long time. Melanie moved her hand to the back of my head, intertwining her long fingers with my hair, deepening the kiss. I roamed my other hand down her back to her round butt, kneading it with my fingers, and she moaned against my mouth. Fuck, the sound of her sweet moans was such a turn-on. I broke the kiss, slightly pulling away, and she looked at me, undone. Thirsty for my touch. Hungry for the pleasure I was willing to give her.

I leaned down to her ear. "I want you so badly," I whispered before teasing her earlobe with my tongue, and she moaned softly.

I lifted her as if she weighed nothing. She wrapped her legs around my waist and I carried her toward the nearest wall, pinning her sexy body tightly against it. I pressed my lips on hers, kissing her hungrily, slipping my tongue past her swollen lips. I was so hungry for her. I wanted to devour her whole. I trailed heated kisses down her throat, and she tilted her head back, resting it against the wall, arching her neck to give me better access. The turtleneck she was wearing was getting in my way, so I grabbed the top of it and tore it down with one swift move, exposing her bare skin. I ran my tongue up her neck, causing goose bumps to rise on her skin, before playing with her earlobe again, and she clenched her hand into a fist at the back of my hair, pulling me tighter. I tossed her onto the stairs next to us, kissing her demandingly. I undid her bra, cupping her petite breast in my hand. It fit perfectly, like half of a delicious, shapely apple. I let her rest against the stairs while moving down to suck on her hardened nipple, and she sighed in pleasure. Maybe it wasn't the most comfortable place to fuck, but we were so desperate for each other's touch, so in need of one another, that the place or time didn't matter. I was craving her like an addict jonesing for his dose. She was like a drug, intoxicating my every vein until not even one was left sober.

"You're mine," I hissed against her trembling body before undoing her pants.

She propped herself on her elbows, staring into my eyes sultrily as I slowly slid her jeans down her toned legs. I took off a shirt above my head and unbuckled my belt, gazing at my prey, waiting for me to take her, to have her, possess her. She bit her lower lip provocatively, casting her eyes down at the bulge in my pants, and I unzipped my fly, freeing my hard cock. She moved closer to kneel in front of me before she wrapped her warm lips around my length and a loud growl escaped my throat.

"Fuck," I grunted, weaving my fingers in her ponytail.

She kept pulling her head back and forth, teasing me with her wet tongue, and I barely restrained myself from fucking her luscious lips, fiercely, rough. I barely tamed the wild, wicked lust. But I didn't want to rush. I wanted to take my time with her, worship her, and make her scream in pleasure. Not use her like any other. I grabbed her chin with my fingers and tilted her head back. She looked at me with her big, sultry eyes, slowly pulling back. I helped her to her feet before crashing my lips onto hers, pressing her body tighter to mine. I kissed her down her throat, spinning her around so that now her back was pressed against my torso. I slid my hand down her flat belly, moving it lower into her panties. I rubbed her sensitive bud with my fingers, kissing and licking her neck. I watched her naked chest moving up and down as she breathed heavily, filling the entire hallway with her sweet moans. I slid my hands lower, slipping my fingers through her wet center. She was so warm and wet, I growled, and my dick twitched against her arched back. I teased her sensitive areola around her erect nipples while pushing my fingers in and out between her thighs. She leaned her head back, letting it fall onto my bare torso as she started moving her hips to ride my fingers, losing herself to the pleasure I was giving her. She started moaning louder, her breath ragged, and I knew she was close. In one swift move, I turned us toward the wall so that she could rest her hands against it. I slipped my fingers out of her, covered with her juices, before I brought them to my mouth, licking her sweet taste. Then I put my hand on her neck and wrapped my fingers around it before entering her with my full length, and she let out a loud sigh. I slid my other hand around her belly, holding her in place, and thrust deep and forcefully inside her. Melanie tried to fight her escalating moans, so I leaned down to her ear and growled as I kept thrusting, harder and deeper, "I want to hear you screaming my name when I fuck you."

She followed my order like a good girl and lost herself in the wicked pleasure with no restraints. "Shane…" she moaned my name repeatedly as she came.

"Now, that is the sound I wanted to hear," I whispered against her ear, her body shaking against mine and the cold wall as an intense orgasm whipped through her.

She turned around to face me, her cheeks flushed, hair a mess, and chest rising up and down heavily. "That was…" she breathed, but I cut her off.

"I'm not done with you," I said, supporting her chin with my thumb. Her eyes grew wider, and I smirked before lifting her again. Instinctively, she wrapped her hands around my neck and legs around my waist, and I kissed her lustfully while carrying her upstairs to my bedroom.

We sat by the bonfire we made on the beach by my house, chatting and laughing carefree. I watched Melanie's beautiful face gleaming under the moonlight and lit by the fire. The image of her as she lay under my duvet after a marathon of sex still on my mind. I smiled, satisfied I made her come in every possible position, in every wicked way. Several times in the bedroom to finish together in the shower. I could swear this woman put a spell on me and definitely had me in overdrive. I could not tame my desire around her.

She grilled some veggies, wearing an oversized grayish sweater and black leggings to her white sneakers. She joked she was glad Mrs. Dorothy bought different types of clothes because after I tore her turtleneck apart, she would have to wear my shirt again. Not that I would mind. She also offered to return the money that Mrs. Dorothy spent on the clothes, which wasn't an option, but it surprised me how humble, pure and innocent she was. She was a complete contrast to what I had assumed about her before meeting her.

"Shane?" she said softly, snapping me back from my thoughts. "What's the reason for that war between our fathers?" She tilted her head to the side, expecting an answer.

I took a heavy breath, once more stunned at her innocence. I scanned her face, realizing she genuinely didn't have the slightest idea about any feuds between our families. I picked up on it before that Dedrick kept her in the darkness, only using her whenever he pleased, but this added to my conviction.

"Your father never told you?" I asked, despite knowing the answer.

"You know my relationship with my father is complicated, to say the least." She sighed, avoiding my gaze.

"Hey." I grabbed her chin with my fingers, and our eyes locked. "You don't have to be ashamed, Melanie. I understand. More than you know."

She nodded, pressing her lips together, forcing a smile.

"We don't have to talk about it," I said softly, sliding my hand at her back, comforting her.

"He's never loved me." She released a heavy sigh, resting her head on my arm. "It hurts, but it's the truth. He's never loved my mother either. I don't know why she's stuck with him for all these years, especially since she knows damn well he's cheating on her on a daily basis."

For the first time during our short yet intense relationship, Melanie opened up to me, which blurred the lines between the plan looming over me like a dark cloud, and what I felt for her. I felt like a fucking asshole for letting her trust me, of all people. At the same time, I knew that at this point, I'd stop at nothing to keep her safe.

"Did he ever hurt you? Or your mother?" I asked, my voice dark like the memories of him hurting my mother. Deep down, I asked myself the question, *How could life be so twisted as to let me develop feelings for the daughter of a man I despised with a passion?* —a man I'd kill in a heartbeat.

"Yes," she said shakily.

I closed my eyes, clenching my teeth, and I felt my blood boiling in my veins. "What did he do to you?" My voice was low, deadly. If words spoken could kill, Dedrick Atwood would be a dead man.

"He hit her and me. Both of us. Many times." Melanie's voice was trembling, and even though I couldn't see her face, I was damn sure her eyes were welling up with tears.

"I swear I'm going to kill him," I hissed, clenching my fists forcefully, trying not to lose composure.

I heard quiet sobs, realizing Melanie was trying to hold back the tears desperately wanting to stream down her beautiful, sad face. I stood up and gently grabbed her arms to help her to her feet. I held her in my arms and pulled her fragile body against me gently as if she were made of glass. As if she was about to break, shatter into thousands of pieces. I knew I couldn't let that happen because I wasn't sure if I would be able to glue her pieces back together.

"What else did he do?" I asked, feeling in my bones it wasn't the whole story. Something had been telling me that Melanie suffered way more than she cared to admit. I knew it by the way she was. Broken. Fragile. All alone with her pain.

"I'm so ashamed, Shane," she whispered, her tears soaking in my T-shirt. I slid my hand to the back of her head and caressed her hair, hoping my touch would comfort her. Wishing I could somehow take her pain away and throw it into the ocean ebbing and flowing beside us.

"You have nothing to be ashamed of, baby," I stated firmly, yet with a soft tone.

"I'm so weak," she sobbed, her words breaking my heart.

"Bullshit," I opposed. "You are the strongest woman I've ever known. I admire you, Melanie. Do you hear me?" I cupped her cheeks with my hands and looked into her sorrowful eyes.

She nodded, overlapping her hands on mine.

I took a deep breath. "What else did he do, baby?"

"He's always used me for his benefit. I was nothing more than just a pawn in his wicked games. He—" She paused, and I knew I wouldn't like what I was going to hear. "He's arranged a relationship for me already in the past."

"You mean before your relationship with Ledford?" I was confused about how someone could be so twisted.

"Yes. I was sixteen and not aware it was arranged either. I feel so stupid. I let my father trick me twice." She looked away, avoiding my gaze again—shame written all over her face. "I felt so broken when I learned about that contract with the Ledfords. And even though Theo knew about how my father treated me, he still agreed to his stupid games. I was always just a contract, a pawn in someone's game, Shane."

I clenched my teeth. Anger stirred within me. I brought my lips to her forehead, kissing it tenderly. "Don't torture yourself, Melanie. It's not your fault, and most definitely, you aren't stupid for trusting your parent. Or wanting to trust him, no matter the monster he is. And your ex…" I paused to put a filter on the words springing to my lips. "Was a fucking loser not to see the amazing woman he had."

I tried to comfort the broken woman whose life I was supposed to destroy—burn to ashes. How ironic was that? I could feel my heart breaking in two, listening to what Melanie had to endure. She led a seemingly perfect, luxurious life, while behind closed doors, all she had were lies, pain, and even more lies. She lived as a captive in a carefully crafted facade of abuse and deceit called her life. I knew this was not a justification at all, but agreeing to my father's plan, I wasn't aware of how her life looked. I was driven by revenge. It was all I knew. Retribution. Vengeance. But the more I got to know her, the more she taught me life wasn't always black and white. The more I got to know her, the more I knew my job was to protect her. It was now my job to make sure whoever tried to harm her failed, and I knew I would stop at nothing, go against anything and anyone, break any rule and burn the whole world to the ground to keep her safe. I was ready to go against my own father and his empire if I had to.

"They were both plain dumb not to see your worth, Melanie," I said, and she chuckled softly.

She smiled through her watery eyes, but she didn't look like someone who had just had a massive weight lifted off her shoulders. She looked like someone still keeping a nasty secret that was eating her alive from the inside. I brushed her hair behind her ear, scanning her face with my fingers.

"There's more, am I right?" I asked, hoping my intuition led me astray this time.

"My ex-boyfriend," she started, her voice breaking. "I mean my former ex-boyfriend, David…" She took a deep breath, struggling to speak, her gaze dropping to the ground.

She didn't have to continue for me to figure out the possible scenario. She had it written all over her face. I inhaled heavily, clenching my jaw. "Please tell me that's not what I think it is?" I hissed, hoping I wasn't right, hoping to hear her object.

"That's exactly what you think," she whispered, still looking down, and I shook my head, my blood boiling. "He… drugged me and took advantage of me. I don't even remember that night, but I knew it happened because…" She paused, and I was fighting my towering rage, clenching my fists. "I was a virgin… before."

"He's a dead man," I stated, meaning every word.

Knowing everything Melanie had experienced tore my heart out, filling it with unearthly fury. I swallowed hard, barely keeping my composure. I wasn't sure if my growing anger outweighed the pain I felt after hearing what that son of a bitch had done to Melanie or the other way around. But I was sure that if this fucking asshole was anywhere around me now, I would've killed him with my bare hands.

"Did you report it to the police?" I asked, my voice dark.

Melanie refused to look me in the eyes. "No. I didn't."

"What?" I couldn't hide my frustration. "What the hell, Melanie? Why not?"

She was silent. She wiped the tear dripping from her cheek away, and I took a heavy breath. I was fucking mad at myself that I couldn't keep my emotions in check.

I took her chin with my fingers and gently tilted her head back, and our gazes locked. "I'm sorry. I don't mean to scare you."

"You don't scare me, Shane," she muttered. "I'm just ashamed of being so weak. My father…" She paused again, escaping my gaze. "I'm sorry. I shouldn't have mentioned it. I don't know why I told you my darkest secret no one knows about."

"No," I opposed, tilting her chin gently so that she looked me in the eyes again. "I'm glad you told me. It means you trust me, Melanie."

"Can I trust you, though?" she whispered, slightly furrowing her dark brows.

"Yes," I stated with no hesitation.

She let out a heavy breath, directing her gaze to the ocean. It felt like she was ashamed to look at me for some reason. I couldn't grasp why, though. None of what had happened was her fault. And she was wrong if she believed she was weak. She was one of the strongest people I knew. She endured all this pain and went through hell with no one by her side, and it didn't break her. She was standing there right in front of me, fighting her own battle like the true warrior she was. Many would give up, but not her.

Melanie might have seemed fragile like a rose, but sure as hell, she was fierce like its thorns.

"Your father took care of it, I take it?" I carried on, fooling myself by assuming Dedrick would do the right thing for once.

"No," she said dryly before looking back into my eyes. Her long black eyelashes wet, tears streaming down her face. "It was my father who forbade me to speak of this."

That son of a bitch.

I took a deep breath, clenching my jaw hard. My anger built up as Melanie's words echoed in my mind, burning me inside out. I didn't want Melanie to see the fury in me. I didn't want to scare her, but it took every bit of my willpower to keep the anger bottled up. I felt like I was screaming deep within, but no sound would force its way from my mouth. The rage was growing inside of me, unleashing my demons. Demons driven by revenge—craving my own kind of *justice*.

"I've heard enough," I hissed, plotting the way I'd teach these motherfuckers a lesson in my head. "Give me his full name."

"David's?" She frowned. "No, Shane. I don't want you to do anything you'll regret doing later." She shook her head, giving me a perturbed look.

Regret? I would fucking put a bullet between his eyes without batting an eye.

"Melanie, please. You know that if you don't tell me, I'm gonna find out on my own," I said, and her eyes darted between mine, bewildered.

"David Leighton," she breathed out.

I nodded before kissing her forehead softly as I held her in my arms.

David Leighton, I'm coming for you.

THIRTEEN

Melanie

I woke up in Shane's bed, stretching out under the duvet, imbued with his intoxicating scent throughout it. I reached my hand to his side, jonesing for his body warmth, but he was nowhere to be seen. I sat up, rubbing my eyes, yawning. I didn't remember falling asleep last night. I remembered snuggling into his broad chest that felt like home and talking—talking for hours. The memory of how he caressed my arm still lingering on my skin. I felt so safe in Shane's arms, so right. He was like medicine for my pain. My drug of choice. My drug I could never resist. All that in such a short period of time.

"Hey." His low yet soft voice reached my ear as he lurked in the slightly ajar door. "You're up?"

"Yeah." I smiled. The sight of this man would always brighten up my day. "Where have you been?"

He walked in, leaving the door ajar before moving closer and sitting on the other side of the bed. "My father called me," he said, his voice dry. "He'll be hosting an annual charity event in New York in a couple of days. It's a fancy event that became a tradition for him."

"I know," I said softly. "I've read about it in the newspapers. So what about it?"

He covered my hand with his, caressing it with his thumb. "You know, as my father's heir, I have to be there."

I nodded, and my stomach dropped at the thought of Shane leaving for New York. I knew this couldn't last forever. At the same time, I wished it could. I let out a heavy breath, realizing how addicted I was to Shane Vergoossen, the last man I should've fallen for. Ironic how something so *forbidden* felt so fine.

My nemesis became my savior.

The question was... would he be my downfall or the reason for my uprising?

"Melanie?" His raspy voice brought me back to reality. I glanced at his perfect face and smiled, drowning in his sky-blue gaze.

"Hm?" I muttered, clinging to his electrifying touch as he brought his hand to my cheek.

"I want you to go with me," he said softly, a mischievous smirk curling up his lip. "As my date."

I straightened up, staring into his eyes, bemused. "But... what about our fathers? You know that my father will never let me go."

"Actually, my father wants to invite your parents this year, too."

"What?" I raised my brow, taken aback. "He's never invited them before. What has changed now? Is it because of you?"

"Maybe," Shane muttered, a sly smirk curled up his lips.

I let out a deep sigh. "Shane… and the press? If we show up there together, we'll make front-page headlines. Especially since I broke my engagement off just recently."

"Do you care?" Shane whispered, leaning closer so that our lips were only inches apart. "Because as long as I have you by my side, the world could be crumbling down, and I wouldn't give a damn."

I slid my hands around his neck and pulled him in for a kiss. We fell back onto the bed, Shane resting his body weight on his elbows above me. I draped my fingers down his back. His muscles began to tense. I saw the effect my touch had on him, but it felt like Shane was holding himself back for some reason. He trailed kisses down my neck, but they felt different. Considerate and gentle and not savage and rough like before.

"Shane," I whispered, and he slowly pulled back to look at me. "I want you."

He smirked and leaned down to kiss me, gently running his hand up my thigh. "I'm all yours, baby," he whispered against the shell of my ear, teasing me with his tongue.

He slid his hand underneath the oversized shirt I wore to sleep, his touch tender, and I whined, undone, "I meant I want *you*."

He pulled back again to look into my eyes, this time a little puzzled.

"I want the passionate, wild, and rough you," I stated, grinding against his rock-hard bulge in his pants, desire surging through my body. I rolled over so that now I was on top of him, straddling him. I glided my hands down his naked torso, biting my lower lip provocatively. "I want your fierce kisses, wicked touch." I leaned down to his ear and sucked on his earlobe before hissing seductively. "I want you to fuck me, Shane."

A deep growl escaped his throat while I licked his neck, nibbling it teasingly. He propped himself on his elbow, sliding his other hand around my bare waist underneath the woolen fabric. His touch sent shivers down my spine, and I moaned against his lips as he kissed me demandingly. I moved my hand to the back of his head, pulling it closer as I intertwined my fingers in his hair, deepening the kiss. He sat up, and I was still straddling him as his hands roamed up and down my body before he tugged the T-shirt I wore over my head, exposing my naked body. Not breaking our hungry kiss, I helped him get rid of his pants, and he ripped my panties apart before I even knew it. He licked the sensitive skin of my neck the whole way up to my chin, and I tilted my head back, giving him better access. He grabbed my hips with his hands, and a loud moan filled the room as he pressed me into him, dipping deep inside.

But even though we had sex that day, he didn't fuck me. That day, he made love to me.

I guess it was then when we slowly started blurring the lines between raw lust and pure love.

"Are you sure you have to go back home?" Shane asked, staring at me with his black brows furrowed. One of his hands on the steering wheel and the other on my knee.

"I can't keep crashing at your place like that. It feels like I moved in with you," I joked, and he chuckled.

"Not that I would mind." He smirked wickedly to the side, and I bit my lower lip. God, the effect this man had on me. His mere smirk was enough to set my body on fire.

"You're unbelievable." I giggled. "We've known each other for a few days."

"So?" he teased before focusing on the road.

I couldn't fight the broad smile desperately forming on my lips as I watched the man of my dreams casually shifting the gears. He wore a slightly unbuttoned shirt, perfectly embracing his toned muscles, a silver ring on his little finger, a cross chain underneath the black fabric of his shirt, and a brow piercing he always wore. His dark hair was shaved short on the sides, longer on top, going to the left side, and dark sunglasses hiding his azure piercing gaze, which I loved the most.

"You're doing that again," he said teasingly.

"I'm doing what again?"

"Drooling over me." He lowered his sunglasses to wink at me, grinning.

"You cocky bastard," I gasped, rolling my eyes before chuckling.

"You love it, babe," he teased, and we both laughed.

He was right, though. In my own twisted way, I found it attractive. The way self-confidence radiated from him miles away drew me in like a magnet. I loved his alpha male attitude. I loved his courage and confidence. I loved the fierce spark in his eyes and the indomitable spirit.

I realized I was falling for this man. *Hard.*

And there was no turning back.

BEFORE I KNEW IT, we parked in the driveway of my father's mansion. I glanced over at the vast white building surrounded by a stunning stone fence and a well-maintained vivid garden with a fountain in the front yard and exhaled heavily.

"We can still go back to my place," Shane said as he took my hand, leaning toward me.

"It's okay, Shane. It's still my *home*," I replied, my tone on the verge of sarcasm and sorrow.

"If it was up to me, I wouldn't let you go." He pressed his lips softly to my forehead before I pulled back, unfastening the seat belt. "Just promise me you won't let him mistreat you, babe."

"I've learned how to deal with him." I forced a smile. "I may look vulnerable, but I'm stronger than you think."

"I know, Melanie," Shane said softly, caressing my cheek. His piercing eyes set on mine. "That's my girl."

I kissed Shane goodbye before getting out of the car. I walked toward my home, looking back to send a smile to the man I wished I had stayed with. But I knew I couldn't. Life wasn't a fairy tale, and as much as I didn't like it, I had to face my reality. I took a deep breath before entering the luxurious home, reflecting my father's love for splendor.

"WHERE THE HELL HAVE YOU BEEN?!" I jumped, gasping at the harsh tone welcoming me as soon as I stepped inside.

I examined my father, who, at first glance, in his tailored suit and grayish hair neatly combed back, looked like a trustworthy man. My gaze moved to my elegant mother standing next to him in her favorite navy knee-length dress, with a black belt around her waist. Her usually wavy, shoulder-length sunny-blonde hair was pulled back in a low bun. They both had their brown gazes focused on me, except my mother's was troubled and my father's vexed.

"I asked you a question!" he shouted, giving me a spiteful look. "You haven't returned for the night, didn't answer our calls. Your mother was worried!"

"I was with Shane," I said dryly.

"You slut!" my father hissed angrily. He wanted to proceed with giving me shit, but my mother intervened.

"Dedrick, please!" she said pleadingly.

"I'll go to my room." I felt resentful that all she ever did was plead with him, only to prevent a situation like this one from escalating. But she was never more than that. It hurt that my mother had never been my rock. I always envied the mother-daughter bond my friends had with their mothers, but I'd accepted it for how it was. Maybe I shared the blame because I never tried harder. Nonetheless, she never taught me that. She never showed me I could have a bond with her, so the idea of having it felt so distant.

I turned on my heel and headed toward the stairs. I wanted to be above him. Them. I wanted to avoid any unnecessary drama. But then I heard him again.

"If you don't stop slutting yourself with the fucking Vergoossen, I'll throw you out on the street where you belong."

I closed my eyes, inhaling deeply before turning to face him. "I almost forgot, *Daddy*. Karl Vergoossen invited us to his annual charity event. But I'm sure he'll send formal invitations," I said, my tone dripping with sarcasm, and my father's face went pale. I knew his weak spot was Karl Vergoossen. I had no idea why he hated him so fiercely, but I knew a mere mention of Karl would drive him mad. "I'm leaving with Shane a few days prior to the event to spend some time with his family." I faked a smile, savoring the hideous facial expression of my father. I couldn't tell if he was more furious or dumbfounded, but the sight was priceless. But then my mother said something that threw me off the scent.

"Melanie, you can't go. He doesn't care about you. All he wants is revenge," she said frantically. "They blame your father for—"

My father cut her off, taking a firm grip on her wrist. "Celine!"

"Blame you for what?" I insisted. It was now crystal clear that they were keeping a secret from me—a secret I had to learn.

My mother glanced at me, terror in her eyes while my father threatened her, his voice harsh. "If you say a word, Celine, you're going to regret it."

"Stop it, you monster!" I ran toward my parents with the intent of separating them, but my father instinctively turned to me and slapped me, and the room fell silent, with only the sound of my mother's gasp echoing through the walls. I held my cheek with my hand, looking into the eyes of my oppressor. "I've had enough. I'm going to ruin you." I cold-bloodedly threatened him. I decided to fight him using his own methods, but I didn't consider the horrid consequences it entailed.

"You wouldn't dare." He shook his head, staring at me with rage.

"Oh, I would," I retorted and turned to climb the stairs, but instead of scaring my father, I only rattled his cage, unleashing the true beast in him.

He followed me up the stairs and grabbed me by my elbow, squeezing it forcefully.

"You won't go against your own father. We both know that!" he screamed in my face in a frenzy of rage.

"I will!" I shouted back. "I'll tell the world the truth and ruin your flawless reputation!"

"You spoiled brat!" he yelled in my ear, yanking my arm with a forceful grip that hurt.

I wanted to snatch my arm and escape that hell, but the next thing I knew, I was falling down the stairs. My mother's terrified voice shouting my name was the last thing I heard before I hit my head, and everything went black.

FOURTEEN

Shane

The night before, after Melanie confessed her dark secret, I ordered Callan to get me an address on David Leighton. We had some scores to settle, and I wanted to deal with this piece of shit without undue delay. I told Callan to come to LA immediately. As my stay here was extending, I needed my best man around. And so, I was just picking him up from the airport.

"Get in," I said as I rolled down the dark-tinted window, smirking at the sight of my right-hand man and best friend.

"Long time no see, boss." He grinned before getting in the car.

I drove away, leaving the sound of tires squealing behind. I took a turn to get on the highway, speeding up as we headed to San Diego.

"So, boss?" Callan asked, staring at me with a perky smirk on his face, and I realized I missed his annoying ass.

"What?" I asked, my gaze on the road.

"Melanie Atwood?" His tone was sarcastic, but then again, when wasn't it? This man was a walking tease. "Atwood?" he repeated, emphasizing his point.

"Life's full of surprises, isn't it?" I glanced at him for a short moment before focusing on the road again.

"Holy fuck, you're serious?" Shock flooded his eyes. He ran his fingers through his blue hair, adjusting himself on the seat. "What about your father?"

"Don't you worry about my father. I'm a big boy," I teased, despite being well aware of the meaning of his words.

"Yeah, but y'know. Your father is, well… dangerous."

"So am I," I said coldly.

"Wait a minute." He took off his dark sunglasses before staring at me. "Are you tryin' to imply you'd go against your father for the daughter of your worst long-term enemy?"

"If necessary, then yes," I asserted firmly.

Callan raised his left brow. The scar he had right above it reminded me of a nasty fight he had two years ago with my former right-hand man who went against my order, betraying our family in the process. I remember like it was yesterday how Callan's zealousness, courage, and devotion impressed me, and with no hesitation, I made him my right-hand man right after I put a bullet in the traitor's head. I had no tolerance for treachery.

"But you're his favorite," he stated, racking his brain to determine if I was being serious. "And you're the heir to the Vergoossen legacy."

"It was never about me, Callan. It was about my mother," I clarified, but a rush of regret washed over my body. I could never speak of my mother without feeling the pain all over again. The pain I was desperately trying to hide underneath a mask of an emotionless, ruthless, cold bastard.

Callan tilted his head, scanning my face as if trying to find a clue.

"I'm the only living thing he has, reminding him of her. He loved her deeply, truly. He never loved like this after. No one. Not even me," I said, clenching the steering wheel. One thing Melanie and I had in common was the feeling of not being worthy of love. Although I was my father's favorite, and in his twisted way, he loved me, I never got to know what love is. There was no place for love in a world where all that mattered was power.

"Didn't your mother die because of Dedrick Atwood?" Callan asked, slightly hesitant. Despite being my best friend, he respected the boundaries I set as his boss.

"She did." I clenched my teeth, trying to keep my rage leashed. "And I can't let history repeat itself."

"What do you mean?" I didn't have to look at him to sense the confusion written on his face.

"I can't let Melanie die."

"I can deal with him on my own," Callan said, loading his gun.

"No. I want the pleasure myself." I slid the gun underneath my belt at my back and fixed the black leather jacket I wore. "I want him to look me in the eyes when I finish him. Let's go."

Callan nodded, not questioning my motives or actions. He led me toward the back entrance of a modern loft. After my call, he sent Franco, one of my men stationed in LA in case of any emergency, to check out this place. We'd always been prepared for any possibility. We had men in every state, in every corner of the country. Callan disarmed the alarm and gave me a sign we could go in. I sneaked inside, and he followed, covering my back. I searched across an empty living room with a dim light and a glass of scotch on a wooden table standing in front of a bottle-green couch. A twisted idea weaved into my mind. I slowly approached the sofa and sat in the middle of it, stretching my arm on its backrest, my leg bent. Callan looked at me with his brow raised, and I shrugged, tilting my head to the side, and a wicked smirk curled up the corner of my lips. I reached for the glass of scotch, and Callan shook his head. He knew my twisted ways by now. He stepped toward the door leading to another room and hid behind the frame, standing by.

I drummed my fingers on my knee until, a short moment later, a chocolate-haired man entered the room, his green eyes wide in fear, looking at me as if I stole his last breath.

Callan jumped behind him, pointing his gun at the back of his head. "Don't move, so maybe I won't shoot."

"What do you want?" He breathed heavily, his body sweating.

I drank the glass of scotch, amused at the growing fear in the motherfucker's eyes. I put the glass back on the table before getting up. I slowly approached the good-looking boy and looked into his scared eyes. "You hurt someone I care about," I said coldly, my gaze deadly.

"Wh—What?" The rich boy struggled to speak, his body shaking.

"Melanie Atwood ring a bell?" I tilted my head to the side, my hands crossed behind. "As far as I know, you hurt her in a fucking disgusting way." I kept my composure, although the rage was tearing me apart from the inside out.

"N-no," he stuttered. "She wanted it. She begged me for it."

"Tsk-tsk." I shook my head, and the guy was shitting his pants. "You should've told the truth. I don't like liars." I took out my gun and cocked it before his eyes.

"I-I'm sorry." His lip was shaking as he spoke. "I did it. I did it. I'm so sorry. Tell Melanie that I'm sorry."

I grabbed the man by his jaw, squeezing it hard with my fingers so his mouth opened. I pushed my gun down his throat, and the sound of him choking filled the empty room. "Time for apologies is up. Now you have to pay," I said sarcastically, and the man pleaded, choking on my gun barrel.

"Please, mercy."

"No one hurts my woman like that and lives," I said and pulled the trigger.

I took a deep breath, wiping my gun with a tissue.

"Get rid of the body," I said harshly, and Callan only nodded before I left for the car.

I LEANED AGAINST THE CAR, staring at my phone screen like a fool. I waited for Melanie to answer my text. I had a weird feeling that something had happened because usually, she would text me back within minutes.

"Boss?" Callan's voice snapped me back from my thoughts. I looked at him, and I knew something was off. I could read his facial expressions like an open book.

"What is it?" I asked, dryly, impatiently.

"We have a problem." His tone gave away that shit just hit the fan.

"Cut to the chase."

"I ordered Franco to monitor the situation at Atwood's, and he just called me. Melanie is on her way to the hospital. He doesn't know in what condition."

"Get in the car." I jumped inside, shutting the door. I started the car engine, and after Callan got in, I drove away faster than a speeding bullet.

"Boss, slow down! You're drivin' like a madman," Callan commented as I was speeding up the highway, overtaking any car on my way.

"I can't, Callan!" I hissed, my gaze never leaving the road. "Melanie is in danger."

"What makes you think so?" He frowned.

"It's the perfect opportunity. He's gonna kill her."

"Who?"

"My father," I breathed out. "He wants Melanie dead."

Callan's phone rang, and he quickly glanced at the screen. "It's Franco," he said before answering the call. "Sup?"

I felt my heart pounding rapidly, adrenaline rushing through every single vein. I didn't remember the last time I was so scared. It must've been so long ago because I already forgot how dreadful the feeling of the scare was.

I wasn't sure how long Callan's phone call took, but to me, every second lasted an eternity. He ended the call before turning to me, saying in his Aussie accent, "Would ya slow down? She's stable."

I let out a heavy breath.

"Franco said she has a concussion, but she's fine. She'll stay in the hospital for the night. Now relax, mate, and for God's sake, slow down."

"Good," I rasped. "Did he tell you what happened?"

"Well, the official story is that she fell down the stairs."

Official, huh?

"She fell?" I tried to stay focused on the road, but the rage flowed through my system like a hurricane. "Or someone pushed her?"

"Can't say. Franco isn't sure. He only overheard a convo between Melanie's parents and the doc."

"Hold on tight, *mate*," I said before slamming my foot on the accelerator.

ABOUT TWO HOURS LATER, I rushed into the hospital, straight toward Melanie's room. Thanks to Franco, who followed the ambulance and sneaked in after the paramedics, I knew where she was put. I ran through the white hallways, passing doctors and patients whose heads turned after me, confused. I might've looked a little odd in the black clothing I only wore for special occasions like today, for instance. But I didn't give a fuck. All that mattered was Melanie.

"What the fuck are you doing here?" I hissed as I nearly bumped into none other than fucking Ledford.

"Evenin'," Callan threw out, casually walking a few steps behind me.

I looked around and saw Melanie's parents standing by the door to Melanie's room with Victoria and Robert Ledford. All four of them gave me indignant looks. I rolled my eyes before turning my attention back to the golden boy standing before me with his arms crossed.

"I came to see my fiancée," he stated, and I scoffed.

"You're off the wall, dude," I retorted. "She's not and never has been your fiancée."

He clenched his jaw, narrowing his eyes at me as if it would scare me.

I tilted my head slightly to the side, looking deeply into his eyes. "But she'll be mine soon."

"What did you say?" He moved away, completely astonished.

"That you're a pain in my ass," I hissed before walking past him. I didn't have time for this shit. I needed to see Melanie.

I approached the Atwood-Ledford gang, guarding the door to the room Melanie was in, looking at me like an intruder they had to get rid of.

I rolled my eyes, exhaling deeply. "Step aside."

"I'm not your errand boy. I won't let you boss me around," Dedrick whined. "Stay away from my daughter, Vergoossen!"

At this point, I was so fed up with his shit that I lifted the bottom of my jacket slightly, exposing my gun. "Don't make me use it." I tilted my head to the side, watching him.

Victoria grabbed her husband by his arm and pushed him to the side, muttering something under her breath. Celine stood still by her husband, but I saw the fear filling her eyes.

"Dedrick, please," she pleaded, her voice trembling.

Dedrick hesitated, swallowing hard. "I'll fucking ruin you," he hissed before stepping aside to let me pass.

I smirked, grabbing the doorknob, but before entering the room, I turned and winked at Dedrick. "That will be fun, father-in-law."

"Melanie?" I whispered as I entered the room, quietly closing the door behind me.

I approached the bed and sat on the chair beside it. Melanie was asleep. She had a few bruises on her hands and a bandage on her head. I took a deep breath, running my fingers through my hair. An ice-cold shiver swept down my back at the thought of what could've happened. At the thought that I could've lost her this very night. It was a frightening thought, and I wasn't the type to get scared easily. In fact, I wasn't the type to get scared at all. In the dangerous world I lived in, where I had to face death nearly every day, you get numb, and even the thought of death doesn't scare you anymore. But the idea of losing Melanie… was fucking terrifying. It was even more frightening than the fact that I got so attached to her in such a short time, despite that being the last thing that was supposed to happen.

I grabbed Melanie's hand and gently held it in mine, exhaling deeply. Despite her condition being stable, I knew she still wasn't safe. There were people who wanted her dead, including my father. And all I wanted at this point was to protect her. I already had a plan forming in my head. I knew what I had to do in order to make her untouchable. I knew there was only one way to protect her from my father.

She has to become one of us.
She has to become a Vergoossen.

"M…" she muttered, bringing her hand to her head, and I straightened up. "My head."

"Melanie?" I fixed the pillow for her. "Careful, baby."

"Where am I?" She struggled to speak, probably still feeling groggy.

"You're in a hospital. You're safe."

"In a hospital?" She could barely keep her heavy eyelids open. "Why? What happened?"

"You don't remember?" I was slightly confused and disappointed. I was hoping I'd learn the truth about this *incident* from her.

"I don't remember anything."

"It's okay. What matters is that you've woken up. I was so damn worried." I sat on the edge of her bed, leaning down to kiss her forehead. "I'll call your doctor. He should examine you."

She furrowed her brows, staring at me intently. "Wait… who are you?" she whispered, and my blood ran cold.

I froze. The world around me stopped turning. I looked into her eyes, terrified. Her voice kept ringing in my ears. Was it possible that she didn't remember me? Was the concussion so bad? An overwhelming feeling of regret and angst flooded my veins.

I lost her.

She didn't remember me. The moments we shared. The undeniable attraction pushing us toward each other like magnets. The effect she had on me. The effect I had on her. It was all gone.

I cleared my throat, trying to stay in control of my emotions. "You don't know who I am, Melanie?"

"I'm sorry," she said softly, and my heart dropped to my stomach.

Fuck.

FIFTEEN

Melanie

I stared at the devilishly handsome man before me. His eyes filled with a mix of dismay and fear. He was rooted to the spot, frozen. My head was pounding, my body sore. But even that didn't stop me from pranking. I sat up, adjusting myself on the hospital bed. It was dark outside, and the room was dim. Thank God because my eyes hurt at the slightest trace of light. I pressed my lips together, fighting a smile.

"I'm sorry, Shane." He frowned at me, confused, tilting his head slightly to the side, his mouth partially open. "I guess it was a bad joke."

He gave me a puzzled look before shaking his head. A faint smile curled up his lip. "Bad joke?" He narrowed his eyes at me. "You're an evil woman." His tone was teasing, and I chuckled.

"Please, don't make me laugh. I'm all sore."

"You started it." He shook his head, now smiling broadly. "You frightened me to death."

"Are you mad?" I asked, making puppy eyes.

He brought his hand to my face, caressing my cheek. "I couldn't be mad at you. I'm over the moon that you woke up." He leaned into my ear and lowered his voice. "I'll punish you later."

He winked at me before leaving a soft kiss on my lips before our eyes locked.

"For a moment there, I thought I lost you." His tone was low, soft. "And it was the worst feeling I've ever experienced."

I drowned in his ocean-blue eyes, butterflies dancing in my belly. I wanted to tell him that I was falling for him or that perhaps I already had, hard. But I couldn't. The words wouldn't come out of my mouth. I was scared it was too soon, and I would scare him off, lose him, and that thought was frightening. Shane slid his hand to the back of my head, gently leaning in to kiss my forehead.

"I'll call a doctor," he whispered, and I shook my head, yes, breathing out heavily. I hadn't found the courage to tell him that I loved him.

"EVERYTHING SEEMS FINE," the doctor, a pleasant Hindi beauty, stated as she wrote her notes down on the patient record. "You'll be good to go home tomorrow. We'll keep you for observation for the night."

I nodded, acknowledging, smiling at her. Despite that being her job, I was grateful for her help. Shane was standing beside me, resting against the wall next to the window, his hands crossed on his abdomen. It was only then that I noticed he was dressed in an unusual way. He looked like a gangster that just dealt with something dangerous, shady. I scanned him carefully all the way from his heavy black boots up to his black leather jacket, wondering what secrets he had. What dark things I didn't know about the man I was falling for.

"Your family is waiting outside to see you," the doc's soft voice snapped me out of my thoughts. "Do you want me to let them in?"

I glanced at Shane, who stood by my side like a bodyguard, taking a deep breath. As much as I didn't want to see my father, I knew it was inevitable. "Yes, let them in, please."

The doctor nodded and gave me a polite smile before she left. I heard her soothing voice through the door she left ajar, updating my parents about my condition before telling them they could come in.

"Melanie, darling, thank God!" My mother ran through the door, reaching her hand to hug me. "Are you okay?"

"Yes, Mom. Just… sore." I felt uncomfortable in her embrace, and I wasn't exactly sure if it was because she would rarely hug me or because I was in pain.

"We were so worried about you." My father's stern voice rang in my ears.

Wow… he really has some nerve.

Mom sat on the edge of my bed, caressing my hair, staring at me with her brows furrowed and a worried gaze. "The doctor said we can take you home tomorrow. We'll take care of you. I promise."

An image from my quarrel with my father flashed before my eyes and an uneasy feeling of anxiety rushed through my body, and I flinched. I looked over at my father and Shane. They were exchanging deadly stares. Shane's eyes narrowed, his jaw clenched.

"You should leave now," my father shrieked, still staring at Shane. "Melanie's with her family, and her boyfriend is waiting to see her."

I couldn't believe the audacity of this man. Even after everything that happened, he still wanted to use me, pushing me into the arms of the man who cheated on me. The man who was responsible for everything that had happened since. Maybe I should thank Theo because if it weren't for his betrayal, I wouldn't have met Shane.

"Are you serious?" I winced. My mother straightened up, swallowing hard. She looked like a scared puppy, afraid to even open her mouth.

"Come to your senses, Melanie," my father hissed. "Don't throw your whole life away because of… *him*." He barely refrained from showing his true colors again.

"No, you know what? You leave." I shook my head, a wave of resentment rushing through me. I looked to the side to see Shane, who respected my need to talk to my parents even though I knew how much he despised my father, especially after I confessed to him the night before. He glanced at me fleetingly, instantly knowing what I needed. He read me like an open book. He understood me without words, and that made our bond so special.

"I think that's your cue to leave, Mrs. and Mr. Atwood," he stated, his voice calm yet firm.

He came closer to my bed, covering my hand with his, and in an instant, I felt safe. Shane's presence made me stronger and braver, not afraid of my father. I looked out of the window, refusing to look my parents in the eyes. My mother cleared her throat before walking out of the room, and my father muttered something under his breath and followed. I didn't have high expectations when it came to my father but knowing that my mother gave up so easily overwhelmed my soul with desolating despair.

Shane sat beside me, pulling me between his muscular arms for a comforting hug. I took a deep breath, inhaling his addictive scent that kept me sane.

"Move in with me," he whispered.

I slowly pulled back to look at him, our eyes locked, and I couldn't hide the astonishment.

"I'm not saying forever, but at least until you're fully recovered. Or until my father's charity event." His voice was so soothing it was like a palliative remedy for my pain, a cure gluing my broken heart back together. "I have to go back to New York, at least for some time, and I don't want to leave you here. Come with me. Please."

I was at a loss for words. The idea of flying to New York with Shane was something I wanted the most. But it was all happening so fast, and I was afraid that one day I would drown in the deep sea I was thrown into. Just a couple of days ago, I had a long-term boyfriend and a life I'd known. It wasn't perfect, but it was familiar. Shane, in contrast, was new territory for me. The question was... did I want to explore that new, uncharted territory?

"Okay." I nodded, unable to fight the smile curling up my lips.

Shane looked at me, startled, as if he didn't expect me to agree. A broad grin formed on his face, showing off his gorgeous white teeth. He chuckled softly before embracing me, his arms felt like home. I realized home isn't a place. Home is where you feel safe, loved, at your best, where you want to be, and where you want to return after a long, bad day. And for me, it was *Shane's arms*.

"Boss?" A vaguely familiar male voice reached my ears as a tall man dressed exactly like Shane lurked at the entrance of the room, peeking through the slightly ajar door.

The first thing that caught my eye was his slicked-back dark-blue hair and multiple cartilage ear piercings. I couldn't see his eyes hidden behind dark sunglasses. It was funny that he wore dark sunglasses inside and in the middle of the night, but there was nothing funny about that man. Shane switched his attention to his friend, employee, or whoever the man was, and the blue-haired man stepped inside the room, closing the door behind him. A dangerous kind of darkness emanated from him in the exact same way as when I first met Shane. I tilted my head to the side, scanning the man with my eyes inch by inch. I had a feeling we'd met before but couldn't recall where. Until he took off his glasses, revealing his hazel eyes, and the world stopped turning.

"Callan?" Shane asked somewhat impatiently.

"I just wanted to check in, see if you needed anything." He cleared his throat, avoiding my gaze.

"No. You may leave. I'll stay here for the night," Shane stated, searching his pockets.

"Shane, you don't have to stay here." I squeezed his hand, smiling at him comfortingly, but he only smiled back, leaving a gentle kiss on my cheek before approaching his friend.

"Here. The keys to my place. You'll stay with me there until we fly back to New York."

"Gotcha." He nodded, fleetingly peeking in my direction. "Get well, Miss Atwood."

"Thank you, Callan." I barely managed to say his name out loud, giving him a faint smile before he walked out of the room.

Shane took off his leather jacket and threw it onto the chair before sitting on the bed next to me, resting his back against the wall and sliding his arm around my shoulder.

"I'm right where I want to be," he said softly, kissing the top of my head.

I sank into his arms, making myself comfortable. I was more grateful that he stayed than I cared to admit.

"Who's he to you?" I asked a little too quietly.

"Callan?"

I nodded.

"He's my right-hand man."

"Right-hand man? As in helping you with business?"

Shane took a deep breath before replying, "Yeah. With business. He's also my friend."

I inhaled deeply.

Well, that complicates everything.

SIXTEEN

Shane

For the next couple of days, Melanie stayed with me. I was surprised how good it felt having her around, waking next to her every morning, making love to her. I never thought that I could actually make love with someone. It wasn't in my nature, but after what Melanie confessed to me and after the concussion she had, I couldn't help but be a little too overprotective. *Fuck me.* I hadn't expected that from myself, but she had that effect on me. For her, I'd die. We even created our little routine. I would drop her off and pick her up at the university. We would eat every meal together and work out together. It was just a few days, but I got so attached to her that I couldn't imagine my day without seeing her. She was like a dose of my favorite drug—a drug I desperately needed.

There were days when I had to leave her alone for some time to take care of work-related stuff. And considering my profession and her identity, it was too dangerous to let her tag along. In her eyes, I was a successful businessman, which was partially true. But the companies my family owned were mostly just covers for our Mafia. We had to have an explanation for our wealth, position, and connections, and it was the best way to blindside ordinary people. Although Melanie suspected something, I knew I would have to confess to her the truth eventually. She was a clever woman, and I'd rather have her learn that from me. There was just one thing that alarmed me. Melanie seemed tense whenever Callan was around. And Callan wasn't himself around Melanie. I caught them exchanging secret looks as if they had a history together or shared a secret, but for some fucked-up reason, I kept pushing that thought away.

Melanie agreed with her professors that she would be taking online classes for the time being. Less than a week later, we landed in New York. My drivers were already waiting for us at the airport. Melanie and I got in my black Lamborghini Veneno Roadster and headed straight to one of my penthouses at Park Avenue. Callan left with Wyatt, my second-in-command's right-hand man, who would take care of my orders whenever Callan wasn't available, and the driver took them to their places.

"Wow, I love the view!" Melanie ran through my living room to the window showcasing the view of Manhattan as soon as we entered my eight-thousand-square-foot penthouse on the very top floor of the skyscraper.

"Yeah, it's pretty impressive from the ninety-sixth floor." I embraced her from behind, admiring the view I'd never really paid much attention to.

My phone rang, and Melanie turned to nod, smiling as if giving me a sign it was okay if I answered. I took my phone out of my pocket to see Elena's name on the screen—my stepmother. Elena was my parents' close friend who started an affair with my father shortly after my mother's death. I wasn't sure if she was just a rebound for him, helping him get through the hard time after my mother passed away, or if he had any feelings for her. But things escalated quickly because barely a year after my mother's death, Elena gave birth to my half brother, Anders. I was six at that time. I couldn't blame my father, though. He was just a thirty-four-year-old man left alone with a son, and Elena was a beautiful ten-years-younger woman with a heart of gold. She cared for me like I was her son, supporting my father ever since. I had to admit that she tried her best to be like a mother to me, and although I could never forget my birth mother, I had a great bond with Elena.

"Elena?" I slowly walked toward the hallway.

"Shane, I hope I haven't interrupted anything?" I heard her warm voice through the speaker.

"No, of course not. We just entered my apartment."

"Oh, I won't take much of your time. Karl and I would like to invite you and your friend for dinner tonight." *My friend, huh?*

I turned back to glance at Melanie, who was texting on her phone. Probably her friend, Scarlett, because she told me she promised she would message her first thing after landing. I took a deep breath, knowing my father was watching my every step, and he didn't approve of my relationship with Melanie. I assured my father I was doing all of this to get closer to Dedrick and that I had every intention of sticking to our plan, but I knew it was just a matter of time until he would see right through me. Therefore, I had to be prepared day and night for every possibility because I wouldn't know what he was planning behind my back. And my father was the kind of man who always had a card up his sleeve. But so was I.

"We'll come. Thanks for the invite." I figured it would be best if Melanie met my family before the charity event we were supposed to make an appearance at. Besides, I knew I had to face my father sooner or later.

"Wonderful! We'll be expecting you at six. Bye, Shane."

I ended the call, turning to Melanie. "Elena, my father's wife, invited us for dinner at six. I said we would come if that's fine with you?"

"Sure," Melanie said hesitantly. "That's kind of her."

I approached Melanie and slid my hands around her waist. "I know my father is intimidating, but I'll be right next to you. You're safe, I promise. And you'll love Elena and Aaliyah."

"Aaliyah?" She narrowed her eyes.

"My half sister. She's only twelve, but she's adorable."

"I had no idea you had a sister." Melanie seemed abashed.

"Yeah, and a half brother."

"Wow." She bit her lower lip anxiously. "That makes me think I don't know much about you, Shane. Except for a few details anyone could Google."

I leaned into her ear, whispering, "You know way more about me, Melanie. I assure you."

She smiled before looking into my eyes, her tone seductive. "Is that so, Mr. Vergoossen?"

"Yes." I ran my thumb over her bottom lip. "Besides, we'll have eternity to explore each other."

"Eternity? Those are big words, mister."

I smirked, looking at her angelic face. Fuck, she was so gorgeous, intoxicating. "Let's start now."

"What do you mean?" she said softly, slightly narrowing her eyes.

I grabbed her hand. "Come with me. I want to show you who I truly am," I said calmly despite deep down being faintly anxious. Anxious that after revealing my dark side to her, she would leave. But I knew it was time to come clean. Especially before I implemented my plan in life, she had to know who I really was. She had to be aware of what kind of man she was falling for.

I led her to the library off the main living room. Its design was dark, unlike the rest of my apartment. There was a fireplace, a glass table in the middle, and a comfy cream-colored leather couch—a seemingly ordinary room.

"So?" Melanie asked, looking around the place. "Am I supposed to know who you truly are because of the library?"

I chuckled before moving closer to the wall perpendicular to the fireplace or the couch and opening a small recess with a biometric technique allowing fingerprint and retina scanning. I pressed my thumb on the biometric before it scanned my retinas, and the wall started to move. I glanced at Melanie, who was stunned at the sight of dozens of different types of weapons hanging in the secret storage compound.

"What the hell?" she whispered, her eyes and mouth wide open. She looked at me, confused, I could tell the adrenaline was rushing through her veins as she swallowed and her breath quickened. "Who are you?"

I slowly took a few steps toward Melanie, expecting her to be scared or even run. Instead, she stood there observing me. Her eyes didn't fill with fear but rather confusion and anticipation. "I'm involved with the Mafia," I said darkly. "My whole family is, with my father being the boss, and I, his heir."

"I knew you weren't normal," she whispered, still dazed. "Are you going to hurt me?"

I shook my head, frowning. I slid my hand around her neck. "Of course not. I won't let anyone hurt you. I'll keep you safe, Melanie."

"I thought I was crazy," she said softly, not breaking eye contact.

"Why?"

"Because I knew it from the day I met you."

My eyes darted between hers. Now I was the one puzzled.

"I felt it, Shane," she continued, her voice strong, without a trace of fear. "Then, after that incident with your father…."

"Yeah, he's not too subtle about it."

She chuckled. "No. Definitely not."

"So, aren't you scared? Mad?" She handled the news way better than I had imagined. Actually, she dealt with the news so well that I was taken aback.

"I am not scared, Shane." She slid her hand to the back of my head, our gazes locked. "You're going to protect me. You promised."

I nodded faintly, caressing the soft skin of her neck with my thumb. "I will protect you, Melanie. You're my priority now. But you have to know that my lifestyle is dangerous. I *am* dangerous."

She let out a deep sigh. Her gaze dropped down for a short moment. "You could be a serial killer and I still wouldn't let you go," she whispered before her eyes moved up to meet mine. "I can't help the attraction toward you.

Call me crazy, but I'm addicted. You're the drug I can't resist."

"I feel the same way. Nothing in this world intoxicates me as you do, Melanie. You're like a drug flowing through my veins. And I don't want to sober up. I want to overdose on you."

"I already did." She sank into my touch, biting her lower lip before standing on her toes to reach my ear. "Now, I want you to show me how you really are. No limits."

"What do you mean?" I growled as she provocatively sucked my earlobe.

She looked into my eyes, her hands around my neck. "Forget everything that happened. Everything that I told you. Don't define me by my past, and I won't define you by the prism of your… profession. Let's start from a blank page."

"Okay," I whispered, our lips only inches apart. "Blank page."

"Good." She intertwined her fingers with my hair, pulling me closer, so our lips were parted only by the mesh of our heavy breaths. She slid one of her hands underneath my shirt, scraping my abs with her nails, causing my muscles to tense. Her eyes still locked with mine, biting her lip sultrily. "Now fuck me. Rough. Wild. Just like you like it."

"You asked for this," I growled before crashing my lips onto hers to kiss her, rough, demanding.

Not breaking our heated tangle, I led her toward the couch before, with one swift move, turning her body back on me. I brushed her hair away and tore the white woolen dress she wore apart, and she gasped. I moved my hand up her bare back, sliding the other around her waist, and bent her against the leather backrest of the couch.

"I'm going to be rough," I said, my tone low. "Are you sure you want this?"

"Yes," she breathed, her round breast pressed against the leather fabric.

I spread her legs with my hand, moving it between her thighs. She was so wet, so eager for me. I pushed my finger through her juices, and a sweet moan escaped her lips. In the meantime, I unbuckled my belt and undid my fly, freeing my hard cock from my pants. I gathered her hair into a ponytail with my hand and pulled her head back, causing her back to arch as I entered her, rough, deep. A louder moan escaped her luscious lips for which I had sinful plans right after I took her the way she wanted.

"You're late," My father's stern voice rumbled through the hallway as Melanie and I entered his mansion. "What took you so long?" He frowned, stopping a few steps in front of me.

"You know." I cleared my throat, barely hiding the amusement. "Traffic."

Melanie's cheeks flushed a cute shade of red, giving away we had spent the last two hours in a delightfully wicked way.

"Traffic," he said, nodding. "Obviously."

"Ah, finally!" Elena sauntered in our direction, a charming smile on her face. Her black chin-length hair was tucked behind her ear, and her lips were painted a carmine red. She wore a black silk dress with sleeves reaching her elbows and a silky red belt around her waist, matching the shade of her lipstick. As per usual, her outfit was complemented with golden jewelry. My father also wore formal clothing: a black shirt, a gray vest, and a carmine-red tie. Melanie and I weren't dressed so formally but not casually either. I wore a shirt with a few buttons left undone, just the way I liked it the most, and Melanie wore a stunning teal blue, as she called it, dress with semilong sleeves and her blonde waves falling down her revealed arms. She looked ravishing. I couldn't take my eyes off of her.

"Hi, dear. I'm Elena." She extended her hand toward Melanie. "Shane's stepmom," she added as the ladies shook hands.

"Good evening, Mrs. Vergoossen. Thank you for the invitation," Melanie said, her tone warm and polite.

"The pleasure is all ours." Elena smiled broadly. "Let's all get on a first-name basis, shall we?"

"An excellent idea, my love. I like to keep things straightforward," Karl commented, his voice toneless.

"It's a pleasure to meet you, Elena." Melanie sounded timid, but she handled it all so well. She peeked at my father, slightly intimidated. "Karl."

"Make yourself at home, Melanie." My father nodded at Melanie before switching his attention to his wife. "Darling, could you please accompany Miss Atwood? I have to steal my son for a moment. We have to talk about some boring business stuff." He gave me a stern look. "In private."

"Of course, my love." Elena smiled. She knew her way around my father. "Melanie, please follow me. We'll be dining on the patio. I'll show you the garden while we wait for our men to join us."

"I'll be right there. I promise you're in good hands," I whispered to Melanie, and she gave me a comforting smile. She turned to my stepmother, and they walked down the hallway, chatting like they'd known each other for ages. I was calm about Melanie. I knew Elena was easy to get along with, warmhearted, and considerate.

"Follow me," my father said in a flat tone.

I rolled my eyes, prepared for this conversation I'd been expecting, and followed him to his office.

"CLOSE THE DOOR BEHIND YOU," Karl rasped, staring at me coldly. He sat back in his plush leather armchair, his arms on both sides of the richly padded armrests with stylish redwood accents matching his sophisticated wooden desk. Black velvet curtains were covering the massive west-wing window. I closed the door and took a seat in front of him on an upholstered caramel leather chair. We exchanged stern gazes before he spoke in a tone as emotionless as his facial expression. "Knowing you, son, I thought you just wanted to bang her."

I clenched my jaw, trying to stay poised. He was testing my patience, but I'd known better.

"But over time, I've started to believe that you want something more than just sex from her."

I did not respond. I stared into his empty eyes, my face unreadable.

"Tell me, Shane. Tell me I'm wrong." He stood from his chair, leaning against the redwood top of his vintage desk. "Tell me we're still on the same team, son."

I heaved a deep sigh, tilting my head to the side. "Have I ever failed you?"

He narrowed his eyes. "No."

"Then trust me and let me do my job."

He let out a heavy breath before straightening up. "Very well. I hope you know what you're doing because I wouldn't want to be your enemy, son."

SEVENTEEN

Melanie

I chatted with Elena mostly about Shane and his half-sibs. She had so much love for Shane, who wasn't her biological son, and I could tell she was an incredible woman full of grace and charm. She told me a few stories from Shane's childhood and how he'd always been a protective big brother to her children. She said after Shane's mother passed away, he became very mature and responsible and had stayed that way ever since, but he was also distant and closed in himself and that she had never seen him shed a tear. She joked he had been a tough man since he was a little boy.

"Ladies," Karl's voice rumbled from behind, and I turned back to see him walking alongside Shane. "Please, take your seats. Let's eat."

Elena led me toward the vast table in the middle of the beautiful patio decorated with flowers and candles and a variety of food. Shane pulled out a chair for me, and despite a polite smile, I noticed something dark in his eyes.

"Is everything okay?" I whispered, scanning his face as I took a seat.

"Yes, don't worry," he replied, sitting beside me. He grabbed my hand and squeezed it in his, and we shared a brief look.

"It's the first time Shane's brought a woman to our home," Elena commented, a genuine grin on her face, her eyes gleaming. "He has never introduced us to any other woman before. You must be special to him, Melanie, have him under your spell."

Karl cleared his throat, clearly not being content with his wife's remark. I was aware he disapproved of my relationship with his son because of who I was—his sworn enemy's daughter. I bet he'd rather have me dead than date his son. I wondered what he told Shane when they went to talk in private. I assumed he had reprimanded Shane, trying to convince him *we* were a *bad* idea.

"Shane!" A girlish voice caught everyone's attention. All at the same time, we turned to see a beautiful girl with raven-black braids running toward Shane. Her sand-brown eyes were beaming with excitement as she threw herself into Shane's arms.

"Hey, little one," he greeted her with a warm hug and a gentle kiss on her prominent cheek. For the first time, I saw Shane smiling genuinely. His face brightened as he looked at the girl I assumed must've been Aaliyah, his little half sister. The girl looked like Elena, two peas in a

OVERDOSED

pod. Both had the same lovely smile and stunning Indian beauty. "How have you been, hm?" Shane asked, holding her hands in his.

"I missed you, big bro!"

"I missed you, too." He chuckled. The sight was so heartwarming I couldn't fight a broad grin forming on my face. "I want you to meet someone, okay?"

The girl nodded, blushing as she peeked at me.

"Aaliyah, this is Melanie. Melanie, this is Aaliyah," she introduced us to each other, and I reached my hand to greet her.

"Hey, Aaliyah. Nice to meet you."

"Nice to meet you too." She smiled before switching her attention back to her brother, whom she clearly adored. "So she's your girlfriend?"

Shane turned to peek at me, smirking as if to check in with me. We had never talked about it. *We* kind of... just happened. "Yes. Melanie is my girlfriend." He focused his gaze back on the lovely girl.

"She's pretty." She winked at him teasingly, and we chuckled. She had the charisma of her father and the charm of her mother.

"Oh, I know," Shane answered before tickling his sister, and she giggled loudly. It was so sweet to watch.

"Come, honey, join us. We're about to eat." Elena pulled the chair for Aaliyah next to her.

"Will Shane's brother be joining us too?" I asked while the household staff served the meals.

"No, he's out of the country," Elena replied. "However, he's on a plane as we speak. You'll meet him at Karl's charity event tomorrow."

"So, does he live abroad?" I couldn't help my curiosity. The Vergoossen family was like a mystery to many, including myself.

"He's studying business and management at Oxford in England," Elena clarified. "I think you're his peer."

"Miss Atwood is one year older," Karl added, his tone dry, his eyes watching me closely the whole time.

"Oh, you're right, honey. Anyway, let's eat." Elena smiled, and Karl nodded before we started dining.

THE EVENING WAS PASSING BY in a surprisingly lovely atmosphere, mainly thanks to Elena's charm. It felt like she was bringing so much joy to the Vergoossen family, and knowing the real, dark side that being a Vergoossen entailed, I must admit, she was handling her role as a wife to a Mafia boss perfectly. Nonetheless, I didn't fully understand back then what it meant to be a woman of a Mafia man, a criminal, a gangster. I was only about to find out now as it was just the beginning of my story. I was just exploring the tip of the iceberg. To this point, their lives seemed normal to me. We had an enchanting dinner and mainly chatted about funny family stories, just like ordinary people. And that misled me into believing that was what their lives looked like. In the meantime, Aaliyah got bored with our conversation and excused herself to her room. Before she left, Karl gave his daughter a warm kiss on her cheek, shocking me with a vestige of humanity in him I'd assumed didn't exist.

"Melanie," Karl started after taking a sip of the red wine. "We keep talking about our family. Maybe you would tell us something about yourself?"

Shane adjusted himself on his seat, drinking his wine in one go. I could tell he didn't feel comfortable having his father around me.

"I told you already. I'm a law student at Stanford, an only child. There's nothing much more to tell, Mr. Vergoossen," I replied, reaching for the glass of wine, but I didn't drink. I wrapped my fingers around the stem to keep my hand busy. It was my way of coping with my nerves.

"Karl," he corrected me.

"Karl," I repeated, nodding. I couldn't get used to calling him by his first name. For some reason, it didn't sit right with me. Unlike Elena, with whom I had no issue chatting as if we'd known each other for ages. "Besides, I'm sure you know more about me than I do myself, Karl," I added with pure sarcasm oozing off me, and I could swear I saw a tiny trace of a smile forming in the corners of the emotionless man's mouth. *Did I impress him?*

"Now I see what my son sees in you, Miss Atwood," Karl retorted.

"Melanie," I corrected him, a satisfied smirk curled up my lips.

"Melanie," he reiterated, the smile broadened on his face. He took a long sip of the wine. "So, Melanie, I've heard your middle name is *Rose*, is that correct?" He looked at me as if he was waiting to beat me in the game of chess we were playing.

"Yes, that's right," I stated, suddenly feeling oddly uneasy.

"Did you know that Shane's mother's name was Rose too?" His eyes screamed checkmate, but I wasn't quite sure why.

"No, I didn't know," I said softly, realizing Shane had never told me anything about his mother, and I didn't pressure him to because I thought it was just something too intimate and painful for him. I didn't want to pry, and I didn't want him to relive the tragedy of losing his mother as a little boy once again.

I started linking the dots in my head. All I knew was that my father insisted on naming me Rose despite knowing that, for some reason, my mother despised that name. I thought it was just a whim of my father's to play on my mother's nerves, but now I wasn't sure. Was it possible my father had something to do with Shane's mother, and that was why they became enemies?

"We should get going." Shane's cold tone snapped me out of my thoughts. His sudden change of heart only added to my conviction that something was off. "It's getting late. It's been a long day. I'm sure Melanie is exhausted after the flight."

"Of course." Karl sent his son a mischievous smirk before raising the glass of wine as if to toast before he took yet another long sip of it, his eyes fixed on Shane's. Suddenly, the atmosphere became so tense you could cut it with a knife, and there was something eerie in the air, something that sent chills down my spine.

"Thank you for the lovely evening," I said, breaking in on the building, invisible tension between the two dangerous men.

"The pleasure is all ours." Elena eased the dark looming tenseness with her charm. "We'll see you tomorrow at the charity."

"Of course." I smiled. "Good night."

I WATCHED SHANE driving his car with overwhelming darkness in his eyes. He'd never been the type to show much affection, but he'd never been so cold and distant either. I recalled the past events to a moment when his behavior had changed. It was precisely when Karl touched upon the topic of Shane's mother and the name we share. I observed his face, inch by inch, as if looking for a clue. A clue that would help me figure out if it was because it brought up the painful memories of his mother's death or because my name had actually had more meaning to the story. I had a sneaking suspicion that it was the latter, especially that Karl mentioned that, and knowing the man he was, he did everything for a reason.

"What is it, Melanie?" Shane asked, his gaze still focused on the road. I was amazed he knew I was watching him without even looking in my direction to check.

"Why?" I asked, still scanning his face. That man was like an unraveled mystery to me.

"You keep watching me." His lips curled into a soft smile. "You can ask me."

"Ask you what?" I frowned. I was slightly annoyed that he could read me like an open book while I couldn't figure him out.

"Whatever it is that you want to ask."

"How do you know I want to ask you something?"

"You do that whenever you have a question, but you're not entirely sure if it's okay to ask."

"Do what?" I leaned back, taking a better look at the man who analyzed me so intuitively without looking at me.

"You watch me." He glanced at me with a faint smile. "As if looking for a clue."

I raised my brows, amazed and annoyed because he was right.

I cleared my throat, hesitant. "I'm wondering what happened to your mother. You never told me how she died."

Shane took a heavy breath, his eyes on the road, but I could see the pain on his face.

"She committed suicide," he said dryly, and I instantly regretted asking.

"I'm so sorry, Shane. I shouldn't ha—"

He cut me off, peeking at me briefly, pressing his lips together into a forced smile, his voice soft. "It's okay, Melanie." He switched his attention back to the road. "It's a heavy topic. Let's not spoil the rest of the evening. The night is still young. We can do something much more entertaining than that. What do you say?"

I swallowed the lump that had formed in my throat at the thought of what Shane had to go through. Not to mention I was even more confused than before asking the question. Why would Shane's mother commit suicide? As far as I was concerned, she had a loving husband, a beautiful son, and a good life. What pushed her to take her own life?

"I'm up, Mr. Vergoossen," I said, trying to dispel the dark thoughts running through my head. "Actually, I have a surprise for you once we return to your place."

"A surprise?" Shane smiled, his tone slightly seductive. "Do I get a clue what it is?"

"Nope," I teased. "Let me be the mysterious one for once."

He chuckled, and his face brightened up. I was glad I managed to lighten up the mood. He grabbed my hand, squeezing it in his, and we drove back to his penthouse, surrounded by the gleaming lights of Manhattan.

EIGHTEEN

Shane

Melanie went to freshen up, and I poured myself a glass of whiskey. I stood by the window in the living room, staring numbly at the Hudson River, sipping the brown liquor. The images from my childhood flashed in my mind with a heavy weight on my shoulders. I missed my mother. She was so gentle and loving, always cheerful. Melanie reminded me of her, just a little bit. Not her appearance. My mother had black hair and blue eyes as I did, but her personality. They both seemed fragile at first sight but had the fierce soul of a warrior. Perhaps that was why Melanie had me at hello. I let out a deep breath, gulping my drink in one go. I knew I had to tell Melanie the truth about me, my father's plan, revenge. I was so fucking scared, though. I was scared she wouldn't understand it, and I would lose her. I was afraid of letting her go, and maybe, that would be for the best. Perhaps if I hadn't been so selfish and stayed away from her as I should have, we could have avoided the upcoming disaster.

But I couldn't resist her—my forbidden temptation.

"Shane?" I turned back to see Melanie. She smiled at me in the most seductive way I'd ever seen. She bit her lower lip, painted red that night and slowly, sultrily, walked closer to me.

"Damn…" I whispered, stunned, as she slowly untied the silk belt of her black robe and slowly took it off of her, letting it fall on the floor. Her big brown eyes fixed on me.

My gaze dropped to the floor seeing the silky robe that pooled around her black high heels before I slowly scanned every inch of her sexy body, starting from her long, toned legs, up her flat belly, round breasts to her beautiful face. She looked dark, sultry. She had dark makeup, and she wore lacy lingerie. It was a transparent one-piece. I swallowed, devouring her with my eyes, my body set on fire. I put my hands on her hips, pulling her closer to me.

"Ah, ah, ah." She shook her finger no. She slid her hand around my neck, and shivers swept the length of my spine before she whispered in my ear, her tone seductive. "You may watch, but you can't touch."

I was intrigued by that side of her. The dark and sultry side of her I had not explored yet. She bit my earlobe, and a deep growl rumbled down my throat. She then grabbed my hand and led me toward a chair, turning to look at me as she walked, provocatively swaying her hips and smirking, sin gleaming in her eyes.

"Sit down," she ordered as we approached the leather armchair. "Tonight, you're at my mercy, Mr. Vergoossen."

Although I was already hard as a rock, fighting the temptation to throw myself at her like a beast and fuck her hard and rough, I was enjoying this side of her, eager to explore it. I sat on the chair, and she walked around me, her hand on my torso, sliding beneath the black fabric of my shirt.

She leaned down to whisper in my ear from behind. "Your hands back. Now."

I growled, savoring her warm, wet kisses on the side of my neck as I slid my hands to the back of the chair.

"Don't move," she whispered before I heard the clicking of her heels and the sound of her pulling out a drawer, and then again, the clicking of her heels against the wooden floor.

I felt something cold around my left and then my right wrist, and I quickly figured out Melanie cuffed my hands. She walked to stand in front of me, letting me admire her sexy body covered only with the transparent lacy fabric of her tight lingerie. She seductively bent down to put aside the champagne bottle and cubes of ice she held in her hands and grabbed the remote from the glass table to turn on the music. I bit my lower lip, gawking at Melanie, who provocatively swayed her hips to the sultry beat, roaming her hands up her curves. My blood drained to my dick, twitching against the zipper. My breath became heavy and ragged, my eyes black with sheer wild lust.

"Melanie," I hissed, my voice raspy and tone low.

She smirked faintly, yet satisfied at the effect she had on me. She slowly approached me, bending down to look into my eyes, her hands resting on both sides of my chair.

"I'll make sure you never forget this night," she whispered before licking her lips, squeezing one of her hands on the growing bulge in my pants which drove me mad with desire. If she hadn't cuffed me, I'd be fucking her hard against the wall by now. She slowly unbuttoned my shirt. Her eyes never left mine before she turned around to reach the champagne and ice, giving me a perfect view of her round ass.

"Fuck," I growled, barely staying still. I was burning, craving her body like a madman.

Melanie poured the champagne into the glass that was standing on the table and reached for one ice tube before she walked closer to me, setting the glass on the floor beside the chair I sat on. She brushed the ice cube against her slightly parted lips, watching me sultrily. She then bent down, resting her left hand against the armrest, and she leaned in to kiss me, putting the ice cube gently to my neck, causing goose bumps to rise on my skin, and I growled. She slowly moved the ice down my neck, torso, and abs, trailing warm kisses down the path where she'd put the ice until she kneeled between my legs and looked up into my eyes. I loved the confidence in her eyes, the mischievous spark gleaming in her gaze. She unbuckled my belt and undid my zipper, wrapping her hand around my hard cock. Her eyes never left mine as she leaned down to take my entire length into her luscious mouth.

A jolt of pleasure whipped through my body as she encased my cock with her warm lips and wet tongue, slobbering up and down my shaft. I watched her head moving up and down. My breath was ragged and heavy until she slowly pulled back, letting my cock pop out from her lips. I watched her, clenching my fists, burning. She reached for the glass of champagne and took a long sip, but she didn't swallow. Instead, she took my dick back into her mouth. The cold sparkling bubbles combined with her warm lips sent a wild sensation through my body. She sucked my cock, tightening her wet lips around it. Drops of champagne dripped down the corners of her mouth. She pulled back again, focusing now on the tip, licking it with her warm tongue. My muscles tensed, and I felt the growing ecstasy as I clenched my fists tighter. Melanie took a deep breath before moving her head down, taking my length deep down her throat. She gagged a little, gripping her throat muscles around my shaft, and I growled at the rush of pleasure. She kept bobbing her head up and down, pushing me to the edge.

"Melanie, I'm close," I hissed, warning her, but she only moaned loudly as if in agreement, speeding up the pace. "Fuck," I growled, and Melanie slowly pulled away so that she held only the tip of my cock in her mouth as shot after shot of cum began flowing out of me. Melanie swallowed each spurt before letting my cock pop out, stroking its tip against her lips.

She wiped her lips before taking a long sip of the champagne. I watched her hungrily with my breath ragged. She walked around the chair to uncuff my hands, leaning down to reach my ear from behind, whispering seductively. "Just for the record, it was the first time I've done that. And I wanted it to be with you."

The thought that she was exploring her sexuality with me was such a turn-on. The moment she set my hands free, I turned around, and with one swift move at full force, I threw the chair away. I grabbed Melanie by her waist, pushing her against the wall behind her. "I'm going to fuck you now," I hissed, hovering over her. I slid my hand up her inner thigh, her body trembling. She was wet. Dripping wet. I stroked her sensitive bud with my fingers through the thin fabric of her lingerie. She pressed her body against the wall, arching her back as she gasped, and I whispered, watching her quivering in need. "In every possible position. But first, you're going to ride my face." She swallowed hard, breathing heavily, her lips parted as she looked up into my lustful eyes. I crashed my lips onto hers, kissing her demandingly before I lifted her princess style and carried her to the bedroom.

I woke up to the sound of my phone vibrating. I glanced at Melanie. She was asleep. Her naked body was covered by the silky duvet. I gently kissed her arm before reaching for my phone. It was twelve past four in the morning. I opened a text from Callan that said *BLACK*. It was our code for emergencies. Different colors for different cases. Black meant that he had something essential to tell me, that there may be a life-threatening danger. I got up from the bed and quietly went to the library.

"Boss?" I heard his deep voice through the speaker.

I stood by the window, gaze fixed on Manhattan that never sleeps. "What is it?" I said, my voice lowered.

"Sorry to disturb you at this hour, but we have a situation."

"What kind of situation?"

"I have intel from my source that Ax's gang is after Melanie."

"What?" I frowned, concerned.

"Allegedly, someone paid them to get Melanie. I suspect they may try their chances at the charity event."

"Someone?"

"We haven't established that yet."

"I want to know who. I want details, Callan."

"Sure, boss. I'm on it."

"Reinforce the security for the event. I want my people there," I said, my voice commanding. "Tell Wyatt to track them down. It's time to put my plan into action, and I want no interruptions, clear?"

"Clear," he replied, his tone serious.

OVERDOSED

I hang up the phone, running my fingers through my hair. I took a deep breath, putting together the pieces of my strategy. I knew what I had to do to keep Melanie safe. And I was determined to succeed, no matter the price. She was my woman now, and I'd kill for her. Die for her.

A FEW HOURS LATER, every station was airing the news about my father's annual charity event. I walked out of my bedroom, buttoning up the formal black blazer, and as I approached the living room, the voice of the lady on the news was becoming louder. I heard my last name mentioned a few times as she clarified that the funds raised from the event would go to a wide range of charities, primarily in support of medical science to help children with cancer, their mental health, and resilience. She couldn't miss out on the gossip that I was supposed to make an appearance with Melanie, the daughter of our family's long-standing enemy, as she said it. I rolled my eyes and switched off the TV. I checked the time on my watch. It'd been nearly two hours since Melanie and a stylist I hired for her locked themselves in one of the bedrooms. I knew this evening was going to be unique, so I hired a stylist to help Melanie get ready for the charity. I wanted her to feel special for the occasion. I wondered what the hell was taking them so long. It took me half an hour to take a shower and jump into the tuxedo I wore.

The sound of the knocking snapped me back from my thoughts. "Boss? It's me, Callan." His voice rumbled through the door.

"Come on in, dude."

"Sup, boss?" His vibrant voice filled the living room as he entered, dressed up.

It was the first time I'd seen him in a suit, and I couldn't help but tease. "Who are you, and what did you do to Callan?" I said, my brow raised as I checked him, head to toe. He wore an elegant navy-blue suit matching his hair.

"Very funny." He rolled his light-brown-with-a-hint-of-green eyes.

I chuckled, amused at his annoyance. I knew he wasn't the type to dress up. He preferred a street gangsta style. "What? I never thought I'd see you so posh."

"Please, just drop it." He let out a sigh. "You know it's just to blend in. I hate suits. Or ties."

"You're not even wearing a tie," I joked. It was way too amusing to see him irate because of a suit. "The thing you have around your neck is a bow tie."

"Yeah, whatever. Same shit."

I shook my head, grinning. "Alright, enough." I cleared my throat. "We need to be focused. Are our men here?"

He nodded.

"Good. I don't want any surprises. Today is the day. I'm going to finish all of this," I stated, and Callan frowned.

"What exactly is your plan?" He tilted his head, watching me. His hands clasped on his abdomen.

"You'll see," I replied. I hadn't told anyone about my plans, not even Callan. I couldn't let it leak, and walls have ears. Growing up in a Mafia environment, you take every possible precaution. You are never safe. Adrenaline accompanies you even when you sleep. "Your job is to guard her, Callan. With your life."

He nodded, fully aware of the responsibility he was accepting.

"Mr. Vergoossen. We're done." I turned to face the pink-headed woman with a pixie haircut, smiling at me politely. She held a bagful of brushes and some other unknown-to-me objects in her hand.

"Thank you, Kate," I said, handing her the envelope. "Here's the check."

"Anytime." She smiled before making her way out.

I wanted to go to the room where Melanie was getting ready, but I stood frozen in time as she walked into the living room. My eyes grew wide as I watched her casually swaying her hips as she took slow steps. She was wearing a full-length sparkling nude dress with a high cut on her left thigh. It had a plunging cutout narrowing down on her belly, with skin-like, transparent sleeves with shimmering embellishments. Her thick waves were left to hang loose, bouncing up and down as she walked. I was mesmerized by her beauty, and apparently, so was Callan. I glanced at him from the corner of my eye. He was speechless, looking at Melanie in a way I found disturbing. As if he wished she were his.

"Cat got your tongues, boys?" Melanie said teasingly, a broad smile forming on her glossy nude lips.

Callan cleared his throat. His gaze dropped to the ground for a short moment before he looked at me. "I'll be around, boss." I nodded, and he set his gaze on Melanie. His body was tense: "You look gorgeous, Miss Atwood."

"Thanks, Callan," Melanie said softly, and Callan pressed his lips together, nodding, and his gaze dropped again.

"Excuse me," he said before leaving, avoiding both of our gazes.

I found the situation weird, but I assumed he was just intimidated by Melanie's presence or her angelic beauty. Or at least, that was what I wanted to believe.

"Is it just me, or is it getting hot in here?" I said, walking toward Melanie with a provocative grin on my face.

"Forget it, Shane!" Melanie exclaimed, her eyes brightening up. "I won't let you ruin my look."

I chuckled, sliding my hands around her waist. "You know me too well."

"Mm-hmm," she muttered, wrapping her hands around my neck, our eyes locked.

"You look stunning," I whispered, stealing a kiss from her lips. "We should get going because if we stay here any longer, I might rip that dress off of you."

"You're unbelievable!" She giggled before I grabbed her hand and led her downstairs, where Callan, who was our driver and Melanie's bodyguard for the night, was waiting for us.

NINETEEN

Melanie

I held Shane's hand as we entered the prestigious Waldorf-Astoria Hotel and headed to the venue where Karl's charity event was taking place. I looked around the grand high-ceiling room. Dozens of round tables were beautifully decorated with white roses in high golden vases and four lit candles in each bouquet. The place was extravagant and opulent, exactly how I imagined an event hosted by someone like Karl Vergoossen would be.

"Good evening, Melanie."

Speaking of the devil.

Karl greeted us with Elena by his side, both wearing broad smiles on their faces. I could tell they both were in their element.

"Son," Karl added, nodding politely at Shane.

"Good evening, Karl. Elena," I said, and Elena hugged me as a welcome.

"Elena, you look ravishing," Shane stated as they exchanged a cheek kiss.

I wasn't sure if I was more dazzled by the remarkable venue or the hosts. Both Karl and Elena looked straight out of a magazine. Karl wore a white shirt under a worthy-of-a-king, black-damask tux with gold lapels and a bow tie, and Elena, a splendid long-sleeve velvet red ball gown with gold crystals worthy of a queen.

"Thank you, Shane. You're so charming, as always." Elena chuckled, snapping me out of the awe.

"Your date looks bewitching too," Karl commented, his eyes on me, and I wasn't sure if his remark was intended more for Shane or me. "No wonder my son is head over heels for you, love," he added, smiling slyly before the waiter offered us a glass of champagne.

I felt weak in my knees and nearly dropped the glass to the floor when I spotted my parents heading our way. I knew Karl sent them an invitation, but never in a million years did I think they would accept.

"Ah!" Karl exclaimed the second he noticed my parents. "What an extraordinary evening! What a sight to see the Atwoods family attending one of my legendary charity balls."

My parents approached us, both of their facial expressions so dark and gloomy as if they were attending a funeral. My mother nervously swiped the nonexistent dust from her emerald-green dress while my father sent Karl a death stare.

"Celine, my dear," Karl continued, his tone as cheerful as ever. "You look gorgeous. You don't look too bad either, Dedrick. It's been ages, hasn't it?"

Despite the show Karl decided to put on, the atmosphere was so tense and dreadful it was painful to watch, and even worse, to be a part of this ridiculous facade.

"Thank you for inviting us," my father finally spoke, his tone as cold as a North Atlantic iceberg. "It's a… pleasure to be here tonight."

"Sure it is." Karl smirked, sipping his drink. I had the impression that, for some twisted reason, he found this amusing. "The pleasure is all mine. Enjoy your evening," he said before he excused them and left with Elena on his arm to greet other guests.

"Good evening, Mr. and Mrs. Atwood," Shane tried to sound as polite as possible despite his hatred for my father.

My parents weren't so well mannered because they both ignored Shane as if he were thin air or a ghost. I was annoyed that they couldn't forget their judgments and be human for once.

"How are you doing, Melanie?" my mother asked, her brows furrowed and eyes filled with concern. My father, in contrast, didn't even try to look bothered.

"I'm doing fine," I said dryly, unable to fight the irritation. If I had to choose, I prefer Karl's sarcastic games rather than my parents' brusque behavior. "Better than ever. Would you excuse us?" I added as I grabbed Shane's hand, and we moved to the other side of the room.

We sat at the table prepared especially for us, and I caught myself staring numbly at the man playing the piano on the stage; its sound soothed my nerves.

Shane overlapped his hand with mine, leaning toward me. "I know how it feels, baby," he whispered, smiling softly. He put his hand on my cheek, stroking it gently. "I know it feels like you're all alone fighting against the world."

"How do you know?" I said softly, my brows furrowing faintly.

"I feel the same way. It may not seem like that, but it's exactly that way," he replied, his tone low and subtle. "But hey, now we have each other."

I couldn't fight the smile curling up my lips. It felt like Shane was the cure, taking all my worries away, medicine for my pain. I looked into the eyes of the man I was falling in love with more and more with each passing day, grateful that he swooped into my life, apart from the undeniable physical attraction and lascivious desire that I felt for Shane. For the first time, I felt precious and loved.

Shane kissed my cheek before saying, "I forgot to tell you. I booked you a session with a fortune-teller. It's in half an hour."

"A fortune-teller?" I was puzzled.

Shane chuckled softly. "Yeah, my father hired a fortune-teller for tonight to add variety to the event."

"Your father loves being extravagant, doesn't he?"

"Oh yes, he does." Shane grinned, shaking his head.

"But I wouldn't peg him as someone who believes in fortune-tellers," I stated. It didn't fit the Karl Vergoossen I knew.

"He doesn't. It's just for fun. Also, to raise more funds apart from the auction," he clarified. "What about you? Do you believe in fortune-tellers?"

I tilted my head slightly to the side, pondering. I'd never really thought about such things. I always assumed everyone was in charge of their destiny. On the other hand, I did believe some things were meant to be. "Hmm… no, I don't believe someone like a fortune-teller can predict your future. But I do believe some things are written in the stars, as they say. You?"

Shane smiled. "No. I'm a practical and realistic type of man. I believe in hard facts."

"So I thought," I joked, and we both chuckled.

Suddenly, his mood changed, and within a fraction of a second, he went from joyful and relaxed to serious and tense. His gaze followed a short brunette in an alluring asymmetrical long-sleeve black lace mermaid dress. A pinch of jealousy rushed through me, but I didn't want to be an obsessively jealous woman who would jump to conclusions or feel threatened. I trusted Shane. Despite knowing him for just a few weeks, I trusted him more than anyone else in my life.

"Excuse me for a moment." He pressed his lips together, forcing a smile, but his dry tone gave away that the woman wasn't just anyone.

"Okay," I said softly. "Just don't make me wait for too long."

"I would never." He kissed my hand, giving me a charming smile before he headed toward the table with refreshments where the brunette beauty with hypnotizing russet eyes and tanned skin was sipping her champagne.

I watched Shane talking to her, he was tense and deadly serious, unlike her. She seemed relaxed, her sex appeal radiating miles away. I wondered who she was and, most importantly, who she was to Shane. Was she someone from his past? Was she someone important? An ex? A lover? A relative? No, definitely not a relative. She was too seductive around him to be his relative. I felt an unpleasant pang of jealousy at the thought that Shane could've had an affair or maybe even a serious relationship with the sexy Spanish beauty.

"Good evening, Miss…?" I instinctively stood up and turned to meet the face behind the silvery voice that rumbled from behind, completely distracting me from my thoughts about the mysterious brunette.

The man looked at me, and his chestnut eyes seemed familiar. I scanned his face, trying to recall if we'd met before. Judging by his asking tone, we hadn't. But there was something weirdly familiar about him. He was handsome, very handsome. His spiked brown hair was neatly brushed back. His olive skin tone contrasted the white shirt he wore under his black tuxedo. It finally hit me. It must've been Anders, Shane's half brother. He looked like a perfect combination of Karl's strong features and Elena's charming beauty.

"Atwood." I extended my hand to greet him.

"Ah, Melanie Atwood." He shook my hand, but a weird chill swept the length of my spine as a sly smirk appeared on his face when he heard my name. Now, he looked just like his father, with a kind of shrewdness gleaming in his eyes.

"You must be Anders," I said, intimidated by his presence.

"Anders." Shane's deep voice reached my ear while he held me around my waist. It was incredible how Shane's mere presence made me feel safe, boosting my confidence like nothing else. I clung to his touch, drowning in his husky voice. "I see you already met Melanie."

"I've just had the pleasure." Anders smiled, this time in a polite, acknowledging way. "I'll leave the two of you alone. I'll say hi to my parents. It was nice meeting you, Melanie."

"It was nice meeting you, too, Anders."

The Vergoossen brothers exchanged sinister gazes before Anders sized me up, head to toe which made me feel uneasy before he turned on his heel and disappeared in the crowd of elegantly dressed people.

"He doesn't like me, does he?" I turned to look at Shane.

He clenched his jaw, letting out a quiet sigh. He didn't have to say anything because I already knew the answer to that question.

"Because I'm an Atwood?" I pressed my lips together.

Shane grabbed my chin with his fingers, lifting it gently so that our gazes locked. "It doesn't matter, Melanie. They don't understand that a name doesn't define a person. They just need more time to see *you* for who you are and not through the prism of your father."

"What did my father do to your family that they hate him that much?"

Shane smiled faintly, caressing my cheek with his thumb. "We'll talk about it later, okay? Now it's your turn to see the fortune-teller."

"Sure," I agreed despite not being satisfied with his sly way of avoiding the topic.

I ENTERED THE ROOM decorated with purple fabrics with stellar constellation patterns. The thing that caught my attention, though, was the crystal ball sitting in the middle of a round table surrounded by tarot cards and candles. I found it funny, and I didn't take the whole thing seriously because it all seemed too extra. The room was dim, and there were also two purple chairs. I sat in front of the older lady with burgundy hair reaching her chin, pale complexion, and icy-blue piercing eyes. Her lips were painted a deep shade of purple, and she was dressed in a black turtleneck with a heavy, layered stone pendant around her neck, matching the color of her eyes, and a floral wraparound skirt.

"Hello, dear," the lady spoke, her voice modulated. "I'm Aura."

"Melanie," I replied, skeptical about the whole experience.

"Let's unravel your future, Melanie. Please let me see your hand, dear."

I cleared my throat, adjusting myself on the chair before I stretched my hand out to her. I thought she would be looking at the crystal ball or using the tarot cards, but instead, she gently took my hand and carefully scanned it for a few seconds before speaking.

"I see a thrilling time in your near future," she started with such a cliché phrase that I barely fought the smile desperately forming in the corner of my mouth. She seemed very serious, though. She looked at my hand intensely as if she was hypnotized. "Something unexpected will happen tonight. It'll usher in the dawn of a new era in your life. You have a secret admirer at your fingertips who helps you when you need it. His intentions aren't clear to me, though." As she continued, she kept proving me right when all she would say were the typical things said by someone like her until she said something that piqued my interest, making my hair stand on end. "Blood-related men fighting for your affection. I see forthcoming nuptials, but they are blurry. I see darkness approaching you. A storm, a devastating hurricane. A new life overlapping with death."

I snatched my hand away, looking at the lady with anger in my eyes. That was not what I was expecting to hear. It was supposed to be fun, not terrifying. "Okay, that's enough." I shrieked, abruptly getting up from the table before I rushed out, my heart pounding.

I stormed out to the hallway, breathing heavily. Luckily, it was empty as everyone had a scheduled appointment with the fortune-teller, and mine ended early. There was only Shane waiting for me. He was on the phone when I left, but as soon as he noticed me, he frowned and ran toward me with concern written all over his face.

"Are you okay, baby?" He put one of his hands on my arm and the other under my chin, watching me carefully.

"Yes," I replied, a little out of breath. I didn't want to worry him with something as ridiculous as a fortune-teller's predictions, most likely a bunch of horseshit she repeated to everyone else. "It was just too stuffy in there. I couldn't breathe."

"Are you sure?" My explanation didn't seem to convince Shane, but I put a forced smile on, hoping I would sound more assured this time.

"I'm fine. I just need some fresh air. Can we go outside?"

"Of course, babe. Let's go." He took my hand, still scrutinizing me as he led me down the hallway.

AMELIA KAPPE

SHANE AND I stood on the hotel's balcony above the gleaming Park Avenue. I inhaled slowly, intensely focusing on the starlit sky, and then exhaled a few times. I couldn't get the fortune-teller's words out of my head.

A devastating hurricane?
Life overlapping with death?

I shook my head, dispelling the haunting thoughts.

"What happened in that room, Melanie?" Shane's husky voice reached my ear from behind as he slid his hands around my waist, kissing the top of my head. "You got scared, didn't you?"

I let out a quiet sigh. "Maybe a little bit."

"I'm sorry, Melanie. I shouldn't have booked you a session with her." His tone was apologetic. I turned to face him, our gazes locked.

"No, Shane. I shouldn't have taken her words so seriously."

"What did she say?"

I frowned, shaking my head slightly, my lips curled up in a soft smile. "It was some rubbish talk. Never mind."

Shane tilted his head to the side. His eyes darted between mine. He rested his hands against the railing behind me, trapping me between his arms. "Melanie," he started, his voice low and tone soft. "No matter what she said, I'm here with you. For you."

I nodded, appreciating his words that meant a little too much to me. Shane bit his bottom lip as if slightly nervous. I frowned, watching him carefully because it was something new to me. He put his fingers under my chin, tilting my head back.

"Melanie, I fell for you," he whispered, looking deeply into my eyes, and my heart skipped a beat. My eyes wandered all over his face as if looking for some kind of confirmation that it wasn't just a dream and I wouldn't be waking up in a moment. I brought my hand to his face, gently caressing his cheek. My breath was ragged and heavy, the excitement, a feeling of unearthly joy rushing through my veins. Shane covered my hand with his, turning his head to the side to leave a soft kiss on my hand that he kept holding in his. He focused his eyes back on me, running his teeth over his lower lip. "I fell pretty damn hard, and there's no turning back for me. And it scares me…."

"Scares you?" I asked quietly, startled.

He softly nodded his head yes. "I've been stone cold my whole damn life. Immune to that shit they call love. I thought it didn't exist… until I met you." He paused, our eyes connecting. "You're like a fire melting the ice I've surrounded myself with. And it scares me because, at this point, I can't imagine my life without you in it."

I looked at the devilishly handsome man before me, feeling like the happiest woman on earth. Shane was a perfect balance between a big bad wolf, who'd kill for me in a heartbeat, and a Prince Charming, who knew how to make me feel like the only girl in the world. Add to it a perfect lover—*quite a deadly combination.* I fell for him too. I fell for this dangerous, reckless man, a criminal.

Unconditionally. Irrevocably. I fell for him despite knowing the risk that love could entail. But I didn't care. Shane knew how to make me feel alive. He knew how to embrace the demons lurking inside me so that I forgot they existed. I fell for him, despite knowing this love would be a constant dance with the devil. Yet, I couldn't resist him. I was willing to take the risk because before him, I didn't live. I only existed.

"I can't imagine my life without you either, Shane," I whispered before he crashed his lips to mine like the hungry wolf he was.

We were kissing each other demandingly, fiercely. Shane put his hand on my thigh, sliding it up underneath the fabric of my dress, kneading it, and a sigh of pleasure escaped my lips, and Shane pulled away, breaking our fervent kiss. He looked at me. His eyes were black, filled with sinful lust, his breath ragged. He slid his other hand up my neck, stopping at my jawbone, tilting my head back, and our eyes locked again. I was breathing heavily, squeezing my hands on the railing behind me.

"Spread your legs and don't make a sound," he said, his tone low and demanding.

His commanding tone was such a turn-on, his touch set my body on fire. At the same time, my heart was pumping heavily and adrenaline was flowing through my system. "Shane, there are people everywhere. And reporters. What if someone catches us?" I whispered, my brain turning into mush from his mere touch.

"I don't care," he hissed, his hand roaming up, higher and higher. "I could be front-page news tomorrow and I wouldn't give a damn," he whispered into my ear, his voice low and husky, before he brushed his lips against the sensitive skin of my neck, causing goose bumps in their wake. "Now, I gave you an order. Spread your legs."

I did as he said, and he moved his hand higher, reaching the soaked fabric of my panties, stroking it with his fingers, and my muscles tensed. I looked into his black eyes, barely containing the moans desperately wanting to escape my lips as he pushed my panties to the side, sliding two fingers inside me. My fists tightened around the cold railing as he kept fingering me with a hungry gaze that never left my eyes. I wasn't sure if it was the rush of adrenaline that we were doing something so wicked in a public place or his authoritative, dominant tone, but I was burning. I closed my eyes, feeling an intense wave of pleasure rushing through my body.

Shane growled, sliding his thumb between my slightly parted lips. "Don't close your eyes. I want you to look at me when you come."

I followed his order with no objections. I found this dark, dominant side of him extremely attractive. I opened my eyes to meet his hungry gaze, devouring the sight of me coming undone because of him. I bit his thumb that he drew between my teeth, fighting to contain the sounds of pleasure that whipped through my body as I orgasmed.

"Good girl." He smirked, satisfied, before slowly pulling his fingers out. He licked his fingers off, growling, and I watched him, panting. He looked around and spotted a table a few steps from us. He walked over there to grab a napkin to wipe his hand. He fixed his tuxedo and approached me before leaning in to kiss my cheek. "We have to go back to the party. My father will give his speech in a few. We need to be there," he whispered as if nothing had happened and took my hand as we went inside.

"Callan?" I barely vocalized his name, rooted to the spot.

How long has he been here?
Did he see us?
Did he watch us?

My heart was pounding wildly, and I attempted to swallow around the dryness in my throat. I felt dizzy at the thought that he'd been there the whole time, watching us.

"Callan?" Shane frowned, slightly abashed. "What are you doing here? I ordered you to wait downstairs."

"I did." Callan cleared his throat, his face unreadable. "I just got here. Your father sent for you."

I wanted to believe that he just got there, but there was something ominous in his gaze that told me it was a lie. I turned my head to the side, avoiding his gaze, although I was sure my cheeks flushed red.

"We're coming," Shane said, his tone flat, and Callan nodded before stepping aside to let us pass before he followed us, and I could feel his burning gaze on my back.

"Thank you." Karl's low voice, followed by a wave of clapping, snapped me out of my thoughts.

I took a deep breath, searching across the crowd of people. I didn't catch a single word out of Karl's speech. I was too dizzy after the wicked moment I had with Shane and even worse after Callan's unnerving gaze. I shook my head, waking up from the haze. I stood on the stage a few inches above the floor of the banquet room, next to Shane, between Anders and Aaliyah and Karl and Elena. All eyes were on us. I knew I had to grin and bear it. Shane insisted on me joining them, and although I thought it was a little out of place, I couldn't say no to that man. The clapping eventually faded away, and Shane stepped up, clearing his throat.

"I'd like to take this opportunity to announce something," he said loud and clear, and the room fell silent. I frowned, watching him, a little confused. I didn't expect he'd be making a speech too. "There's a woman by my side tonight. A special woman." He smiled as he turned to look at me. "It's not only because she's incredibly stunning, and damn, is she." He peeked at the guests, and they chuckled. "But because she doesn't pretend. She doesn't play any games. She's unapologetically herself," he stated, the last part slightly softer as if it was meant only for me. As if he didn't care about other people in the room, only me. His eyes locked with mine as he continued. "I love that woman. With all her worn edges, fractures, scars."

My heart skipped a beat, and my breath became heavy and slow. I looked at Shane with my eyes growing wide. He reached his hand to me, and I took it as if in a trance. I took a step toward him, everyone watching us with anticipation.

"Melanie, you're a warrior. I know it." Shane's tone was low. "You're the strongest woman I've ever known. You don't need a man to bring the world to its knees. But I don't want you to fight the battles alone anymore. In this crazy, fucked-up world, I'm willing to be there for you for the rest of my life."

"Shane..." I hesitated, my lips parted in awe.

Shane reached into his pocket, a mysterious smirk on his face. He opened the black velvet box, and a huge diamond ring glittered before my eyes. I looked Shane in the eyes, completely taken aback, before he dropped down on one knee. "Melanie Rose Atwood, will you marry me?"

TWENTY

Shane

Everyone gasped as I dropped down on one knee, holding the ring box in my hand. My eyes were on Melanie, who was looking at me like she was hypnotized, her lips slightly parted, confusion written all over her beautiful face. I was sure my father was boiling inside, and so were Melanie's parents, but who would give a fuck? When you find a love like this, nothing stops you; you fight for it, taking all the risks in the world. And for Melanie, I was willing to take the risk. I was willing to risk it all, including my life.

"Melanie Rose Atwood, will you marry me?" I said, looking into the eyes of the woman that managed to burn down the thick walls I'd surrounded myself with and find her way in, engraving her name forever in my heart.

She was speechless, and I couldn't blame her for that. She didn't expect any of this. Not so soon. I knew we'd only known each other for a couple of weeks, but did the time have any meaning? I was sure I wanted to spend my life with someone like her. Yes, maybe it was a bit rushed, but not hasty. I thought everything through. Not once, not twice. Over and over again, and I knew to protect her, I had to make her a Vergoossen. That way, I wouldn't have to worry about the most dangerous man I'd ever known—my father. He was twisted, but he had rules he would never break. He protected us Vergoossens. For him, the family came first. Always. Whether by blood or bond, a Vergoossen was a Vergoossen, each equally important and valuable. Untouchable.

"Shane," she whispered, her sweet voice a little shaky. I got nervous that she would say no. After all, she was only nineteen, and we'd never talked about marriage. She opened her mouth, ready to give me an answer when a gunshot sounded loudly through the room, and everyone screamed, looking around in fear.

Just my fucking luck.

"Security!" Karl shouted, frowning angrily. He stepped before Elena and Aaliyah, covering them with his body. People started freaking out, creating a fuss that wasn't helpful at all. "Ladies and gentlemen, please remain calm." His voice was commanding.

Melanie's eyes grew wide, and she struggled to catch a breath. I got up to embrace her. "Calm down, baby. I'm here," I whispered before kissing her forehead.

I was sure the gunshot came from the hallway. I quickly scanned the room and noticed Callan was missing. It didn't take long to connect the dots.

"Fuck," I hissed.

"What is it?" Melanie asked, her body shivering.

"Anders, take care of Melanie," I said to my brother, who nodded, not questioning my intentions. We might not have had the best relationship, but in life-threatening situations, we had each other's backs, and I knew I could trust him.

"Shane, please, don't!" Melanie shouted after me as I ran toward the hallway.

MY BLOOD RAN COLD when I saw Callan's body on the hallway floor, surrounded by a puddle of blood. An icy shiver swept down my back, and I hurried toward my friend. "Hold on, man." I slid my hands under his head, lifting it gently. He barely kept his eyes open, mumbling something under his breath, but I couldn't catch a word. I assessed his body, spotting the gunshot wound inches below his heart. I placed my hand there to put pressure on the wound. "Don't you dare leave me," I pleaded, even though I was sure he couldn't hear me. I was scared I could lose my friend and fucking furious that the security let this happen. There were dozens of men in every corner of the building, and yet an intruder got in and shot my most important man. I swallowed, wondering if the bullet was meant for Melanie, and my hair stood on end.

"Callan!" Melanie's voice rang through the hallway. I turned to see her running toward us, fear in her eyes. She managed to keep cool, though. She quickly reached for her phone and called 911.

"Mr. Vergoossen." One of the bodyguards sprinted in our direction, and a bunch of others followed.

"Surround the building," I hissed, rage thundering inside me. "Get the shooter and bring them to me. Alive."

They nodded and dispersed to follow my order.

Melanie put her hand around my arm. "The ambulance is on its way," she whispered, but even her soothing voice didn't ease my pain.

I FOLLOWED THE AMBULANCE with Melanie by my side. She refused to stay behind. She was a real queen, fearless and fierce, not leaving the side of her king. She squeezed my hand as we waited in the hospital hallway for who knew how goddamn long. I took a deep, heavy breath, running my fingers through my hair. I was drained. Not a single day could go smoothly. I peeked at the TV screen hanging on the wall in the waiting room right in front of us to see the whole situation had already leaked to the media. I watched the pale-skinned man with a neat haircut moving his mouth with a *Breaking News* bar at his waist height, saying: *Shane Vergoossen's proposal to Melanie Atwood was interrupted by a gunshot.* I rolled my eyes, shaking my head. Fucking press. Had they no dignity at all? The man was fighting for his life, and all they cared about was a fucking scandal that would sell well.

"Mr. Vergoossen?" An Asian man in his forties, dressed in blue scrubs, approached.

"Yes." I nodded as I stood up from my seat. So did Melanie.

"I'm Dr. Zeng. Are you a relative to Callan Sinclair?"

"I am his employer. He doesn't have any relatives," I stated. For a short moment, my mind drifted to the time when I met Callan. He was just turning nineteen, all alone after the tragic loss of his father in a car accident, only he survived. He was lost, getting involved with the wrong crowd. I found him beaten up on a street after he involved himself in a fight with one of the gangs that used him to deal drugs, but something got fucked up, and they wanted to get rid of him. I didn't have the heart to leave him there on the street to die. My men dragged him to the car, semiconscious, drugged. After a few days, when he got better, I offered him a job as one of my errand men at first. He proved himself worthy, loyal and eventually replaced my former right-hand man. Ever since, I had felt responsible for him as if he was my brother. We had a special bond. *Or so I thought.*

The doctor nodded. "He lost a significant amount of blood. He needs a transfusion. ASAP. Do any of you have O negative blood type? In this case, only the same blood type is compatible."

"I do," Melanie said, our eyes locked.

It felt like one gaze was enough for us to understand each other. No words were needed. A faint, reassuring smile appeared on her face, and she squeezed my arm. I slid my hand at the back of her head and pulled her closer to kiss her forehead.

"Please, follow me, miss," the doctor stated, and Melanie hurried after him. I watched them leave, their voices fading. "We'll ask you some questions and run a quick test to make sure you're safe to donate."

I ran my hands over my head, trying to stay sane. I reached for my phone and searched for Wyatt's number.

The ring echoed in my ears before I heard a deep voice through the speaker. "Boss?"

"What's the status? Did you get the perp?" I asked, my tone dark.

"Not yet, boss."

I clenched my teeth, taking a deep breath. "Send someone to the hospital. I need someone to watch over Callan twenty-four seven. I'll text you the address."

"I'm on my way, boss. I'll be there in fifteen. I figured you'd need me there."

"Thanks, Wyatt." I hung up the phone, but I didn't even have the time to put it away before it rang in my hands.

"Fuck me," I hissed, seeing my father's number. He was the last person I wanted to talk to right now. I exhaled deeply before answering, "Karl?"

"How's Callan?" His tone was flat. I was surprised he even asked.

"He needs a blood transfusion."

"At least he's not dead."

No shit.

"Is that all?" I asked, glaring at the city that never sleeps through the hospital window.

My father scoffed. "Don't fuck with me, Shane. You know the reason I'm calling."

Of course, I knew. The moment I saw his name on my phone screen, I knew it was about Melanie. Or rather about me proposing.

"Can we not have this conversation right now? Over the fucking phone while my friend is fighting for his life," I hissed, anger rushing through my veins, but I kept my cool.

A few seconds passed before I heard his voice again. "Dedrick Atwood is coming to the hospital to take Melanie. He raised hell after you left. Obviously not too fond of the idea of you being his son-in-law," he said sarcastically, and I started to believe Karl could approve of my plan after all.

"I'll deal with him," I replied dryly.

"Good. We'll talk about your misdeed in private. After all of this calms down."

Misdeed? He's fucking ridiculous.

"Wait. There's one more thing," I stated, looking around to see if Melanie was in sight. "Did you invite Sofia?"

"Son." He didn't have to answer. I knew him far too well. I was boiling inside. I knew my father was wicked, but I didn't think he would bring my ex back for whatever reason. "I thought the sight of her would help you remember you shouldn't trust a woman."

I nodded, clenching my teeth before ending the call. He was such a hypocrite. He would stop at nothing to get what he wanted.

"You okay, boss?"

I turned to face Wyatt, who watched me clenching my fist as I fought the rage growing in me. I knew my father wouldn't approve of my relationship with Melanie. And I knew he would try his twisted games to separate us, but that was a fucking stab in the back.

"I'm fine," I growled.

Wyatt knew me quite well. He was my second most important man after Callan. He could read me and learned when to speak and when to let go.

"How's Callan?" he asked, diverting the topic.

"He lost a lot of blood. Needs a transfusion. What blood type are you?"

"*O* negative," he replied.

"You're a match. Go check in with the doctor. Melanie's there, but maybe they need more blood."

Wyatt nodded and headed toward the designated room. At that exact second, I noticed Melanie's parents heading toward me, both with frantic looks on their faces.

Fuck me twice!

I took a deep breath, preparing myself for the tantrum they were about to throw.

"Where is my daughter?!" Dedrick roared, seething.

"She's being examined by the doctor," I replied dryly.

"Why? What happened?" Celine's eyes grew wide in horror. I glanced at her, narrowing my eyes. I was wondering why she never stood up for her daughter. She clearly cared for Melanie, yet for some reason, she chose an abusive husband over her only offspring.

"She's okay." I calmed her down. "She's going to donate her blood. My friend needs a transfusion."

Celine breathed a sigh of relief. She sat on the chair, rubbing her temples. She wasn't as strong as her daughter. Maybe that's why she'd never found the strength, the courage to be in charge of her own life.

Dedrick's harsh voice snapped me out of my thoughts. "Once they're done, Melanie is going back to California with us."

I tilted my head to the side, looking Atwood straight in his raging eyes before saying, matter-of-factly, "She's not going anywhere with you."

He gave me a spiteful look. "How dare you speak to me like that! I'm her father, and you? You don't own her, Vergoossen!"

I scoffed. "I'm aware. Unlike you."

Dedrick was the type of man who couldn't take being challenged. He locked his hands into fists and hissed through clenched teeth, "She's coming back home with us."

"I'm not going anywhere." Melanie's soft voice caught everyone's attention. I looked back to see her closing the door to the room before she approached me. Celine stood up, her hands shaking, and moved to her husband's side. Melanie stood beside me, staring at her parents resolutely, saying, "I'm staying here. With Shane."

"I'll never approve of your relationship!" Dedrick yelled, still clenching his fists. Celine watched the whole commotion, her brows furrowed in concern. She barely held her tears back.

"I don't need your approval," Melanie retorted. "Nor permission. I'm staying here where I belong."

"Melanie, please. You can't," her mother pleaded, shedding a tear. "What about your life? Your studies?"

"My life?" Melanie scoffed. "My studies? It was all yours. I've never had my own life until I met Shane. I can start over. Here in New York, on my own terms."

I silently watched Melanie, proud of her. This was the first time she'd been so determined, as if something had changed. I thought it was because of the proposal or because I confessed my love to her. She felt more secure knowing she wasn't just a game to me. And partially, I was right. *Partially*.

"If you stay with that man," Dedrick started, boiling inside. "Or worse, marry him, you can forget you ever had parents!"

"Dedrick," Celine gasped, her eyes wide.

"Okay," Melanie stated, her tone barely above a whisper. She nodded, looking at her parents, her eyes welling up with tears. "It's not like I've ever had real parents anyway."

I reached for Melanie's hand and intertwined her fingers with mine. I saw how hard it was for her to have this conversation, and I wanted her to know she wasn't alone. She had me, and I would stand by her side no matter what.

Celine burst into tears, covering her mouth with her hands. Dedrick, in contrast, smiled cynically, scoffing, "You'll regret your decision faster than you think, Melanie. Apparently, you don't know who you want to marry. You're not aware of what kind of people the Vergoossens are."

Melanie didn't speak. She pressed her lips together, fighting back the tears before she cleared her throat and squeezed my hand, giving her parents a stern look.

"Don't bother coming home," Dedrick threw out harshly before grabbing his wife by her elbow. "Celine, let's go."

"But Dedrick!" Celine cried out.

I couldn't understand why she let that abusive motherfucker rule her like that. And I couldn't stand the power he had over that broken, intimidated woman. I focused my gaze solely on Celine. "You're welcome to stay with us, Mrs. Atwood."

Melanie glanced at me, a spark of hope gleaming in her eyes, but it was killed faster than it appeared.

"If you stay with that spoiled brat, then don't bother coming back home either," Dedrick hissed into her ear, and she gave Melanie an apologetic look before turning on her heels and, with no words, walked away beside her toxic husband.

I swear I could hear Melanie's heart breaking in two as she watched her parents walking down the hospital hallway until they were no longer in sight. She bit her bottom lip, inhaling deeply as a single tear dropped down the corner of her eye, and Melanie quickly wiped it away. I slid my hands around her trembling waist and pulled her in for a hug. I held her in my arms, caressing the back of her head.

"I'm so sorry, baby," I whispered, wishing I could take her pain away.

Melanie inhaled deeply, rubbing her eyes. "It's nothing. I'm used to it."

"It's okay, babe. You can cry," I said, cupping her cheeks in my hands, our eyes locked.

"They're not worth my tears," she stated dryly. I could tell she was hurting, but she didn't want to show it. She didn't want me to pity her.

"You're right. They're not." I stroked her cheek with my thumb, and she smiled through her watery eyes. She was so strong. I admired her. Many would break, but she didn't. Every time she fell, she rose. Stronger, more determined. Despite people stripping down her soul, she kept moving forward like the true warrior she was. But everybody has their limits. It was just a matter of time until she would reach hers. And by the time one reaches their limits, their heart turns into ice so that nothing and no one can hurt them ever again.

"You should rest," I said, realizing she'd just donated her blood and must've felt dizzy. "Did the doctor say anything about the transfusion? Is Callan better?"

Melanie's eyes darted between mine before she replied, "I… didn't donate my blood." She seemed abashed, and I frowned. "It turned out I have…" She hesitated. She didn't sound convincing at all and to be fair, I got suspicious. "A minor infection and they didn't want to risk transmitting the virus."

I nodded, deciding it'd been a hell of a day for both of us. I didn't want to add more stress than she already had to cope with. I didn't believe in the minor infection because, first off, I spent the past few days with Melanie, and she seemed perfectly fine. Second, she was a bad liar. But I couldn't deny she got me worried. "Is it something serious?"

"Nothing to worry about." She forced a smile. "I'm glad Wyatt showed up. He's a match, and the doctors went with him. I was worried they wouldn't find another donor fast enough. Wyatt was like a gift from heaven."

"You're very concerned about Callan," I stated, and Melanie seemed perplexed.

"He's your friend. Of course, I worry about him."

"Mr. Vergoossen." Dr. Zeng's voice caught our attention, and we both turned to face him. "We managed to stabilize Mr. Sinclair's state. We took out the bullet and stopped the internal bleeding. The blood transfusion went well. He's stable now."

"Oh, thank God," I said with relief. It felt like a huge weight was taken off my shoulders. "Thank you, doc."

The doctor smiled, shaking my hand before he headed for one of the rooms. Melanie's eyes brightened, and she smiled, looking at me before I hugged her.

"I love you, Shane," she whispered as I held her in my arms. "I love that you care about your close friends. That you aren't entitled like other people in our society. I'm in love with you."

I gently pulled back to look into her eyes that were gazing at mine with relief. "I'm in love with you, too, Melanie."

After my men arrived at the hospital, Melanie and I went back to my penthouse. Melanie was oddly quiet on our way back there, and I wondered what was on her mind. Ever since she left the doctor's office, she seemed pensive. I assumed it was because of the bitter goodbye she had with her parents. Melanie went to the bedroom to change, and I threw the tux jacket I'd worn on the couch. I got rid of the tie. I swear I'd been counting down the minutes until I could take it off. I hated ties. I undid a few buttons and rolled up my shirtsleeves before pouring myself a glass of whiskey when my phone screen on the table lit up.

"What now?" I breathed out, exhausted with the never-ending issues.

OVERDOSED

I clenched my teeth, staring at the text that made my blood boil.

From: Sofia

I miss you.

Sent Sunday 1:22 AM

I drank the whiskey in one go, anger flowing through my veins. The audacity of that woman, she had no boundaries. I didn't want her in my life. Not anymore. Not after I met Melanie. She was my past, and that was where she should've stayed.

"I'm going to take a shower." Melanie's seductive tone rang in my ears, and I looked at her. She leaned against the wall dividing the living room and the hallway, staring at me sultrily. My gaze followed the length of her body, covered only with a white towel wrapped around her breasts. She was smirking, slowly biting her bottom lip.

"Damn," I whispered, gawking at her like I was mesmerized. I threw the phone away, my anger replaced with lust. "You want to be the reason I go crazy?" I said teasingly, my eyes still on her. "Because you're succeeding."

She chuckled softly, playing with her hair. "I want you to join me," she whispered, her tone provocative as she roamed her hand down her body. "I'm going to be… *wet*." She turned around, letting the towel fall onto the floor before turning her head and winking as she walked to the bathroom, naked, swaying her hips. I was burning. The sight of her round butt was enough to drain my blood straight to my dick. A sly smirk formed on my lips as I shook my head.

That woman will be the death of me one day.

I put the glass I was holding aside and started unbuttoning the rest of my shirt as I followed my blonde beauty.

I STEPPED UNDER THE SHOWER, where Melanie was already waiting for me. I admired her petite naked body, wet from the running water before I slowly lifted my eyes up, and our gazes locked. I licked my bottom lip, watching her hungrily. Her wet hair was pulled back, revealing her gorgeous face. I traced the water drops streaming down her lips, neck, cleavage, belly, and only one droplet remained on her long black lashes. Melanie watched me, breathing heavily as if waiting for my move.

I stepped toward her, the water stream hitting my body. I put my hands on Melanie's hips and pushed her against the glass shower wall, crashing my lips onto hers. I drew my tongue between her mouth, kissing her fiercely, and a deep moan rumbled in her throat. My hand roamed down her body, kneading her thigh while I rested against the wall with the other one. Melanie slid her hands to the back of my head, intertwining her fingers in my hair as she pulled her head back, exposing her neck. I kissed and licked demandingly. I moved my hand up her inner thigh until I reached her core. I rubbed my fingers gently around her sensitive bud, making her pant in need. Then I pushed two fingers inside and she moaned against my ear before sucking my lobe, causing my cock to twitch against her belly, her long nails digging in my back. I looked into her eyes that she barely kept open as I kept fingering her, her lips slowly parted, letting the sigh of pleasure escape them.

"I love you, Melanie," I hissed, her lustful gaze driving me mad.

"I love you, too, Shane," she whispered, her perky breasts moving up and down. "But fuck me like you don't."

I bit my lip, and despite the cold water running down our naked bodies, I was burning. I pulled my fingers out of her, and Melanie groaned, undone. With one swift move, I turned her body back to me, pressing her breasts against the wet glass wall.

I grabbed her hair and pulled it back so that her head tilted back. I leaned to her ear, hissing, "Your wish is my command." And I plunged deep inside her, thrusting fast and forcefully, still pulling her hair until she came, screaming my name before I let myself finish.

TWENTY-ONE
Melanie

I woke up snuggled into Shane's arms. We somehow ended up in his bed, but I couldn't recall how. I traced his naked toned abs with my fingertips, inhaling his addictive scent as if my life depended on it. Intoxicated. That was how I felt. That was what my relationship with Shane looked like. We were intoxicated with lust, overdosing on the euphoric feeling we could get only from one another. Frankly speaking, he had me intoxicated from the moment I first laid eyes on him. And our relationship was mostly physical, with oh-so-good sex being an integral part of it. At first, I couldn't say I loved Shane. I lusted him. Maybe because I wasn't sure what love was. I was deprived of the feeling my whole life, so how could I know what it felt like? Until Shane showed me what it felt like. Until he gave me a taste of the most addictive feeling in the world. But to me, it wasn't *just* a feeling. To me, love was a mix of feelings. A sense of security, affection, and tenderness. Selflessness, because you put the needs of your loved one above yours, but also greediness because you can't stop craving the presence of that one particular person. Sexual desire, attraction. All in one. *Love*. The feeling is so complex. So powerful people are ready to kill for love. Die for love. Now I could understand why. I'd die for him. I'd kill for him—*Shane Vergoossen, my dangerous ride or die, and now the future father of my child.*

I exhaled deeply, and suddenly the feeling of anxiety rushed through me. I bit my lower lip nervously as the events from the previous night flashed before my eyes.

You can't be a blood donor, Miss Atwood. You're pregnant.

The doctor's voice kept echoing in my ears.

It's still a very early stage. Did you know about it?

Of course, I didn't. It was a shock for me. I felt dizzy and overwhelmed with the news. I played the past few weeks I'd spent with Shane in my mind again and again like a tape on repeat. We had spontaneous, unprotected sex many times, and there were chances I might have forgotten to take the pill. Pregnancy wasn't something I planned, at least not so early in my life, and most definitely, not so early in my relationship with Shane. I didn't even know if he wanted to have children or how he would react. I wanted to tell him the first thing after I left the doctor's office, but my parents surprised me with their not-so-pleasant visit. And later… I freaked out. I wanted to wait a few days to make sure it was true. I needed a few days to get used to that thought and decide what I would do about it.

"Are you awake?" Shane growled as he turned his head to me. His heavy lids were still half-closed.

"Yeah," I said softly, indulging in the warmth of his skin.

"What are you thinking about?" He bent his arm, caressing my hair with his fingers, and rested his head on top of mine.

"You."

I didn't see his face, but I could feel a smirk curling up his mouth. "I was thinking about you half of the night. I couldn't fall asleep."

I propped my elbow to look him in the eyes, frowning. "Why? What were you thinking about?"

Shane pulled up so that he was in a sitting position now before reaching out to his nightstand drawer. He looked down at the small velvet box he held in his hand and opened it slowly. I looked at the stunning diamond ring before casting my eyes upward, and our gazes locked. "This ring belonged to my mother. She left it for me before she…" Shane paused, inhaling deeply before continuing, his voice low and husky, so damn attractive. "She left it to me with a note. She said she wanted me to give that ring to the woman who would make my heart bloom like a rose, petal by petal. At first, I thought it was never going to happen. I thought love didn't exist. Until I met you, Melanie. You've proved me wrong. You've proved everything I believed didn't exist exists." Shane took the ring out of the box and grabbed my hand. I felt my heart fluttering like crazy and butterflies dancing in my belly. A broad, genuine smile painted on my face as I looked into the eyes of the love of my life. "Marry me, Melanie."

I shook my head yes, chuckling through tears of happiness. "I will marry you, Shane."

A broad grin formed on Shane's face, and he slowly slid the glimmering oval-shaped ring on my finger before he brought my hand to his lips and kissed it. "I want to spend my life with you," he whispered, resting his forehead on mine. "I love you, Melanie. I have fallen in love with you, and there's no turning back for me."

"There's no turning back for either of us." I slid my hand at the back of his head, weaving my fingers through his hair. "Not at this stage. You're mine, and I'm yours. Forever."

Shane moved his hand to the back of my head, pulling me in for a kiss. He slid the other one on my waist, flipping my body so he was on top of me. In just a short moment, we were in a heated tangle, kissing hungrily, burning with untamed lust, drowning in wild desire.

AFTER AN INSANELY *lovely* morning, Shane and I visited Callan at the hospital. We entered one of the VIP rooms for Vergoossens, where Shane had Callan placed as if he were one of the family members. That was one of the reasons why I fell in love with that man. Despite being a dangerous Mafia heir, he had a heart of gold. Shane once told me that it was the way Vergoossens were. Ruthless with their enemies, ready to die for their family. I thought I was lucky to soon be Mrs. Vergoossen.

I sat on the chair beside Shane and next to Callan's bed. I didn't want to interrupt their conversation. They talked about the events from the previous night. Callan recognized the shooter. He said it was a black-haired female with dark skin, hazel eyes, and a scar above her brow. As soon as Shane heard the description, he assumed that it was a woman called Angelina, and Callan confirmed. Apparently, she was a member of Ax's gang, which I'd never heard of before, and they both suspected someone hired them because, as they stated, they wouldn't go after the Vergoossens alone. I felt lost and nervous. I had no idea who they were talking about but it all filled me with horror. Unwittingly, I started twisting the engagement ring Shane had put on my finger just a few hours before. I didn't have a chance to get used to it, and maybe that was why my thumb automatically rubbed the new piece, or maybe it was my body's response to the anxiety. Most likely the latter. I hadn't realized I was doing that until I caught Callan's eyes gazing at the ring. In an instant, I let the ring be, and for a short second, our eyes locked. A weird shiver ran down the length of my spine as I could see some kind of regret written on Callan's face.

My gaze dropped, and I cleared my throat. "Excuse me. I'm going to get myself a bottle of water. Do you want something?" I said, switching my eyes between Shane and Callan.

"I'll go," Shane stated. "You stay here."

No, that's not what I want!

"It's okay, Shane," I said, slightly embarrassed. "You have things to discuss, and I—"

"Babe." Shane's husky voice cut me off. He stood up and moved closer toward me, cupping my cheek with his hand. I fleetingly glanced at Callan, who looked away the second my gaze met his. "I don't let my woman walk around the hospital with no proper security a day after a shooting at one of our parties. I'll go. You stay," he commanded, and I gave up. I knew Shane was a stubborn man who had to have things his way. I nodded, and he gently kissed my cheek. "I'll be right back."

I followed Shane with my gaze to the door. I felt uneasy being left alone in the room with Callan because he wasn't just anyone. He wasn't just Shane's bodyguard or friend. He was someone from my past, and it felt wrong because I kept that a secret from Shane.

"Congratulations." Callan eventually spoke, breaking in on the dreadful silence, his tone flat.

I turned to look at him. He sat on the hospital bed in a white, loose shirt and shorts. The jewelry from his piercings had been removed, probably because of the surgery. His dark-blue hair was a mess and his face held no trace of emotion. He didn't resemble the eighteen-year-old boy I used to know.

"Thank you," I replied softly.

"Are you happy?" He stared at me piercingly as if trying to see right through me.

I nodded as I whispered, "Yes. Yes, I am happy."

He sighed deeply. "I regret I couldn't give you what *he* gave you." He intonated the sentence in a way that made me shiver. As if Shane was the enemy that took his life away from him.

"Don't do this, Callan." I shook my head, furrowing my brows, my tone firm.

"Do what, Melanie?"

"Don't ruin it. You're his friend."

Callan took a deep breath. I walked toward the chair and sat, leaning toward him.

"Let's leave the past behind, Callan. We were just kids."

I wasn't sure if those words hurt him, but his face fell, and so did his gaze. He looked down, nodding regretfully. It seemed like he wanted to say something, but the door swung open, and Shane walked in, holding two bottles of water.

"There you go." He fetched me one of the bottles, a genuine smile on his face, lightening up the gloomy atmosphere looming over the room. "And this one's for you, mate," Shane said teasingly, handing the other bottle to Callan.

"Thanks, boss."

"Today, I'm not your boss. I'm your friend." Shane winked, and I couldn't fight a smile.

I admired the bond they had. Maybe that was why I didn't tell Shane about Callan. To me, Callan was just a memory. Someone from my past. Someone neutral to me now. But I had a haunting impression that if I told Shane we had a history together, it could ruin their friendship. And that was the last thing I'd want. Besides, I considered the relationship I had with him in the past as a completely closed chapter of my life, meaningless to my present or future.

Shane turned to face me again, his husky voice snapping me out of my thoughts. "My father called me. He wants us to come for dinner tonight." His gaze was serious as his eyes darted between mine.

"It's okay, Shane. We'll go," I stated. I was expecting this, knowing that Karl didn't approve of our relationship, and now we were engaged. Nonetheless, I was ready to face any obstacles. I was ready to fight the world by Shane's side.

"Trouble?" Callan questioned and Shane turned to face him.

"Nothing I can't handle," Shane said firmly, reaching for my hand. "Take care, Callan. I'll see you soon."

We were sitting by the high-end wooden table in the Vergoossens' residence. This time we ate in the bright, elegant dining room with its style being on the verge of modern and vintage with plenty of natural light and a charming fireplace. I squeezed Shane's hand, and he smiled, soothing my nerves. The atmosphere was tense. I caught Karl sending me a sinister gaze several times, but it wasn't that that made me uneasy. It was *Anders*. I was racking my brain, wondering what his issue was. He was ten times worse than his father. Whenever I spoke, he would scoff or mock me. He looked at me as if I was his worst nightmare. I got it that the Vergoossens weren't too enthusiastic about me because I was an Atwood, but it felt like it wasn't the case for Anders. There was something more than that. I knew it. Eventually, it floated to the surface.

"Well." Karl's stern voice snapped me out of my thoughts. His gaze was focused on my glimmering diamond ring. "I suppose we should congratulate you on your engagement."

"You've got to be shitting me," Anders snapped, drawing everyone's attention to him. "Are we seriously going to play a happy family now? With her?" He looked at me, furrowing his brows, his eyes filled with hatred.

"Watch your mouth," Shane hissed, although keeping his composure.

"Or what?" Anders retorted.

"Anders," Karl started, but his younger son cut him off. It seemed he didn't respect his father as much as Shane did. He was more rebellious and reckless.

"No, don't try to shut me up," he shouted. "Let's face the truth. If I brought Atwood's daughter home, you would bury me alive."

"Atwood's daughter?" Shane scoffed, clenching his fist. "Melanie is so much more than that. Don't define her by her last name."

"Oh, right. Because now it doesn't matter whose daughter she is," Anders continued. His tone was a mix of sarcasm and towering rage. "Might I remind you that just a couple of weeks ago, you saw her as—"

Shane stood up, slamming his hands against the table. "You better stop, Anders. I'm warning you," he vocalized. His voice was so dark and cold that it sent chills down my body.

Anders clenched his jaw, nodding while staring into Shane's eyes. He took a deep breath before turning his gaze to his father, who watched the whole commotion with disdain on his face. "Even now, you let him do whatever the hell he wants," Anders hissed, his tone low. "He brings an enemy to our house, and you do nothing. You let him because he's your firstborn. Rose's son. The great heir to your great legacy. A real Vergoossen, flesh, and blood. And I? I'm just the worst version of him."

"You know that's not true, son," Karl rasped. "You are both equal to me. You are both my blood."

"Is that so?" Anders replied mockingly before finishing his wine in one gulp and throwing the glass against the table, shattering it into pieces. "Because it doesn't seem like it," he added as he headed out of the dining room. The room fell awkwardly silent, and I nearly jumped when the loud sound of the door banging echoed through the hallway. Through the big window with the view of the front yard, I saw Anders getting into his car and driving away.

I glanced at Elena, who was inhaling deeply, her eyes closed as if trying to fight back the tears. She seemed hurt and maybe a little ashamed but not surprised. I figured that it wasn't the first time her son lashed out like that. I didn't know the reason for it, but it didn't take a genius to figure out that Anders was envious of his older brother.

"Forgive this disturbance, Melanie," Karl spoke, his tone stern and calm as if nothing had happened. He was spectacular at keeping his composure regardless of the situation. "If you'll excuse us, I'd like to talk to Shane now. In private," he added, turning his gaze to Shane.

I couldn't bring myself to speak and just nodded my head.

"I'll be right back," Shane whispered in my ear before he followed his father.

Elena sighed quietly. "Luckily, Aaliyah wasn't here to watch this."

I reached my hand out to grab Elena's. I could feel the weight she was carrying on her shoulders as the mother and the wife, but most importantly, as just a woman. "Everything will be okay, Elena," I said, instantly regretting my choice of words. I didn't know what to say, so I went with the cliché phrase I'd heard my whole life, which meant absolutely nothing.

"Melanie," she said softly, looking deeply into my eyes. "You are a very bright and charming woman. But I don't think you know what it means to be a part of this family."

I tilted my head to the side. "I don't think I follow." I slowly pulled back, resting against the cream and gold chair.

Elena cleared her throat, fixing her chic white shirt. "You see, there's more to this family than meets the eye. And being the wife of its successor holds some responsibilities."

"You don't have to watch your words, Elena. I know everything about this family. Shane is honest with me," I stated. Shane knew this conversation was coming, and I was glad he had prepared me for it. I was satisfied I'd learned the dark secrets of the Vergoossen family from him.

"Good." Elena nodded, her voice soft. "I hope you know what you're doing."

"I do," I said, determined. At this point, there was no turning back for me. Not only did I fall in love with New York's most dangerous Mafia heir, but I was also carrying his child.

TWENTY-TWO

Shane

I stared at the dark sky through the window in my bedroom, a glass of scotch in my hand. Melanie was already asleep, her sexy body covered with the silky duvet on my bed that now smelled like her. Fuck, I could never forget the scent of her. The scent engraved deeply in my soul. I peeked at her, sipping my drink. She looked so beautiful when she was sleeping. So innocent. I wanted to sneak back into the bed and hold her fragile body in my arms, but I couldn't. I felt guilty and couldn't stop thinking about the conversation I'd had earlier with my father. His harsh voice rang in my ears, and I was trying to muffle it with the sharp flavor of the strong liquor. I'd expected he would be furious after I proposed to Melanie against his will. He demanded I follow the plan or make Melanie our ally in his twisted war against Atwood. I wanted neither, but he threatened he would tell Melanie the truth. The truth about our plan, the truth about my initial intentions toward her, and I felt guilty. I felt guilty for not confessing the truth yet. I knew I had to do it because I didn't want to continue building our relationship on a constant lie, yet I couldn't bring myself to tell her the truth. I was scared I would lose her and didn't want to let her go. She was like a drug to me, and I got addicted. I knew if I ever lost her, I wouldn't be able to fill the void after her.

My phone pinged, snapping me out of my thoughts. I peeked at Melanie to check if it woke her, but she only made a cute sound, stretching as she turned to the other side, still asleep. I walked over to my nightstand drawer and reached for the phone.

From: Wyatt

PURPLE

Sent Monday 0:39 AM

I took a deep breath before finishing the scotch. Purple was our code for completing a task that still needed my call. I figured my men probably caught the perp responsible for the shooting at the charity gala, and I knew I had to leave now. I sat on the bed, caressing Melanie's hair.

"I'll be back soon, baby," I whispered, leaving a soft kiss on her forehead.

"Mm-hmm," she muttered, her eyes closed.

AMELIA KAPPE

I wasn't sure if she heard me, but I hoped I'd get back before she woke up. I went to one of my closets where I kept my equipment and clothes for such occasions. I quickly changed into a black turtleneck and a bulletproof leather jacket before I grabbed my gun and left.

"Well, well, well," I said, slowly walking toward Ax, the leader of one of the gangs in New York, and Angelina, his partner in crime and lover. "What a pleasure to see you both." I smirked sarcastically, tilting my head to the side as I watched them.

Wyatt and my men under him locked Ax and Angelina in one of our buildings underground. It was where we dealt with our enemies or simply executed them. They were both cuffed with their hands above their heads, tied to the ceiling. The place was all concrete and dark with a dual-head floodlight on a stand directed at the captives, its intense light blinding them.

Wyatt already questioned them and established that Angelina was the one who shot Callan. However, she refused to confess who had hired her and who her target was.

I sat by the steel table, throwing my gun on it. "Let's cut to the chase. I value my time. Tell me." I paused, circling the gun on the cold steel top. "Who hired you, and who were you after, and I may spare one of you."

"Angelina, don't say anything," Ax hissed, breathing heavily.

Although Ax was the leader of his gang, I'd always considered Angelina a more dangerous person than her lover. He might've been considered the head leading the gang, but she was the neck turning the head.

I took the weapon in my hand and cocked it. "Speak."

"Fuck you!" Angelina shouted before spitting on the floor.

It was too far to reach me, but it was enough to test my patience. I scoffed, slowly leaving my seat as I approached her. I looked her in her outraged eyes as I pulled the trigger, shooting Ax in his knee. The place filled with the sound of the gunshot, followed by a groan of pain. "Speak, or I'll put the next bullet in his head," I said sternly.

"Angelina, don't," the red-haired man pleaded as he turned his greenish eyes to his love. "He will kill me anyway."

I moved closer, putting my gun under Ax's chin and pressing it to his throat, my eyes on Angelina, who was close to breaking. "Who was your target?"

"Melanie Atwood," she uttered, looking at me pleadingly.

I let out a deep sigh, rage flowing through my veins. I clenched my teeth angrily. "You were supposed to kill my woman?"

"No, only kidnap her."

To me, it didn't change anything. I was breathing heavily, fighting the fury growing inside me.

"Who sent you?" I rasped, pressing the gun barrel under Ax's chin.

Angelina's lips were trembling, and tears started dripping down her face as she watched her man shitting his pants. "Theo Ledford and Sofia Meyers."

My blood ran cold. I looked at her with my eyes wide open. Shocked. I was suspecting Dedrick Atwood, even my own father, thinking it was their twisted way to tear us apart, but I didn't think of her fucking ex, not to mention Sofia, my ex. What was her role in all of it?

Without batting an eye, I pulled the trigger, taking Ax's last breath. His blood splashed on my face. She was supposed to take my woman away from me, so I took her man away from her. Ruthless? No. That was the price for double-crossing a Vergoossen. I had no conscience when someone messed with my family, or even worse, my woman.

Angelina kept screaming and threatening me, but it was all a blur. I already had a plan forming in my head regarding Ledford and Sofia. I looked at Wyatt, who was waiting for my orders. "Get me the phone number for Theo Ledford. Now," I rasped, commanding.

"What about her?" He glanced at Angelina, writhing against the chain she was cuffed to.

"Leave her here. I'll deal with her later."

OVERDOSED

I WIPED THE BLOOD from my face and removed the jacket covered with blood before throwing it into my trunk. I looked over at the sleek beach residence in Suffolk County on Long Island, where I had just arrived. The place had brought so many memories. Some of them pleasant, some others painful. I sauntered toward the entrance and knocked. It was dawn and so peaceful I could hear the ocean waves. I rang the bell and knocked repeatedly. I finally heard a movement, and the porch light went on before the door opened.

"Shane?" Sofia tied a white robe around her waist, her sleepy eyes spread wide open. "What are you doing here? What time is it?"

"Aren't you happy to see me?" I asked, my tone low.

"I…" She hesitated. "I just didn't expect to see you."

I scoffed, walking past her. I knew this place by heart, so I headed to the living room, where I sat on the cream couch, spreading my arm on the backrest.

Sofia watched me, baffled, nervously brushing her deep-brown hair behind her ear as she cleared her throat. "Considering that you haven't answered my calls or texts for the past two years, I assume something has happened. Otherwise, you wouldn't be here in the middle of the night."

"Clever as always," I said sarcastically. The truth was I didn't want to see that woman ever again, and if it weren't for her meddling into my life with Ledford, for whatever reason, my foot would never come through the door of this house. "You know me, Sofia. I don't like wasting my time, so I'll get straight to the point." I got up and walked closer to her. She crossed her arms, watching me anxiously. I knew she had something on her conscience because she wasn't the type to be intimidated by anyone. Not even me. She was challenging and seductive, always playing games. Now when I thought of it, I wasn't sure what I saw in her. She was wicked, dirty—nothing like Melanie.

"Well, what is it?" Her eyes darted between mine with uncertainty.

"Why did you hire someone to kidnap my fiancée?" I tilted my head to the side, hovering over her. She was much shorter than Melanie, maybe five-two.

She cleared her throat before saying softly, "I don't know what you are talking about."

"Don't try to fool me," I scoffed. "I know everything. My men caught Ax and his queen. He's dead, by the way." I took a few steps toward Sofia as I spoke, and she moved back until she reached the wall behind her.

"I did it for us," she admitted, looking into my eyes with regret. "So we could have a second chance. I love you, Shane. I never stopped."

I grabbed her chin with my fingers, tilted her head back, her lips parted slightly, and whispered, "You have a fucked-up way of showing your feelings. First, you screwed my brother, and now you plot the kidnapping of my fiancée." I pulled away, moving back. The images from the night when I caught her riding the cock of my sixteen-year-old brother flashed before my eyes, and I felt sick. She was five years older than him, and I could put her in jail for this or get rid of her in a more dirty way, but I chose to let her live with it and let the karma do its job.

She gave me a confused look, disappointment written all over her face. "Shane, I'm sorry. I told you already. I don't know how this happened. I would nev—"

"I don't care," I rasped. "All I want to know is why you did this and whose idea it was. Yours or Ledford?"

Sofia's gaze dropped, and she bit her lip. "It was his idea." She looked into my eyes again. "He contacted me a while ago and made me believe you don't have any feelings for that girl and that I... that I could win you back if she disappeared from your life."

"Oh, for fuck's sake, did you fall for that?" I rolled my eyes, anger flooding my system. How the fuck did fucking Ledford know about Sofia? But then again, I didn't give a shit. I was furious that he tried to kidnap Melanie. God knew what else he was plotting in his twisted mind. "It was you," I let out a heavy breath as I realized it must've been Sofia's doing that Angelina managed to get inside the charity event. "You helped Angelina pass the security, right?"

"Yes." Her voice cracked.

"For fuck's sake," I shouted.

"Shane, I'm sorry, I did this because I love you. I thought—"

"You thought you could force me to love you again?" I scoffed, irritated. "You and Ledford deserve each other."

"Shane, please. Let me explain." Sofia grabbed my hand, but I snatched it away.

"Stay away from my woman and me," I spoke, heading out of her house. "This is a warning."

I got in my car, checked my phone, and started the car engine. I got a text from Wyatt with the number for Ledford about an hour ago. I was boiling inside, and the pretty boy was lucky he was over 2700 miles away. I started a new conversation and typed a message.

To: Ledford

I know everything. You're lucky you're in *LA,* or you'd be on your way to the hospital with broken bones now. If you ever try to touch my fiancée again, you're a dead man.
Yours truly, S.V.

Sent Monday 4:51 AM

I threw my phone onto the passenger seat and let out a deep sigh. I was tired of all the shit that had been coming up—on the same hand, I determined like never before to fight for my relationship with Melanie. I put my foot down, leaving the sound of the tires squealing as I drove away, heading to the only person that gave my life meaning. I was hoping I'd arrive before she woke up, leaving the darkness of this night behind. Now my only concern was confessing to Melanie the truth.

I ARRIVED AT MY APARTMENT around seven a.m. Melanie was still asleep, so I went straight to the shower, washing the remaining dirt and sins off my body. The cold water helped me cool down. I jumped into a white tank top and gray sweatpants and headed to the kitchen to prepare breakfast. I looked through the fridge to see what we had and decided to make an avocado salad. I knew Melanie loved it. Fuck, I knew everything about this woman. She had me under her spell, wrapped around her little finger.

"Hey." Her soft voice reached my ear, and I looked up from chopping a cucumber to meet her gaze. "Where have you been? I woke up during the night, but you weren't here. Is everything okay?"

I smiled, trying to dispel any of her doubts. I didn't want to tell her any of the fucked-up shit that happened during the night. "Yeah, don't worry. Just work."

"Work? In the middle of the night?" She was rubbing her elbow, leaning against the wall, watching me with her big brown eyes.

I put the knife aside and headed toward her. I grabbed her chin with my fingers, leaning down so our eyes locked. "Melanie, you know what I do. I won't pretend to be someone I'm not, but I don't want you involved in any of this, okay?"

She nodded, letting out a quiet breath.

"Come on, let's eat. I've prepared breakfast," I grabbed her hand and led her to the kitchen island where the almost ready salad was waiting for her.

"Mmm. Looks delicious," she muttered, licking her lower lip seductively as she gazed into my eyes, smirking.

I couldn't fight the smile curling up my lips. "What? Me or the breakfast?"

"The breakfast," she said, drawing her teeth over her bottom lip, her tone teasing. "Obviously."

"You hurt my feelings," I rasped, leaning into her ear, teasing her lobe with my tongue.

A soft moan escaped her lips, and she looked at me with sheer lust in her eyes. She kept glancing at me, breathing heavily before she whispered, "Make love to me."

My eyes darted between hers before, with one swift move, I lifted her and set her on the kitchen counter, shoving away all the things in my way, and they shattered on the floor. We were kissing hungrily, impatiently taking off each other's clothes.

I was so determined to tell her everything that day and finally confess to her the truth. But the effect Melanie had on me broke down every little piece of my will I had collected for the past few weeks to tell her about the revenge that no longer meant anything to me. Instead, I lost myself in the mad lust mixing with my love for this woman. I couldn't resist her. I wanted her so badly. I craved her like a drug. Without her, I could no longer exist.

So I made love to her as if there was no tomorrow, tracing every inch of her perfectly shaped body with my fingertips, memorizing every curve, every way my touch made her naked body shiver.

TWENTY-THREE
Melanie

"What are you thinking about?" Shane's husky voice snapped me out of my thoughts as I snuggled into his arms in his king-size bed, his fingers in my hair that was now a total mess after hours of sex in every position. It felt like I couldn't get enough of him, no matter how many times I had him. It was never enough. The physical attraction between us was insane, inexplicable, inimitable.

"I was wondering…" I hesitated. My heart was pounding like crazy. I knew I couldn't keep my pregnancy a secret from him for much longer. It wasn't fair. I played a hundred different scenarios in my head, with Shane being over the moon in some of them or completely furious and against it in others. But no matter the scenario, I knew what I wanted. "What do you think of having kids?"

"Kids?" I didn't see his face, but I could tell he was taken aback. "I've never really thought about it. Why?"

"Nothing. I was just curious," I quickly replied. I knew it wasn't right of me, but I freaked out again. It was all happening so fast, too fast.

"I like the idea of having a family with you, Melanie," Shane said softly, grabbing my chin with his fingers and gently tilting my head back so our eyes locked. "I think we should first set the wedding date." He kissed the tip of my nose and smiled.

I propped myself on my elbows, resting my head on my hands, not breaking our eye contact. "Do you have a specific date in mind?"

"How about next month?" he asked, dead serious, and I sat looking at him in disbelief.

"Next month?"

"Yeah, why not?" He adjusted himself on the bed to hold me in his arms, leaving a soft kiss on my arm as he whispered. "I can't wait to call you Mrs. Vergoossen."

I felt a weird feeling in my belly. Excitement. Happiness. Butterflies. I felt like the luckiest girl under the sun. It felt like I had everything. Sometimes I was afraid it was all just a dream, and I would wake up to the dire reality I had lived in just a couple of weeks before. But it was happening for real. The feeling was real. Too real to ever recreate it. A love like this only happens once in a lifetime.

"Okay," I said, unable to fight the laughter of pure joy. Everything seemed so easy, so natural with Shane, that I didn't want to wait. I wanted to be his, officially and forever. "Let's get married in a month."

"Are you serious?" Shane looked at me, surprise on his face.

"I am," I whispered, grinning as I kissed him. "I love you."

"I love you, too."

The next couple of days were like paradise on earth. The media reported on my unexpected wedding to Shane Vergoossen, New York's most eligible billionaire and my family's long-term enemy. We were the hot headlines of every newspaper and even got labeled as *Romeo and Juliet*. I couldn't care less. I felt like I was floating on a cloud of bliss. I'd never been happier in my entire life. We set the wedding date, and I dove into everything about the wedding. I managed to forget about my dark past, about all the dreadful things I'd been through, and I started to believe it all was finally behind me. Sometimes I felt melancholic because I hadn't heard from my parents. I felt like they abandoned me only because I was chasing my happiness. But then again, I had Shane, and he made sure to make me feel like the only girl in the world. I thought he was my blessing, my savior, and that I was about to create a new life by my dream man's side. Little did I know, it was the calm before the massive storm.

"What are you doing, babe?" Shane's voice rumbled against my ear as he slid his hands around my waist from behind and kissed my cheek.

"I'm trying to find something to wear. I'm going to be late for my meeting with Scar," I replied, rummaging through the closet Shane had arranged for me in one of the rooms.

"If you ask me, I like you most naked," Shane teased, whispering to my ear as he sucked my earlobe between his teeth.

"Shane!" I laughed. His warm, minty breath caused my body to tingle. "You're unbelievable!"

He twirled my body so I could face him, his hands still on my waist, and I rested against the closet. We both smiled, looking into each other's eyes. "Can you blame me?" he rasped, his tone low and growly. "You're walking sex. Just a glimpse of you turns me on to my limits. And you look so sexy in this lingerie it's driving me crazy." His hand roamed my inner thigh, his touch burning against my skin, and he trailed hot kisses down my neck, making me tremble. He reached the hem of my lacy panties that were a part of the one-piece sultry white lingerie I wore, stroking my sensitive bud with his fingertips. He slowly slid the lingerie strap down my bare arm, kissing it gently, causing my muscles to tense. He continued rubbing my clit through the thin fabric. "Fuck," he growled, his tone low and husky, alluring. He looked into my eyes, devoured me with his hungry gaze, and I was burning. My whole body was aching for his touch. My lips parted slightly, letting soft moans escape. Shane looked down into my eyes, licking his lower lip as he slid my panties to the side, and pushed two fingers inside me. My hips started moving, begging for more.

Begging him to fuck me. "You're so wet," he rasped, his eyes black, filled with savage lust. "You need to get fucked. Hard."

With one swift move, he turned my body so my belly was pressed against the wooden closet door and my backside ground against the growing bulge in his pants. I was panting in need, my legs spread, anticipating the feeling of his hard length shoving inside me, when my phone's ringtone filled the room.

"Ugh," I growled, undone. "It's Scar. I have to go."

"She can wait," Shane whispered, teasing my lobe with his tongue.

I had to use every bit of willpower in me to resist him. I spun around and teasingly tapped the tip of his nose with my finger, "You have to wait for it, Mr. Vergoossen." I kissed Shane's lips, and he growled as I freed myself from his embrace. I cleared my throat, reaching for my phone, trying to extinguish the burning desire. "It's Scar. Shit. She's already at the boutique." I turned to look at Shane, who ran his fingers through his hair, breathing heavily.

"Are you going to leave me like this?"

"Yes." I chuckled. "I'm going to choose my wedding dress now with a friend I haven't seen in weeks. This has to wait," I said teasingly.

"I can't wait for our wedding night." He walked toward me and put his hands on my hips before leaning into my ear. "I'm going to rip the wedding dress off of you."

"Oh, so I better choose wisely." I winked at him, laughing, and kissing him gently, murmured, "Can you drop me off at the boutique? I don't want Scar to wait for long, and I'm already late."

Shane let out a soft sigh, looking at me apologetically. "I can't, babe. I'm sorry. I have some errands. But Callan will drive you."

"No, it's fine," I said softly, but Shane had already reached for his phone and dialed Callan's number.

"Don't worry, babe. I don't need him today. I'm going to my father's company," Shane stated, his phone near his ear as he waited for Callan to pick up. He winked at me reassuringly, and I knew it was pointless to object. Shane was very protective over me, and I knew he would feel calmer knowing Callan was with me. Besides, he liked to have things his way. Although, I didn't like the idea of having Callan with me in the bridal shop. I felt like it would be a little awkward. Shane finished the conversation with Callan and turned to me, kissing my forehead before he said, "Done. He's ready to take you there. Enjoy your day, soon-to-be Mrs. Vergoossen."

"Yeah, you too, Mr. Vergoossen," I replied, and Shane stole a soft kiss before he headed out of the closet.

I inhaled deeply, pulling myself together. I quickly put on a black-floral-print romper that tied at the back of my neck, with a silky belt around my waist, and did my hair into a sleek low bun. I fixed my makeup and headed outside, where Callan was already waiting for me.

LUCKILY, THE BRIDAL BOUTIQUE I had booked myself an appointment at was located on 5th Avenue, so about ten minutes later, I greeted my friend. As soon as we parked by the boutique and I stepped out of Callan's SUV, Scar's face brightened up, and she ran toward me with her arms spread and a broad grin.

"Hey, boo!" Scarlett pulled me in for a friendly hug. "Oh my God, I missed you so much!"

"I missed you, too!" I squeezed my friend in my arms. It felt amazing to have her here with me after so many weeks. We stayed in constant touch, voice messaged, texted or video called each other every now and then, but it wasn't the same. The video calls couldn't replace face-to-face meetings.

Scarlett pulled away and looked at me, still grinning. "You look amazing, Mel! New York does good things for you. Or wait." She leaned to whisper in my ear, her tone teasing, "The legendary Shane Vergoossen does good things to you."

I blushed, chuckling. "You have no idea."

We both giggled, and I let out a sigh of relief. I was so glad to see my friend. "You look gorgeous, too, Scar. This green dress suits you."

"Thanks, babe." She blew me a kiss and winked. God, I missed her easygoing, positive attitude. "So, tell me. Are you pregnant?"

"What?" My heart skipped a beat, and I looked at her with surprise and shock.

"Relax, I'm kidding." She chuckled. "But you have to know that everyone at Stanford gossips about you. Some even make bets whether you went nuts, you're pregnant, or the sexy Mr. Vergoossen is forcing you to marry him."

I burst out laughing. "What? Why?"

"What do you mean, why?" Scar asked sarcastically. "You ran away from your engagement party to Theo just a couple of weeks ago, and a few weeks later, you're getting married to another man. Let's not forget you're only nineteen."

"It does sound crazy, doesn't it?" I furrowed my brows, feeling giddy.

"If you ask me, you lost your goddamn mind!" Scar joked. "But I get it. Shane Vergoossen is a fucking Greek god. I'd lose my mind for him too." She brought her hand near her mouth and lowered her voice. "For sure, I'd lose my panties."

Scar winked teasingly, and I burst out laughing. Suddenly, her facial expression changed, and her eyes grew wide as she gazed at something behind me. I turned around to check what she saw, and I noticed Callan walking around the car before standing right behind me. I instantly figured that Scarlett had to recognize him.

Callan cleared his throat, his hands crossed on his abdomen as he spoke. "I'll be around. Call me when you're done, Miss Atwood."

Feeling awkward, I let out a quiet breath. "It's okay, Callan. You're free to go."

"I'm sorry, Miss Atwood. I'm not allowed to leave. Boss's orders."

I rolled my eyes. "I swear Shane is exaggerating now."

"Can't blame him." Callan lowered his voice. "I would be, too." He nodded before he briefly glanced at Scar, who was watching us, hypnotized. "I'll wait in the car. Excuse me." He walked to the other side of the car and got in.

I turned to look at Scar. She raised her brow, her arms crossed. "Why the hell is your ex-boyfriend your bodyguard now?"

"He works for Shane," I admitted.

"Does he know?" Scar watched me, frowning. I knew she wouldn't judge me. After all, she'd always been the one with crazy ideas and the YOLO mantra, yet I couldn't help but feel judged.

"You mean that Callan was my first boyfriend?" Scarlett shook her head yes. "No. I didn't tell him." My gaze dropped down, and I fidgeted my fingers nervously.

Scarlett sighed. "Mel, why didn't you tell him?"

"It's... complicated. Shane values Callan. He treats him like a brother. I didn't want to ruin it. Besides, that part of my relationship with Callan is in the past. It was just a teenage crush."

"If you say so." My friend took a deep breath, putting her hand around my arm. "Let's go get you a fucking sexy wedding dress." She winked at me, showing off her beautiful smile, and we entered the boutique.

I was enchanted by the sophisticated design of the bridal salon, with a red carpet running through a tasteful white interior. An elegant lady in her forties greeted my friend and me with a lovely smile, offering Scarlett a seat on a grayish padded chair with golden legs while she led me to the fitting room where I was supposed to try on the wedding dresses. I felt like a princess wearing the stunning white gowns, and butterflies were dancing in my belly at the thought of me walking down the aisle toward the man I had irreversibly fallen in love with. I tried a couple of different types of wedding dresses, from lavish ball gowns to unpretentious sheaths. All of them were unique and splendid, but only one of them had stolen my heart.

"Wow," Scarlett whispered. Her eyes grew wider as I came out of the fitting room in a Rhiannon mermaid gown from Galia Lahav's Queen of Hearts collection with a low neckline, pearl detailing at the back, and sheer long sleeves and beaded lace. "You look stunning, Mel. That's the one."

"That's the one," I agreed, smiling as I twirled around.

That evening, I was preparing dinner, smiling to myself as I lit the candles in the dining room and decorated with red rose petals on the floor. I was ready to tell Shane about the pregnancy, and I wanted the evening to have a special charm. I prepared his favorite smoked salmon with lentils and asparagus, bought a bottle of bordeaux, and was anticipating him coming back home. Our home. I was a little nervous but also excited. I checked the time on my phone. It was six thirty p.m. Shane was running late because usually, he'd be back by now. I went to the bathroom to fix my makeup for the fiftieth time. I wanted to look good. Perfect. I wore a black off-shoulder dress with long see-through puff sleeves and painted my lips red, leaving my waves down. I glanced at my engagement ring glittering on my finger and smiled. I heard a bell ring and ran straight to open the door. Although, I found it odd that Shane used a doorbell because he'd never done that before. However, I was too excited to check who it was. I assumed it was my fiancé.

I opened the door, and my enthusiasm level went down. "Callan?" I looked at him, puzzled.

"Melanie, we need to talk," he said, his tone serious.

I frowned. My eyes darted between his. I got a little scared that something had happened to Shane, and my heart started pounding rapidly. An unpleasant lump formed in my throat. "Okay. Come on in."

Callan walked in, and for a second, he seemed taken aback as he scanned the room, prepared for a romantic dinner. His gaze dropped to the ground before he turned to me, setting his eyes on mine.

"What is it, Callan?" I asked impatiently, playing out the worst possible scenarios in my head.

"I can't keep doin' this," he whispered, shaking his head as his brow furrowed.

"Doing what?" I narrowed my eyes, my fingers fidgeting.

"I can't keep pretendin' that you don't mean anythin' to me. That you and me… that there was nothin' between us."

"Callan, but—"

"I know you're off-limits." He rubbed his temples with his fingers. I felt lost and awkward. I genuinely believed it was all behind us, all in the past. "I know you're with him. And I know I don't stand a chance. I mean, what kind of woman would refuse someone like Shane Vergoossen? Rich and powerful, I can't compete with that."

"Callan, you know it's never been about money or power for me. I didn't, and I don't care about it."

"I know, Melanie. I know," he said softly, moving closer toward me, looking piercingly into my eyes. "And I know you should be with him. I know he would make you happy, but I…" He paused as if contemplating his words before he let out a deep sigh. "I can't forget about you. And when I saw the engagement ring on your finger, something broke in me."

"What are you saying? Please don't do that." I shook my head, scanning his face, hoping it was just a bad joke.

"I can't. I'm sorry." He let out a heavy breath, running his fingers through his dyed hair before settling his gaze back on mine, his brows furrowed. "I can't because I never stopped lovin' you. I still love you, Melanie."

I was rooted to the spot, and Callan grabbed my hands in his and started leaning in as if wanting to kiss me. I couldn't move. I was completely shocked and overwhelmed.

Then I heard Shane's raspy voice hissing behind me, and my heart skipped a beat. "Don't. Or I'll put a bullet in your head right on the spot," Shane rasped through his clenched teeth as he put his gun to Callan's temple. His eyes were so filled with hatred and fury that it scared me. Shane cocked the gun, and my body started shaking, and I felt like I was losing the ground beneath me. That was not how he was supposed to find out about my past relationship with Callan. I instantly regretted not telling Shane the truth earlier because now everything was crumbling around me. Shane's trust for me, for Callan, maybe even our love. I fucked up.

"Melanie, step back," Shane commanded, his gaze never leaving Callan.

"Shane, please let me explain." My voice was breaking, and my body was trembling. It felt like my knees had turned to jelly, and I could barely keep standing.

"I said, step back," he hissed. His voice was so cold that it sent icy shivers down my spine. "Well, Callan. What did you just say to my fiancée?"

Callan stood still like a statue. He didn't even blink. He just kept staring at me with regret all over his face until he finally said, "I'm in love with her."

TWENTY-FOUR

Shane

My blood was boiling with savage rage flowing through my every fucking vein. Ever since I met Callan, I'd been treating him like he was my brother. I cared for, hired, befriended, and trusted him with my life. In return, he'd been lying straight to my face, lusting after *my* woman. I inhaled deeply, trying to combat my towering anger. I swear I wanted to put a fucking bullet in his goddamn head right this very second. But I couldn't do it. Not like this. Not in front of Melanie. She was watching me, pale and trembling, and despite also being furious that she hadn't mentioned there was something between her and Callan, I couldn't do anything to her. I loved her too deeply even though she'd hurt me.

"Get out of my sight," I hissed, gritting my teeth.

"Shane," Callan spoke, his tone apologetic, but I cut him off.

"I'm your fucking boss. You should never have forgotten that," I said, low and cold. "Now get the fuck out of here. Don't make me kill you."

"Boss, please let me explain," he pleaded, but with every word coming out of his mouth, I felt sick. The image of him trying to kiss my fiancée flashed before my eyes.

"Get. Out," I deadpanned. "And don't come near my fiancée or me. You're fired."

Callan breathed out heavily, glancing at Melanie, and despite it being just a fleeting glance, it made me sick to my stomach, and I was seething. He walked out of my place, not saying a word, not looking back. I closed my eyes, inhaling and exhaling several times before I gazed at Melanie, watching me with her hands shaking and eyes welling up with tears. I hated it. I hated seeing her like this, but I was also hurt and furious that she didn't tell me about Callan.

"Speak," I ordered. I hated myself for being so cold toward her, yet I couldn't fight it. The rage was stronger than me.

"I wanted to tell you, Shane. I swear," she whispered, looking at me apologetically.

"Then why didn't you?" I hissed.

"I don't know. I thought it wasn't important." Melanie rubbed her temples. A single tear dripped down her sweet cheek.

"Tell me now. Everything."

Melanie let out a heavy sigh, swallowing hard. She focused on the vase in the hallway or just the wall. I was so numb I couldn't tell. "Callan was my first boyfriend."

First boyfriend?

I clenched my teeth as I shook my head, eyes closed briefly. I was jealous. Fucking jealous. He was her first boyfriend, so he had her first kiss. He gave her her first butterflies. He had her love first. And if what they say about first love was true, she had never forgotten him.

Melanie cleared her throat before speaking, snapping me out of my thoughts. "I was sixteen. It was just before my father arranged my relationship with David Leighton. Callan came to California with his father after his mother died of cancer. They moved from Australia, and my father hired Callan's father as a gardener. Callan visited his father often, helping him. My father eventually hired Callan as his errand boy, driver, or whatever was needed. Somehow, we started chatting, hanging out together until he finally kissed me."

"Enough," I hissed, turning to the side. I couldn't listen to this. I was picturing Melanie, the woman I lost my head for, kissing a man who I considered my friend. It was too painful for me. Maybe if they had told me about it right away after the first time they saw each other at the hospital, I wouldn't have been so pissed off. I would understand. After all, it was before I met Melanie, and she had every right to have a past. I wouldn't care. But the fact that they both kept it a secret was like a stab in the back. I couldn't help but be suspicious that maybe they still had feelings for one another. Otherwise, why would they keep pretending they were strangers? But what turned the tide for me was Callan trying to kiss Melanie. "I don't need details. Why did you break up?"

"Because of my father," she admitted, and my heart dropped to my stomach.

That was the last thing I wanted to hear. She didn't break up with him because she stopped having feelings for him, but because someone separated them. She would ask herself the question, *What if?* I asked myself that question.

What if Dedrick didn't separate them? Would she still be with him?

"Why?" I asked, still avoiding her gaze, as she avoided mine.

"He didn't like the idea of his only daughter dating someone insignificant. As you know, he had other plans for me. As soon as he found out about..." Melanie paused and took a deep breath, biting her lip as her gaze dropped to the fingers she was nervously playing with before she continued, her voice cracking. "About *us*. He fired both Callan and his father. You know the rest of the story."

"Do you still love him?" I looked at her. I had to see her reaction and read her body, her eyes.

"No." She didn't hesitate. Her tone was firm and genuine. She cast her gaze upward, and our eyes locked. "I love you, Shane."

I threw away the gun I still held in my hand and rushed toward Melanie. I put my hands on her waist and pushed her against the wall, crashing my lips to hers, kissing her demandingly. *Possessively*. I couldn't stand the thought of another man touching her as I did. I couldn't stand the thought of my close friend touching her as I did. I wanted her all to myself. And only to myself.

"You're mine," I hissed in between our fiery kisses. I took her hands in mine and pinned them above her head. "You're only mine, Melanie." I nibbled her lower lip before trailing kisses down her neck.

"I'm yours," she sighed, breathing heavily.

I lifted her body, her legs wrapped automatically around my waist, her fingers running through my hair as we kissed hungrily. "You're my madness, Melanie. My addiction," I said, staring into her eyes, undoing my fly, our breaths mingling.

"And you're mine," she moaned against my lips as I shoved inside her, thrusting fast and forcefully, slamming her body against the wall.

I FELT LIKE A FUCKING HYPOCRITE. I got angry at Melanie that she hid something from me, while I myself have been keeping a much worse secret from her the entire time. I hid my initial intentions from her. My father's wicked plan. *Revenge*.

I stood by the window in the dining room, sipping scotch. Melanie went to the bathroom to freshen up, and I waited for her. It was about time I confessed the truth to her. I wanted to start over. No lies. No secrets. A blank page, as she called it before. I glanced at the table, the candles and rose petals, wondering how romantic the evening could've been. She had prepared all of this, probably to celebrate something. Our upcoming wedding, maybe? Or just to spend a romantic evening together. Instead, I fucked Melanie against the wall like an animal satisfying its needs.

"Hey." Her soft voice reached my ear, and I turned to face her.

She'd changed her clothes to my shirt and tied her hair into a ponytail. My gaze slowly followed the length of her body. I loved when she was wearing my clothes. I loved when my clothes smelled like her. As our eyes met, she pressed her lips together in what seemed a forced smile, approaching me, and I set the glass aside on the table.

"I'm sorry, Melanie. I acted like a savage." I took a deep breath, collecting the strength in me to finally tell her the truth. To say to her how fucked up I was. Dark and damaged. "I need to tell you something." I looked into her eyes, knowing I didn't deserve her.

"I need to tell you something, too," she expressed, furrowing her brows as she rubbed her elbow.

I frowned, observing her. I thought she had already told me everything. "Okay, who goes first?"

"I want to," she said nervously, peeking at me. "If I don't tell you now, I may chicken out again, and I've been wanting to tell you this for days now."

"Okay," I said softly, moving closer to her. I grabbed her chin with my fingers, caressing her soft skin with my thumb, and she leaned into my touch. "Just know that whatever it is, I love you."

Melanie's eyes darted between mine, and she took a deep breath. "Okay, so… I'm p—"

Melanie and I turned to look at the door as loud banging and shouting coming from the hallway filled the room. "Melanie, are you there?!"

Fuck me!

I gritted my teeth, clenching my fist. As if we didn't have enough issues for one day, Theodore fucking Ledford showed up at my door. He kept banging and screaming, and I exhaled deeply, heading toward the door.

"What do you want?" I hissed, staring at him, outraged.

"Where are your good manners, Vergoossen?" he mocked. "Won't you invite me in?"

I glanced at Melanie, who stood a few steps behind me, her eyes wide. I moved aside, making way for Ledford to come in, still gritting my teeth. I was furious enough already, and the last person I wanted to deal with at the moment was fucking Ledford. I closed the door. Ledford was looking around, a sarcastic smirk on his face.

"You must have a good reason to come here knowing that I want you dead," I rasped, and Melanie winced at me, perturbed.

Ledford turned on his heel, sneering, "Yeah, yeah. You can drop that bad boy attitude now." He glanced at Melanie, checking her out head to toe before he continued, his tone taunting. "Once Melanie finds out about your revenge, I think you'll be the one with something broken. A heart, if you have one."

Revenge.

My blood ran cold as I heard it. How did he find out about it? I clenched my fists, looking at him with rage, breathing heavily. I watched as a sardonic grin formed on his self-satisfied face. I felt as if I was frozen. Unable to move or speak. I could hear my heart pounding in my chest.

Melanie frowned, her eyes puzzled. "What do you mean?"

Ledford tilted his head to the side, his tone condemning. "You're screwing the wrong guy, Mel."

Melanie scoffed, shaking her head, "What?"

"He played you, baby," he continued his mocking game, but at this moment, something in me broke, and I lashed out.

I grabbed him by his collar, pushing him against the wall. "Don't you fucking dare call her baby," I hissed, staring into his face with a deadly fury washing through me.

Melanie came between us, separating us as she shouted, "Stop it!" She pulled me away from Ledford, and he fixed his varsity jacket, clenching his teeth as we both stared at one another with hatred.

"I don't know if you're worth this, Melanie," he spoke angrily, his eyes bouncing between Melanie and me. "But for some fucked-up reason, I had to come here and tell you the truth."

"Don't," I hissed, barely restraining myself. I didn't want *him* to tell Melanie the truth. And I couldn't tell her now either. Not like this. She wouldn't have believed that I was planning to tell her myself just a few minutes before he interrupted us. Fucking shit, he chose the worst possible timing.

"What truth?" Melanie's voice was breaking, her body trembling. Her eyes started welling up with tears as if she saw something bad coming.

I searched for her gaze, breathing heavily. I felt like everything around me was spinning, like I was losing the ground under my feet. I couldn't bring myself to speak, no word would come out of my mouth, and Ledford didn't waste any time.

"Your beloved fiancé showed up in your life only to take revenge on your father. They blame him for Rose Vergoossen's death," he blurted out, and my world collapsed.

I watched Melanie staring at me with disbelief, her lips parting and tears dripping down her face. "Tell me that's not true," she whimpered, her eyes imploring me.

"He can't," Ledford chimed in, and I snapped.

"Shut up!" I wanted to fucking punch him in his smirking face, taking off the shit-eating grin he wore, but I restrained myself. I knew that wouldn't have made the situation any better. I turned to Melanie, wiping a tear from the corner of my eye. "Melanie, I wanted to tell you. I was waiting for the right time. I was about to tell you before... *he* came."

Melanie scoffed, shaking her head as she cried, "Tell me everything. Now."

I turned to Ledford. "Get out. This is between Melanie and me."

"No," she objected. "He's going to stay," she said, crossing her arms as she watched me with hatred in her eyes, and it broke my heart.

I took a deep breath, fighting the storm of emotions within me. "Okay, if that's what you want," I said, looking at her, but she refused to look me in the eyes.

"Speak," she insisted. "Or, you know what?" She looked at me for a short moment, her gaze full of contempt. "You had your chance, and I don't want to listen to any more of your lies." She turned to her ex. "Theo, you tell me."

"Ah, with pleasure," he mocked, and my fist clenched involuntarily with full force.

"Melanie, please. It's between us," I hissed, pleading, but she didn't say anything. She kept staring at Ledford, tears streaming down her face, her body shaking.

Seeing her like this broke me, tearing my soul apart. I wanted to embrace her, hold her crumbling pieces between my arms, so I moved closer, reaching for her hand, but she snatched it. "Don't! Don't touch me," she hissed, refusing to look me in the eyes, gritting her teeth.

Ledford rolled his eyes. He sure as fuck couldn't wait to break my world into pieces. It was his retribution for losing Melanie. "Alright, lovebirds. Let's cut to the chase," he mocked, and my rage was growing with every single word coming out of his cynical mouth. "You see, Mel, you were just a pawn in his twisted game. Twenty years ago, Rose Vergoossen had an affair with your father."

"What?" Melanie whispered, dumbfounded.

"That's not true," I rasped. "That's Dedrick's side of the story. He raped her!" I lashed out. I couldn't listen to his lies anymore. I was shaking and out of control. All I saw was red. All the painful memories kept flashing in my head. The haunting images and sounds of my mother's suffering before she couldn't bear it any longer and took her own life.

"Of course, your father told you that," Ledford taunted. "The almighty Karl Vergoossen couldn't stand that his wife cheated on him. What's more, she was carrying the child of another man."

I lost it. I turned into the savage beast I was and punched him square in the face. The blood spilled all over the floor. Melanie gasped, covering her mouth with her shaking hands before she ran to her ex. Her fucking ex and not me. She helped him get up, looking at me like I was the bad guy. Maybe I was. Perhaps I had always been, and I forgot it for a while. She made me believe I could've been a better person. Start over. Leave my dreadful past behind. Apparently, I was wrong.

Ledford wiped the blood from under his nose, glaring at me angrily, his breath heavy and ragged. "You're done, Vergoossen. You lost."

"Get the fuck out of my house, or I'll fucking kill you," I shouted, the pain and rage tearing me apart from the inside.

"Not until Melanie hears the whole truth. And I want to see your face when she does," he breathed out before he turned to Melanie, ending this. Ending everything. "He wanted your death, Melanie. His mother overdosed on sleeping pills, and he wanted you to do the same so that Dedrick would suffer the same way he did. They're twisted. Sick."

"Theo, take me out of here," Melanie cried, running out of my apartment.

Ledford took one last look at me in triumph, savoring the taste of my failure. "We're even now," he sneered and followed after her.

My world had collapsed. My vision got blurry, turning everything around me to black. It felt like the thick walls I'd surrounded myself with to prevent me from ever being hurt, to numb myself from emotions so that I'd never suffer again after my mother chose to die, were crumbling down. Melanie was the only good thing that had happened to me. She was my only light, showing me the way out of the darkness that surrounded me. And now she was gone. I lost her, and I didn't know if I could ever win her back. But the most painful part was the fact that I broke her. I broke the person who, for the past few weeks, I'd desperately been trying to fix. Maybe I was too broken myself to fix another human being. Maybe I was too damaged to love. Love was something pure, and fuck, I was far from being pure. I didn't deserve her. We were always a losing game. From the first moment I laid eyes on her, we were doomed. You don't build something as rare as this on a lie. Now I knew it, and I had to pay the highest price.

"Fuck!" I shook my head, trying to regain control over my body and start thinking clearly. This was not who I was. I did not give up. I was a Vergoossen, and the Vergoossens fight for what they love. And most definitely, I loved Melanie, and she was worth fighting for. Melanie was the kind of woman I swore didn't exist, and that was why I couldn't let her go.

I grabbed my car keys from the cabinet in the hallway and stormed out of the penthouse.

I'm not letting you go, Melanie. I'm not letting you go.

I WAS SPEEDING UP THE ROAD, following Ledford's red Porsche. Yeah, I was a tad bit twisted and hella overprotective, but I put a tracker in Melanie's phone so that if ever something happened, I'd have a way to track her. When raised in a Mafia family, things like this are essential. I spotted his car, stepped on the gas and sped past them, only to stop right in front of them, forcing Ledford to slam on the brakes.

"Are you fucking crazy?!" he shouted as he got out of the vehicle.

I ran to the passenger seat and opened the door. "Melanie, please talk to me. Five minutes. That's all I ask."

She shook her head, cupping her face in her hands before she let out a heavy sigh and got out of the car.

"Melanie, what are you doing?" Ledford cried out.

"Please, wait in the car. This won't take long," she uttered, and I took a deep breath.

I waited for Ledford to get inside before I set my gaze on Melanie, but she still refused to look at me. Her eyes were swollen, eyelashes wet and heavy with tears. Her body was quivering, and her breath ragged. It was breaking my heart. "Melanie, I love you. You have to believe me," I pleaded. "Everything we've had was true. I wasn't pretending my love for you. If I could go back in time—"

"But you can't," she cut me off, her voice cold and stern. "That's the thing, Shane. You can't!" She started crying, punching my chest with her fists, and I let her. "I hate you! God, I hate you so much! I trusted you. I told you everything I went through, and even that didn't stop you from playing your role! You're sick!"

"Melanie, you know that's not true." I gently grabbed her wrists in my hands, pressing them to my chest. I watched the woman, who I swore to protect, break down. I clenched my jaw, fighting back the tears in my eyes as she desperately cried. I knew I was the reason for it, and I couldn't stand that thought. Her pain was tearing me down. "I've regretted agreeing to my father's fucked-up plan every fucking day since I met you. And I hate myself for it. I'm fucked up. I know that. But I was raised that way. My father was fueling me with goddamn revenge as if it was the purpose of my life. Until I met you." My voice was breaking. I held her hands in mine and, for the first time in twenty years, cried. Last time I shed a tear, I was five and at my mother's funeral. "You freed me from this, Melanie. You freed me from the heavy chains keeping me in the past. And I love you. I so fucking love you, Melanie. You're my life. I'm lost without you."

"I don't believe you," Melanie sobbed, struggling to catch a breath. Fuck, I wanted to take the pain away from her. I just didn't know how. I felt so fucking helpless. I broke the woman I loved the most.

"You have to believe me," I whispered, grabbing her chin in my fingers and tilting her head back so our eyes locked. "Ever since I laid eyes on you, I knew I couldn't hurt you. And you kept proving me right every single day. Everything I've done after was to protect you."

Melanie pulled back, taking a deep breath as she wiped her tears. Her eyes turned black with lethal hatred. "If you wanted to protect me, you should've stayed away from me."

"Melanie, please… give me a chance to prove that I love you." My voice cracked.

"No, Shane. What we had was lust, not love."

"Don't say that."

"But it's true. We've mistaken lust for love."

"No, Melanie. Only love can be this strong. And only love can hurt so damn much that I'm suffocating."

"Well then… Love is lethal," Melanie whispered, staring numbly into my eyes. I didn't understand her words, but I felt cold shivers washing over me. I felt fear.

"Because whatever this was... I overdosed, and it killed me."

I shook my head, her words cut deep like a knife, tearing my heart apart. "Don't say such things."

Melanie looked at me with contempt, her eyes glistened with tears. "Stay the hell away from me," she shrieked before she turned on her heels and got back in the car.

Ledford instantly drove away, and I felt like I was drowning. Suffocating. I stood alone on an empty street, surrounded only by the darkness of the night, immersing in the excruciating pain and questioning every decision I'd ever made that led me to this point. Did I regret anything? Hell yes. Would I change anything? No. If I hadn't agreed to my father's twisted plan, I would never have met Melanie. I knew my father would proceed with his plan anyway, with or without me, but I... I would never have experienced this kind of wild passion and raw desire. I would never have savored the sweet taste of pure love.

Melanie Rose Atwood was the only woman that could change me. The only woman I was willing to change for. I knew this wasn't the end of our story. It couldn't have been.

I lost count of the whiskeys I'd had. I felt like a miserable shit drowning my sorrows in alcohol. I sat on the floor, resting against the couch in my living room with the lights switched off, my head cupped in my hands. Darkness. That was all I knew. It was so easy to indulge in it again. But without Melanie in my life, I didn't see the light anymore. I couldn't get the images of her crying her eyes out, because of me, out of my head. It was breaking me if it was even possible to be more broken than I already was.

I heard the sound of the door opening and then closing. Then footsteps and the sound of someone turning on the lights. I didn't see who it was, not that I cared. I knew it wasn't Melanie. I would sense her presence and recognize her scent.

"Jeez, bro," Ander's voice rumbled in my ears. "You look like shit."

"And that's how I feel," I rasped. "What are you doing here?"

"Father sent me," he stated dryly. I heard the sound of liquid being poured, and I figured he was getting himself a drink.

"And what does he want again? Whose life does he want to ruin now?" I wasn't sure if I was more resentful or sarcastic, and the alcohol numbed the pain.

"He couldn't reach you. Couldn't reach Callan."

"Callan," I scoffed.

Anders continued his speech. He'd never miss a chance to play on my nerves. Not even after he fucked my girlfriend in the past. It still wasn't enough for him. "Call Father. He's shitting his pants that you got killed or something. He's always exaggerating when it's about his firstborn."

"You want my life so bad?" I asked, exhausted, not having much strength left in me. "Take it. I don't care. You'll see, it's not as good as you think."

"What?" I was either imagining things or I picked up a hint of distress in his voice.

"I'm done with this shit. I'm done with Karl fucking Vergoossen."

"Shane." A cold chill ran through my body as I heard a familiar voice.

I lifted my head to see if I was going crazy or if it was happening for real. *Callan.* He was there, standing in my doorway.

"The nerve of you," I hissed as I rushed toward him, letting the anger flow through my veins.

"Wait, it's about Melanie," he exclaimed, and my body refused to move.

I stood still, frozen, looking at him with my heart rumbling in my rib cage. Ironic how, within one goddamn day, I lost my friend and the only woman I ever truly loved. "What is it?"

Callan took a deep breath, his voice cracking as he struggled to speak. "She… Melanie, she…"

"For fuck's sake, speak!" I shouted, shaking and so fucking scared.

He looked me in the eyes, his brows furrowed and his breath heavy and ragged, before he finally blurted out, "She overdosed on sleeping pills."

Love is lethal.

OVERDOSED

To be continued

ABOUT THE AUTHOR
AMELIA KAPPE

Amelia is a hopeless romantic who believes reading and writing are beautiful acts of tasting life you wouldn't dare to live. Forbidden romance, full of angst and twists, is most definitely her favorite trope, and that's what you can expect from her books or stories. She doesn't believe something like perfection exists and therefore, all of her characters are flawed and relatable.

On a day-to-day basis, Amelia is a successful interactive story writer with millions of reads across multiple platforms. Although, she's in her element, writing deep narratives for her upcoming books.

Whenever she's not writing, she's playing out new plots in her head with a cup of coffee she's addicted to. She loves traveling and believes she still hasn't found her place on earth. She feels at home in her husband's arms and next to their adorable furry friend.

Get in touch with Amelia on

Instagram—@akappe.author or TikTok—@ameliakappe

ACKNOWLEDGEMENTS

Thank you to my family and friends who keep supporting me and my passion for writing.

To my husband, who forgives me the evenings he spends alone while I dive into the world of my characters. Love you.

To my dad, who's also my best friend. Your proud gaze after I publish a book is the best reward I can get, Dad.

And most importantly, thank you to my readers who, by choosing this book, boost my motivation to keep going.

Printed in Great Britain
by Amazon